CHILD'S PLAY

CHILD'S PLAY

*Enriching Your Child's Interests, from
Rocket Science to Rock Climbing,
Stamp Collecting to Sculpture*

Monica Cardoza

CITADEL PRESS
Kensington Publishing Corp.
www.kensingtonbooks.com

CITADEL PRESS BOOKS are published by

Kensington Publishing Corp.
850 Third Avenue
New York, NY 10022

All Kensington titles, imprints, and distributed lines are available at special quantity discounts for bulk purchases for sales promotions, premiums, fund-raising, educational, or institutional use. Special book excerpts or customized printings can also be created to fit specific needs. For details, write or phone the office of the Kensington special sales manager: Kensington Publishing Corp., 850 Third Avenue, New York, NY 10022, attn: Special Sales Department, phone 1-800-221-2647.

CITADEL PRESS and the Citadel logo are Reg. U.S. Pat. & TM Off.

Designed by Leonard Telesca

First Printing: May 2003

10 9 8 7 6 5 4 3 2 1

Printed in the United States of America

Library of Congress Control Number: 2002114198

ISBN 0-8065-2338-7

To Avery
And to all adults who share their interests with children

Contents

Foreword

It starts out full of promise. Parents intent on helping their children develop strong self-esteem watch joyfully as their youngsters begin life full of enthusiasm—every one of life's small details is greeted with wide eyes and excited shouts. But no sooner do their children enter elementary school than these same parents find themselves watching helplessly as some inexplicable force chips away at their children's natural sense of self-esteem.

Suddenly, their children are shyer and less sure of themselves. What happened?

In my book *Nurturing Good Children Now: 10 Basic Skills to Protect and Strengthen Your Child's Core Self* is a chapter called "Passion." In that chapter, I write that the world in which we live almost guarantees that children will drift away from not only their family but their natural bents and interests as well. Instead, they are drawn toward peer groups and the pursuit of popular culture. The result is a weakening of children's sense of themselves.

Parents' inclination is to counter these forces by becoming better listeners, doling out positive discipline, and heaping on constant praise—"Good job," we say, or "Nice work." While these actions are all essential to nurturing self-esteem, in my thousands of conversations with parents and children all around the country, I have found that the children who have developed self-esteem from the inside out are those whose parents have helped their youngsters find, select, and nurture a passion.

I call them passions, but you could just as easily call them interests or hobbies. Regardless, they are incredibly powerful antidotes to the popular culture pull felt by most children. And they are something I encourage the families I work with to pursue.

Pursuing a deep-seated passion builds areas of strength such as delay of gratification and the ability to focus and tolerate frustration. Passions give children something to share with their parents. It helps them learn to read and to pay attention to detail. It also strengthens character. What's more, children with passions often have less of a need to acquire materialistic things. That need is fulfilled via the knowledge that they have something else—something more important—inside.

What's surprising about passions is that too few parents try to find and nurture their own children's, despite the fact that it doesn't require specialized expertise or take much time or money. It simply requires guidance to avoid pitfalls, prevent becoming overwhelmed, and keep children focused on what truly interests them. This book contains a road map for finding and nurturing your child's interests, which is why I encourage all parents to pay attention to what's on these pages.

—Dr. Ron Taffel

Preface

A byproduct of having children is a heightened awareness of the goings-on of other children. Three years into my son's life it became painfully apparent that few children possess deep-seated interests—a fascination with kites, for example, or falcons, or anything having to do with the *Titanic*.

Being a writer, I did what comes naturally. I interviewed educators and child experts, all of whom agreed with my observation that few children today have strong passions. They also pointed out that deep-seated interests provide children numerous benefits, including the experience of losing yourself to the all-too-rare pursuit of a passion in a moment of quiet downtime.

Going to the source, I talked to children who have interests, as well as to their parents. What I learned is that children acquire their interests in different ways, but once interests "take," children make them their own. In doing so, these children acquire a strong sense of self, mastery, and wonder.

We can learn a lot from these families, as well as from child experts who have devoted their professional lives to putting the spotlight on childhood interests.

It's for those parents who want to find the one special interest that excites and fascinates their child that I've written this book.

My deepest and most sincere thanks to the parents and children who took the time to answer my seemingly unending questions as I poked into the minutest details of their interests. Like many families whose children possess strong interests, these families believed in the power of this book to unlock the special interest that lies within every child.

Special thanks to those adults who recognize the importance that interests have played in their lives and who seek to pass that excitement along to others: Cindy Ross for proving children are never too young to enjoy the great outdoors; Sharon Lovejoy for planting the gardening seed in young children; Kevin Nierman for molding young students into artists; Richard Starr for smoothing out the bumps for his woodworking students; and Neil Johnson for providing a framework for children interested in photography.

Thanks, too, to my literary agent, Meredith Bernstein, for believing in this project, and to my editor, Ann LaFarge for her brutally honest answers to my questions.

And for my patient husband who endured two years of a paper-strewn office and undecorated house, and our dear son, Avery, whose passion for drawing imaginary creatures brings him comfort and joy.

CHILD'S PLAY

1

High Interest Rates

Monty's first and most vivid childhood memory is sitting on the back of a horse. Martha recalls flipping through seed catalogs with her father. Eldrick wasn't walking when he was introduced to golf.

Besides their notoriety, these three individuals—Monty Roberts, Martha Stewart, and Eldrick "Tiger" Woods, respectively—have something else in common, something few people would not find admirable: a deep love for a particular interest cultivated and nurtured by a loving, engaged parent.

Consider what Roberts writes in his book *The Man Who Listens to Horses* (Random House, 1997):

> I was not like other toddlers, lifted onto a saddle as a diversion or so that a photograph might be snapped. I sat on a horse in the crook of my mother's arm for many hours at a time, while she gave riding lessons at the horse facility where she and my father lived. The feel of leather reins and horsehair, the sound of a horse blowing, the smell of fresh

1

hay and horse lather: my senses first stirred in the world of horses.

Stewart dedicates her book *Entertaining* (Clarkson Potter, 1982), in part, to "My father, for instilling in me a love of all things beautiful." She expands on that thought in *Martha Stewart's Gardening: Month by Month* (Clarkson Potter, 1991), where she acknowledges her father for being "my first teacher of gardening." Her strongest childhood memories, she writes, are of planting seeds indoors with her father and poring over seed catalogs.

And though Woods may not recall sitting in a high-chair watching his father practice his swing, his father does. In *Playing Through: Straight Talk on Hard Work, Big Dreams and Adventures With Tiger* (HarperCollins, 1998), Tiger's father, Earl Woods, writes:

"At six months, Tiger would sit in his high chair in the garage as [I] would practice [my] swing, hitting it into a net.

"From the very start, he was fascinated—he had an incredible attention span of almost two hours, and he never took his eyes off me."

The parents of these three individuals shared something with their children that cannot be bought in a store, can't be learned in a day or a week or a month, and isn't relentlessly promoted during television commercial breaks. These parents shared their time, knowledge, and passions, and as a result passed on their interests so their children could also enjoy them.

As a result of being exposed at an early age to a particular interest, all three individuals embraced their respective interests and grew up to excel at them. The stories behind how their interests were nurtured are as fascinating as the extent to which they have excelled within their fields of interest.

THE GIFT THAT KEEPS ON GIVING

What adult isn't stopped in her tracks at the sight of a child immersed in an interest, whether it's a fascination with stargazing or a love of woodworking or an attraction to all things having to do with insects? We pause, stop and stare in wonder and awe—a refreshing change from observing children sitting transfixed and impassive before a TV screen. When a birthday or holiday rolls around, we readily purchase a gift geared toward the child's interest in the hope that we, too, can be part of the nurturing process.

That's because the older we get, the more we value interests. Rarely do you hear adults say they wished their parents had never encouraged them to embrace an interest. More often it's the reverse case. A familiar refrain goes something like this: "I wish my parents had insisted I continue my guitar lessons." Or "My father makes furniture. I wish I had spent more time with him in his workshop so I could make furniture like he did." Or "My mother is from France, but I never learned the language and rarely visited the country. I should be traveling there with my children and teaching them to speak French."

Our fascination with children who pursue interests and our regrets at having never persevered with our own are so powerful and compelling that more adults are turning their backs on those who say these dreamers are too old to pursue an interest. "What? You're going to take piano lessons, at your age?" they ask incredulously, more out of envy that you're doing something constructive for yourself than out of concern you won't accomplish what you've set out to do. You say you're not planning to become a virtuoso. You're doing it because it brings you a sense of fulfillment and you just plain enjoy it.

INTEREST-RELATED FACT

More adults have taken the better-late-than-never approach to interests, creating a booming adult-education industry. Consider Elderhostel, which offers programs throughout the world for those ages 55 and older who wish to pursue college degrees or explore interests ranging from aviation to furniture making to nature photography. Elderhostel has grown from one educational site and 200 attendees in 1975 to more than 2,000 educational centers with a quarter million attendees.

Adults are also turning to interests to balance their work lives. The trend has prompted workers to request condensed work-weeks that would allow them time to pursue their passions. As part of my work as a business writer, I interviewed the president of a recruiting company. I asked her to describe the benefits companies could offer that would attract the best employees. Without hesitation, she told me, "I have a stack of résumés from experienced people willing to leave their jobs if I can find them a company that offers a four-day, ten-hour-per-day workweek."

INTEREST-RELATED FACT

Pursuing interests later in life is not only enjoyable but healthy. A study conducted by two groups of neurologists from University Hospitals of Cleveland and Case Western Reserve University, both in Cleveland, Ohio, found that people who remain active outside of work by taking up such activities as painting, gardening, or playing a musical instrument are three times less likely to develop Alzheimer's disease as they age than their more intellectually passive peers.

THE TRICKLE-DOWN EFFECT

The focus on pursuing interests later in life is having a trickle-down effect. If pursuing an interest makes me feel so good about myself, the thinking goes, then it would be equally advantageous for my child to pursue an interest.

Parents want for their children what they themselves didn't have. In this case, it's instilling a lifelong love of a particular interest. But beyond the personal satisfaction derived from pursuing interests, consider these additional reasons many parents have for wanting to help their children discover an interest:

• *Pursuing an interest is a slow process.* Nurturing an interest is a process that stands in stark contrast to our fast-paced lives. It offers a haven from the demands of homework, errands, and school or day care. Pursuing an interest enables us to sit back and concentrate on one thing.

• *Children left to their own devices wind up with some less-than-inspiring interests.* Wondering if I could pick up tips on how parents share interests with their children, I visited various parenting web sites. In each site, I performed a search using the keywords "interests," "hobbies," and "activities." What I got back was shocking, and spoke volumes on the state of interests among children and teenagers.

Many sites contained messages from parents concerned about their children's lack of interests. A typical message went like this: "My ten-year-old son shows no real interest in acquiring proficiencies outside of computer games and socializing."

Another site contained a forum on which young people could post information about themselves, including their interests. One young teen wrote that his "favorite activities" included watching television, socializing, and playing computer games. And this wasn't just one instance of a teenager with downright uninteresting interests. This was the norm.

Looking on the bright side, you could say that the above-mentioned teen had—or at least thought he had—interests. Many children don't have any, and by now we know all too well what children who have no interests do. We read about young teens resorting to vandalism all in the name of "boredom" and of having nothing better to do than hang out at the mall.

• *Pursuing interests enhances learning.* It's been said that the pursuit of an interest results in a complete education. A child interested in rock climbing continually tries to find out more about his hobby, and thus develops reading and research skills. He searches for new places to climb, polishing his map-reading skills. He explores nature and learns about the environment. He figures out how pulleys work; thus physics plays a role. His interest compels him to seek information from experts, developing his social skills.

The link between interests and learning has long been acknowledged by developmental theorists. American philosopher John Dewey (1859–1952) believed in gearing educational content to individual interests. And Swiss psychologist Jean Piaget (1896–1980) asserted that all learning rests on interests.

INTEREST-RELATED FACT

Interests fall halfway between play and work, noted developmental theorist Anna Freud (1895–1982), the youngest of Sigmund and Martha Freud's six children. Like play, interests are pleasurable and relatively pressure-free; like work, they require cognitive and social skills, including planning, delay of gratification, and exchanging information with others.

HIGH GRADES FROM EDUCATORS

Acknowledging the positive benefits attributed to pursuing interests, many educators have woven interest-based learning into their curriculums.

Home-schooling parents have long used interests to guide learning. Instead of marching to the beat of a conventional curriculum, they incorporate into their studies texts and courses that focus on their children's natural talents and curiosities. So Sheila's love of underwater creatures is incorporated into her English studies, and Alexander's fascination with ships becomes the basis of a geography lesson. Chris writes reports on subjects of his choosing, such as his latest on Mongolia. Sara can put aside her math book to step outside and crush rocks to see what's inside.

Gifted-child organizations have also endorsed the notion that interests have a place in academia. To that end, they advocate programs that train teachers to nurture the interests of all students, from the learning-disabled to the gifted. The theory is that by weaving students' interests into the curriculum, children who master their schoolwork faster than their classroom counterparts remain excited about learning.

"We can say, 'Okay, you've accomplished what you need to do in half the time of other students, so what else do you want to do? What interests you?' " asks Sally Reis, president of the National Association for Gifted Children, Washington, D.C., and professor of educational psychology at the University of Connecticut, in Storrs, Connecticut.

However, a scarcity of resources coupled with a singular emphasis on developing basic skills makes this all but impossible in most educational systems. "Prescribed standards and high-stakes testing are driving interest-based learning out of the curriculum," says Dr. Joseph S. Renzulli, director of the National Research Center on the Gifted and Talented at the University of Connecticut. "The kinds of learning that are engaging, efficient and enjoyable—what I call the three E's of education—are being held hostage to the kinds of trends going on."

Fueled by the focus on standardized testing, many parents have themselves become engulfed in a kind of academic teaching frenzy. "Too often I see parents more interested in cramming content than in developing interests," says Reis. "Rather than buy your kids phonics books and books on math and reading, take your kids to a museum or read to them on a broad range of subjects."

If a book or new experience sparks an interest, embrace it, say educators, regardless of how unconventional or trivial it may appear. When Reis's daughter Julie developed a fascination with all things having to do with the *Titanic,* several years before the feature film on that fateful ship hit movie screens, Reis encouraged it. "If I weren't in the education field," she notes, "I'd be saying, 'Why not do something else?' But because I know what I know, I offer to purchase a kit with actual photocopies of *Titanic* documents."

AN INTERESTING TREND

Interests lend themselves nicely to a trend in which parents are trying to regain some of the time they've lost to schools and outside activities.

Some parents have successfully lobbied principals to cut the generous amounts of homework allocated each weeknight. Parents United for Sane Homework, a group of parents and educators, strives to give parents a say in the amount of homework their elementary-school children receive. Founder Daria Doering writes on the group's website, www.sanehomework.com: "I do have several deep and everlasting academic regrets from my childhood, but they do not involve lack of homework! My regrets are that I didn't persevere with music lessons, and that I didn't study as many languages as possible, as early as possible. I am sure that the abilities to play music beautifully and to speak foreign languages fluently would bring me great pleasure, if I possessed them."

Other groups have sought to reclaim family time by scaling back on after-school activities. Putting Family First is one such group. Based in Wayzata, Minnesota, the grass-roots organization jump-started a national movement in 2000 in which families were asked to scale back on outside activities, television, and the Internet in order to spend more time on family-oriented activities. The group's web site is www.puttingfamilyfirst.us.

My town took up the challenge and declared March 27, 2001, Family Night—a night to pursue family activities. The problem was that many eager participants didn't know how to go about doing this. In fact, the woman behind the idea found herself fielding calls from parents worried about what to plan for that night.

It seemed we'd forgotten how to pursue activities with members of our own families. We've become used to relaxing by ourselves with our noses in a newspaper or book. We're comfortable zipping around town to scheduled events, but aside from watching television, what is there to do as a family?

Pursuing interests is an ideal way to fill this time. By their very nature, interests draw parents in like few academic subjects or extracurricular activities. Unlike homework, interests don't pigeonhole parents into the role of a supervisor whose job it is to make sure the work gets done. Unlike extracurricular activities, interests don't relegate parents to the role of sideline observer.

When it comes to helping children pursue their interests, parents play a key role, but it's one that most parents aren't accustomed to playing. When it comes to interests, parents play the role of listener and supporter; children play the role of teacher, instructor, and coach. Not surprisingly, this role reversal may make some parents uncomfortable and many children absolutely exuberant.

What the interest is and how it's pursued spring from the child. As one twelve-year-old boy said when his mother asked him what she had done right in nurturing his interests as well as those of his younger brother: "You never pressured us. . . . You always backed us up."

Think about that the next time your child explains the intricacies of birds' nests for the umpteenth time. The smart parent listens as though hearing about the topic for the first time, then asks questions. What *is* the difference between a blue jay's nest and a star ling's nest? Where do sparrows nest again? What materials could we leave outside to encourage birds to build nests near our home?

THE PUSHY PARENT SYNDROME

Early in my son's life, it became clear that if I didn't try to help cultivate his interests, he stood a good chance of ending up with such "hobbies" as watching TV and playing computer games. Not that he wasn't intelligent enough to pursue an interest. The process just wasn't happening on its own.

INTEREST-RELATED FACT

In *Nurturing Good Children Now*, Dr. Ron Taffel lists interests, or what he calls "passions," as one of the ten basic skills children need to protect and strengthen their core selves. However, he writes, "Over the twenty years I've been in practice, young children seem to be having a harder time developing special interests beyond what the pop culture spoon-feeds them. This is a worrisome and potentially dangerous trend."

I tried to spark my son's interests beyond current fads by sharing my own passions with him. But that didn't work. I realized this when one day he brought home a Mother's Day card he had made in preschool. It contained the incomplete statement "For fun my Mommy . . ." followed by the child's response to the statement. In my son's case, he said, "likes to go to restaurants." I was taken aback. Besides the fact that I'd rather cook than eat out, he didn't mention my writing, or the fact that I'm a black belt in karate. Why didn't he mention that I take horseback riding lessons or that I golf and garden?

I tried to arouse his interests in the martial arts, golf, and gardening. (At his age, horseback riding seemed a tad risky.) And while I wasn't expecting him to take naturally to any of them, I thought he might take a liking to one of them. But I wasn't having any success. Should I simply allow my child's interests to develop naturally? By overseeing his interests, am I not pushing him into areas he might not necessarily want to go?

Apparently I wasn't the only parent with these concerns. "I have a ten-year-old daughter and an eight-year-old son," wrote one woman on a parenting website. "They are great kids and do well in school. My problem is that I am trying to find an outside activity for each of them, but they refuse to do anything I suggest. I'm not a pushy parent and will not force them to join something they don't want to, but I see other kids involved in outside activities, and I think this is important."

Another parent on a different site asked: "How much should we push our son to be involved in extracurricular activities?"

Some parents push their children in many directions in the hope that their youngsters will "take" to something. All too often, however, these parents end up asking themselves the all-too-common question, "I expose my child to everything, so why doesn't he have any interests?"

Some parents push to make up for their own parents' lack of pushiness. A friend of mine recalled, "I always loved fashion, but it never occurred to my mother to help me pursue that interest. Now my sister and I find ourselves pushing our kids into every extracurricular activity, even though we know it's overkill."

Some parents push to satisfy their own unrealized aspirations. For example, Amy has always enjoyed cooking, but was never able to fulfill her dream of attending the Culinary Institute of America, then graduating to become head chef of a four-star restaurant. Therefore, she'll fulfill her dream through her child, forcing him to cook alongside her.

There's also the oft-told story of the father who, having never fulfilled his dream of playing on a professional sports team, enrolls his son in every available sport. Or consider the parent who wants his child to excel at sports in order to obtain a college scholarship—despite the finding that less than one percent of the children participating in organized sports will qualify for a college athletic scholarship, according to the National Center for Education Statistics, Washington, D.C.

Pursuing interests isn't about registering a child for the extracurricular activity of the season. Sure, take your child to a soccer game and ask her if she'd like to join a team. But don't sign her up for the sake of signing her up.

In fact, put interests before extracurricular activities. Rather than encouraging your child to join activities he may or may not like, take the time to learn what excites him, then find an interest that relates to it and pursue it together. It's all about building a passion that will last a lifetime, not a season.

Finding a child's passion requires a large expenditure of time. But the time spent exposing your child to different interests isn't wasted if the exercise reinforces in the child the pleasure that springs from pursuing a passion. If you take the time to find your child's interests, you'll never have to push. In fact, if you succeed in finding your child's passion, he'll be the one pushing you to help him pursue it.

DISCUSSING DOWNTIME

Children spend long days in day care or school. Some have hours of homework every week night, and some spend entire weekends being shuttled to soccer games and other organized sports. Do children really need yet another distraction? Another activity to take away whatever little downtime they have?

Sure, kids need downtime. Time to relax, without the television blaring. But by the same token, it would be a shame to let valuable time go to waste that could be used to pursue an interest that will provide lifelong enjoyment. Besides, how many children enjoy quality downtime—downtime intended to allow them to mellow out, to catch their breath from their busy day? Oftentimes, they wind up watching television or hanging out with friends.

A child who has an interest can pursue it in her downtime. Reading a book about collecting dolls, thinking about how a rocket works, and swinging a golf club are forms of quiet time. And, certainly, a child has to think about something during moments of quiet time. Why not an interest?

And consider this. If parents don't play a lead role in helping to uncover their children's interests, peers or marketers will. By allowing your child to watch TV, aren't you letting marketers shape your child's interests?

In fact, some toy manufacturers would have you believe that finding an interest is as easy as purchasing one of their products. Toy stores have been replaced by "knowledge" and "brainy" stores. There are entire stores that focus solely on science and nature activities for youngsters. Toys are marketed as "activity kits," "developmental tools," and "interactive opportunities." It's enough to make a reasonable parent believe that pursuing an interest is as easy as buying a kit or book, that the child's interests will be magically sparked by the product, which will lead to a lifelong fascination with that interest.

Despite your good intentions, the rocket kit that cost an arm and a leg didn't turn your child into a budding rocket scientist. The bug-catching kit failed to instill a love of nature. In fact, you scolded your child when you saw him using the kit to tote around his collection of small plastic dinosaurs.

Against your better judgment, you become annoyed as the child loses interest in the toy. You glance at the box the toy came in and wonder why your child never approached the excitement of the children pictured on the box, hunched over the kit, all smiles. You vow never to buy another toy until the child learns to appreciate what he has.

Then reality sets in. You realize that the kits, books, and software programs geared toward specific interests won't cultivate interests. You may even wonder whether these toys leave children less interested not only in the toy but in their parents as well.

Some children wear their interests on their sleeve. You've probably heard of a child who takes to an interest with barely a nudge, who out of nowhere develops a love for a particular hobby. For example, the child who picks up a musical instrument and seemingly never puts it down. The child who goes to an aquarium and goes on to major in ocean biology. The child who bakes with his mother and grows up to be a pastry chef.

But these instances are few and far between. For most children, finding an interest is a long-term process and requires a parent who knows the difference between "pushing" and "guiding." It's wrong to push a child into an activity because it'll keep him busy and other children are doing it. Rather, take the time to assess your child's interests, then guide her toward them. In other words, find the interest first. Later on you can find a group related to it.

OF INTEREST

When Jane Goodall, British conservationist, chimpanzee expert and journalist, was four, her family reported her as missing, only to discover later that she had spent hours crouched in the straw observing how a hen lays an egg. When the child returned home, her mother didn't scold her. She could see the joy in her daughter's face; she sat her down and listened to her story. Years later, Goodall's mother was one of her most ardent supporters when her daughter left for Africa.

FROM TOTS TO TEENS

As I write this chapter, I glance out my kitchen window on a Saturday afternoon and see my neighbor's teenage son assisting a carpenter who had done work at the boy's house, and is now working next door. In the five years since moving into my house, I'd never seen the teenager pick up a hammer, much less spend a day carrying around wood and observing a master carpenter. It turns out he was intrigued enough—and not too shy—to ask if he could help.

The anecdote highlights two important points. One, teenagers are as likely to harbor interests as young children. In fact, in many ways it's easier to explore the topic with a teen than with a five-year-old. Two, interests often reveal themselves in subtle ways. As parents, we must always be on the lookout for budding interests, especially in children who seemingly have none. Everyone harbors interests; some people just need more help finding them.

When I was a sophomore in high school, my father took me to a facility in Hoboken, New Jersey, to have me tested for IQ, abilities, and interests. While he was at it, he decided to have my younger sister tested too. His reasoning for such a move was motivated by a concern that college was fast approaching, and his daughters had little idea of what majors they wanted to pursue. He told us he was more than happy to pay our tuition, but he wanted us to study something we liked, could excel at, and could support ourselves with. I remember him saying "You can major in basket weaving, but you should enjoy it and be good enough at it to earn a living from it."

After a weekend of testing, we waited anxiously for the results. When they came in, we found nothing too surprising—in my case, that is. I was of average intelligence and showed strong interest in art, music, literature, and noncompetitive sports. I would do well to major in English or journalism and would more than likely enjoy pursuing a career in those areas. It was partly as a result of the testing that I majored in journalism and gravitated toward the martial arts, eventually earning a black belt in karate and writing a book for women interested in studying the sport.

My sister, on the other hand, tested differently. She was highly intelligent. In fact, the tester stated that she would excel at almost anything she pursued. However, she had no strong interests and didn't know in what areas to focus.

The good news is that there are ways to uncover children's interests, even among those youngsters who don't seem to have any. By taking the time to tap into your child's interests, you'll experience some of the most exciting, fun-filled and satisfying times together. Talk about quality time! Your child will cherish it long into adulthood.

Interests Move to the Fore

- Many adults have come to appreciate the gratification and personal growth associated with pursuing interests. As a result, more adults are pursuing their own.
- The popularity of interests among adults is having a trickle-down effect, with more parents wanting to help find and nurture their own children's interests.
- Many children today categorize as "interests" such activities as socializing, watching television, and playing computer games.
- Developmental theorists have long acknowledged that interests enhance learning.
- Home-schooling parents and gifted-child educators routinely weave their students' interests into the curriculum.
- Regardless of how unconventional an interest may appear, if it sparks a child's passion, it's worth pursuing.
- Seeking more quality time with their children, many parents are calling for less homework and fewer after-school activities. Pursuing interests is an ideal way to fill this newfound time.
- Pursuing interests appeals to children because they select the

interest and determine how to pursue it. It's the parent's role to listen to and support the child.

- For most children, finding an interest is a long-term process that requires a parent who knows the difference between "pushing" a child into an area she doesn't want to go into and "guiding" a child toward areas about which she's passionate.

• Words of Wisdom •

Whether they're called interests or passions, many prominent people have had nothing but positive—and sometimes humorous—things to say about them. Consider the following:

"A passionate interest in what you do is the secret of enjoying life, perhaps even the secret of a long life; whether it is helping old people or children or making cheese or growing earthworms."

—Julia Child (1912–), chef, author

"One thing life has taught me: if you are interested, you never have to look for new interests. They come to you. When you are genuinely interested in one thing, it will always lead to something else."

—Eleanor Roosevelt (1884–1962), lecturer, newspaper columnist, world traveler, wife of Franklin Roosevelt

"A man will fight harder for his interests than for his rights."

—Napoleon Bonaparte (1769–1821), French general, emperor

*"My personal hobbies are reading, listening to music, and si-
lence."*
                              —Dame Edith Sitwell (1887–1964),
                              English poet

"A hobby a day keeps the doldrums away."
                              —Phyllis McGinley (1905–1978),
                              American poet, author

*"The most powerful thing you can do for kids is get them
into something interesting, help them imagine a life doing interesting things. Those are the life-transforming experiences."*
                    —Deborah Meier, acclaimed educator and a
                    MacArthur Foundation Fellowship winner
                    who has opened schools in some of the toughest
                    neighborhoods of New York and Massachusetts

*"Three passions, simple but overwhelmingly strong, have
governed my life: the longing for love, the search for knowledge, and unbearable pity for the suffering of mankind."*
                         —Bertrand Russell (1872–1970),
                         British philosopher, mathematician, social critic, writer

*"When literature becomes too intellectual—when it begins to
ignore the passions, the emotions—it becomes sterile, silly,
and actually without substance."*
                              —Isaac Bashevis Singer (1904–1991),
                              Nobel Prize–winning author

*"Every man without passions has within him no principle of
action, nor motive to act."*
                              —Claude A. Helvetius (1715–1771),
                              French philosopher

"Before he sets out, the traveler must possess fixed interests and facilities to be served by travel."

—George Santayana (1863–1952),
American philosopher, poet

"Judge of thine improvement, not by what thou speakest or writest, but by the firmness of thy mind, and the government of thy passions and affections."

—Thomas Fuller (1608–1661),
English clergyman, author

"He who reigns within himself, and rules his passions, desires and fears, is more than a king."

—John Milton (1608–1674),
English poet, scholar

" 'Know thyself,' said the old philosopher, 'improve thyself,' saith the new. Our great object in time is not to waste our passions and gifts on the things external that we must leave behind, but that we cultivate within us all that we can carry into the eternal progress beyond."

—Edward George Bulwer-Lytton (1803–1873),
English author, politician

2

Stop, Look, and Listen

When her son Thomas was six, Marci checked out from her local library the audiocassette "Sing 'N Learn Chinese: Introduce Chinese with Favorite Children's Songs."

"My husband travels to China for business, and when Thomas was five, he had brought him back a board book containing pictures and the Chinese symbols for those pictures.

"Thomas loved that book," she continues. "So when I saw the tape at the library, I thought, Maybe he'd like to learn some Chinese songs."

Thomas was immediately transfixed by the tunes, which included familiar melodies as well as native children's songs from China. "I'd play them in the car, and we'd sing them together," says Marci.

When Thomas was in first grade, he asked his mother if he could have a play date with Jie, a Chinese student in his class who spoke little English. "Thomas would point to objects in the house and ask Jie to say the Chinese word for them," says Marci. "Then he'd get his book and practice the words with Jie."

Thinking Thomas might enjoy experiencing Chinese culture, the family drove to Chinatown in New York City, an hour's drive from their home. "Thomas was fascinated by the people, food, and scenery," says Marci.

Though materials were few and far between, Marci did manage to find a book called *At the Beach,* which introduces children to ten Mandarin Chinese characters. Thomas would take a black crayon and try to draw the characters.

"Like most kids his age, Thomas was prone to moving from one thing to another fairly quickly, so I thought he'd soon grow tired of this one," says Marci.

To her surprise, however, he didn't. After searching for additional outlets for her son, Marci discovered a children's summer program for learning Chinese. It would mean an hour's drive each way once a week. But if he was willing to do it, so was she.

After his first class, he was hooked.

Thomas came home from class one day and announced that he wanted to go to China. Marci and her husband Rob are planning to take him when he turns ten.

EXPOSE, THEN OBSERVE

According to interest-development specialists, Marci and Rob were astute on two counts. One, they took advantage of the fact that Rob visited China and exposed their son to the country via a Chinese language book for children. And, two, they recognized Thomas's interest and built on it.

"Adults should expose their children to many opportunities, people and places, then observe how the child responds to those events and opportunities," says Dr. Ann McGreevy, enrichment coordinator with the Pentucket Regional Schools, West Newbury, Massachusetts, and professor of education at the former Notre Dame College, in Manchester, New Hampshire.

HANDS-ON IDEA

When exposing your child to new experiences outside the home, keep the event focused. Nature centers, community theaters, and local historic places of interest tend to have fewer distractions than temporary museum exhibits, which attract crowds, and children's museums, whose myriad offerings prevent children from concentrating on any one station. Places that promote their gift shops as much as their main attractions also detract from children's attention and require greater planning to keep the focus on the real reason for the trip.

Had Marci simply asked Thomas if he'd like to pursue Chinese, he might have said no, not fully understanding what it is. "You can ask children what interests them, and you probably should," says McGreevy. "But you also want to observe them. Who do they choose as friends? What do they spend time doing? What toys pique their interest? Such choices determine interests."

Observing children requires little more than time and an eye for discerning how they communicate beyond the obvious. Young children communicate through their eyes, the quality of their voices, their body postures, gestures, and mannerisms. Older children communicate in more subtle ways. In either case, you are your child's most accurate judge and are in a unique position to observe your child's interests. Following are starting points for observing your child·

Observe Play

My former home is located on a dead-end street where on any given sunny Saturday some eight children ages two-and-a-half to eight play together. Watching them is like viewing a Norman Rockwell painting come to life.

Five-year-old Emily has been riding a two-wheeler since she was three. She rides so fast it scares her parents. She scales walls and stands in a wagon as it's pulled by a running child. It strikes me that she might harbor an interest in gymnastics.

Sean, six, is so in love with baseball you'd think his mitt was sewn onto his hand. He's seemingly always wearing it, tossing the ball into the air, then catching it. Offer to pitch him the ball and his eyes light up. Beyond his obvious interest in baseball, where else could it lead? Baseball-card collecting? An interest in the history of the game? In the science behind a curve ball?

Note, too, how children play outside their home environments. Whenever nine-year-old Sarah visits her grandmother, she makes a beeline to the basement. She spends hours there looking for old objects. Noticing her daughter's interest, Sarah's mother bought her a children's book on archaeology. As a result, Sarah has expressed a desire to learn about Native American artifacts.

HANDS-ON IDEA

Explore your child's interests by discussing current events: special occasions, such as the Olympics and presidential elections; scientific discoveries, such as the unearthing of dinosaur bones, the discovery of a sunken ship or new photos of space; and even obituaries. When Fats Waller died, Clint Eastwood's mother bought him several of the musician's records, sparking her son's lifelong love of jazz.

Observe the Use of Materials

Play materials can help children transform feelings into action. Whether they are toys, blocks, sand, paint, clay, wood, paper, crayons, or pencils, materials help children to exhibit their interests.

Noticing that his six-year-old son Chris enjoyed playing with toy soldiers and marching throughout the house banging on a toy drum, Clark took him to some historic reenactments. Chris became so enchanted by the rat-a-tat-tat of the snare drum that he learned to play the instrument. Today, the twelve-year-old is a member of a foot militia and has participated in more than a hundred historical reenactments.

HANDS-ON IDEA

Shoe-box-size plastic storage containers have become ubiquitous in many households with children. Instead of using them to store the usual assortment of toys and fast-food giveaways, fill them with materials your child enjoys or things your child has yet to explore. One mother fills her child's boxes with postcards, stickers, pompoms, ribbons, and objects found in nature. Every so often she adds something new.

Julie likes to make palm-sized books from scraps of paper and tape. She then draws pictures inside to create a story that she reads to her dolls. Robert enjoys designing and drawing inventions. He hoards scraps of wood and pieces of fabric, saving them for future projects. Brian digs for clay in his backyard. Emma makes daisy chains from flowers she picks.

Learn to value the materials your child cherishes. One mother said to me, "Sam is always bringing home things he finds outside—rocks, feathers, bugs. I throw them away when he's not looking." Perhaps a better idea would be to help Sam pursue his interest in natural objects by helping him to organize and identify them.

HANDS-ON IDEA

Make your home a place where interests naturally develop. One parent set up a table in her den for the express purpose of allowing her children to work on their favorite projects.

Observe Relationships with Adults

Children often favor certain adults over others. Note whom your child is fond of and ask her why. My uncle used to give me high-quality art paper, blank canvas, colored pencils, and pastels, and he'd talk to me about art. He was married to an artist, which to me seemed elegant. He was the reason I started oil painting lessons.

Jessica's interest in her Native American background is encouraged and nurtured by her mother, grandmother, and uncle. The ten-year-old's beadwork designs are incorporated into fire bags, which were traditionally used to hold flint and other materials for starting a fire. She exhibits them with her mother and grandmother. She is also an accomplished powwow dancer, and once performed a traditional dance with her uncle at her school.

HANDS-ON IDEA

When purchasing stamps at the post office, avoid buying routine flag stamps. Allow your child to choose from among the latest subjects issued. Beyond the obvious interest in stamp collecting, your child may become intrigued with the subject of a particular stamp.

Think about the hobbies and interests of the adults you know. Tell your child about them and see if they spark an interest. If Aunt Karen took up dancing later in life, tell your child. If she shows interest, perhaps she could observe her aunt in a class. If Uncle Jim enjoys kayakking, tell your child. Perhaps he'd like to accompany his uncle on a short, simple ride.

Listen to Comments

Besides observing children, be attentive to how they perceive their world. Listen to their observations about what they view on television or overhear in conversations between adults, as well as their responses to the thoughts and feelings of others. An interest may lie hidden in a casual comment such as "I didn't know moss could grow on a rock" or a question such as "How fast can a car go?"

HANDS-ON IDEA

Children with interests are natural learners. Awaken your child's sense of learning by asking questions. One mother interviewed for this book remarked that during family car trips she would ask her children such questions as "Why is the word 'ambulance' written backward on that vehicle?" or "Why are there reflective dots in between the lanes?" Such questioning awakens children to a sense of learning that is intuitive and natural.

Ceramics artist and teacher Kevin Nierman says he's impressed with parents who, when they see that their child is interested in working with clay, take the initiative to get the child involved in the art. Each week, Nierman's Kids 'N' Clay Pottery Studio, in Berkeley, California, draws some 200 students, ages five to eighteen.

"They'll say, 'My five-year-old is asking to learn the potter's wheel,' " he says. "I ask, 'Where did she get the idea? How does she know what a potter's wheel is?' They honestly don't know. Often the child will have seen it on television, or they do one thing at school, and they love it."

In the same vein, listen to what others have to say about your child. One mother noted that she had never taken seriously her daughter's fascination with board games. Then one day her daughter's kindergarten teacher commented, "Paulina designed a board game that she and Brian played together. Has she done this before?" The comment inspired the mother to help her daughter invent such games at home.

And don't hesitate to offer your own observations. When my son's friend Matthew came over for a play date, the two of them drew. I was impressed with Matthew's detailed drawing of a machine he'd invented that moved heavy objects, and made a point of showing it to his mother.

Observe Routines

Watch your child's behavior during such routines as cleanup, eating, and dressing. Note specific abilities such as tying shoes. If Scott enjoys tying fancy knots with his shoelaces, introduce him to the art of knot tying. Maybe Jillian enjoyed reading a science-fiction book. Consider introducing her to astronomy.

Note when your child changes routines. I always assumed that bedtime meant reading time. That assumption was proved wrong when my son suggested we alternate with other activities such as making up games, using flash cards, and drawing.

HANDS-ON IDEA

Remove the predictability from routines. One parent occasionally asks her young son what nearby places of interest he'd like to pass on his way to school. His choices have ranged from the train station, a construction site, the high school, the hospital, and a stream.

Note, too, when children become too caught up in their routines. Judith Pellettieri's son was bright, eager to please, did all his homework, and got straight A's. "But he was turning into a schoolhouse gifted child with no sense of self," she says.

As principal of Simonds Elementary School, in New Hampshire, Pellettieri is an unlikely advocate of home schooling. But when she realized that her son "was not finding his passions," she pulled him out of public school and home-schooled him through the sixth grade and part of seventh grade.

Pellettieri wanted her son to have the time to pursue what he wanted—and he did. "He would pedal his bike to a pond and have lunch," she says of his home-schooling experience. "He started charting a blue heron's eating habits." The experience had such a profound effect on him that upon applying to Middlebury College, in Vermont, he wrote his college essay on his year spent home-schooling. He is now studying for his Ph.D. in microbiology at Johns Hopkins University, in Baltimore, Maryland.

Interestingly, Pellettieri also home-schooled her three other sons throughout parts of their education. One studied gymnastics until he was twelve years old. Another started playing the violin at age five and today majors in music at Loyola Marymount University, in Los Angeles. "All my sons developed a work ethic, passion, and a love of learning," she says of their home-schooling experience, adding that "It's not about what you're going to be when you grow up."

Pellettieri stresses parents' roles in fostering their children's passions. "I've seen too many parents handing their child over with blind faith to a kindergarten teacher," she says. "Parents are their children's first teachers."

Pellettieri's home-schooling experience was so positive that she encourages parents to do the same. "By sixth grade, every kid should be able to say, 'I'm good at this.' If that takes parents pulling their child out of school for a year to sail around the world, I say more power to them."

RECORDING INTERESTS

Interests develop slowly, change course, and sometimes disappear altogether. By recording interests, you keep them alive, track their progression, and encourage the pursuit of additional interests.

I tried using a notebook to track my son's interests. The effort was sporadic at best. Also, because he was too young to record his own interests, the activity became a one-sided event. But even among children who can write, I would wager that few have the patience and discipline to keep an interest journal. Fortunately, there is a tool, designed by gifted-child educators, that involves both parents and children and isn't limited to jotting down observations and ideas in a blank notepad. It's called a total talent portfolio.

A total talent portfolio is nothing more than a compilation of information that reflects a child's strengths and interests. It can be as simple as a letter-size manila folder or as elaborate as an artist's portfolio containing pages with plastic sleeves to protect its contents.

At Southeast Elementary School, in Mansfield Center, Connecticut, a total talent portfolio consists of a 9½-by-11-inch folder with eight sturdy pages each containing a pocket to insert papers. Students decorate their portfolios and store in them papers related to the subjects they like, listings of extracurricular activities, descriptions of hobbies and collections, drawings, awards, photos, and even computer disks. An original poem, a letter to the editor of a newspaper, and a collection of information on sea turtles are all fodder for a talent portfolio.

HANDS-ON IDEA

If your child's school doesn't explore students' interests, find classmates or neighborhood children who have hobbies. Then expose your child to those people, regardless of their ages. Younger children are often impressed by older children who practice an interest.

Your child's home talent portfolio might also contain your comments based on your observations—how your child likes to play, with whom he plays, the materials he uses. If your child is older, note her remarks. If she has set a goal for herself, note it— "I want to create a fashion design and enter it into a contest" or "I want to join the swim team at the Y." Observe the steps your child has taken to accomplish her goal.

I purchased a twenty-five-cent pocket folder in bright red to store my son's drawings of imaginary creatures. It soon became stuffed, so I purchased a clear plastic storage bin for his works. It's kept beneath his bed where it's always in plain view, and has come in handy as his creatures have taken on a three-dimensional proportion in the form of clay.

Susan Irvine, the enrichment teacher at Southeast Elementary, notes that she's seen more parents doing something similar to the talent portfolio at home. "When we first started using talent folders, students with the thickest folders were the ones who didn't do this at home," she says. "Those whose portfolios weren't so thick didn't need to collect this information, because it was already being collected at home."

In addition to enabling parents to see patterns develop, a portfolio can revive an interest that's stalled. When your daughter expresses frustration with her interest, you can whip out the portfolio. You might choose to spend this time with your child complimenting her on the progress she's made or suggesting related interests.

"MY BOOK OF THINGS AND STUFF"

While a portfolio is great for tracking current interests, more formalized tools are useful for uncovering untapped interests. One such tool for sorting through interests is "My Book of Things and Stuff: An Interest Questionnaire for Young Children."*

The sixty-page workbook contains about fifty questions, and is targeted to children ages six through eleven. I posed the questions in it to my five-year-old. The questions help children explore their passions and discover their "learning styles," or the method by which they best master concepts. For example, if your child is interested in bats, knowing that she likes to listen to CDs or tapes and work with other people might lead you to have her invite a playmate over and allow them to listen to an audiobook of a story about a family of bats.

"The questions contribute a foundation of parents' understanding of their children's bents and interests," says Dr. Ann McGreevy, the workbook's author. "There's enough in there that could act as a catalyst for discussion for parents and children to get to know each other better."

---

*Ordering information can be found in the Resources section.

FIVE TIPS FOR INQUIRING MINDS

"My Book of Things and Stuff" prompts parents and children to think about subjects and activities they may never have considered. Most important, it encourages parents to ask substantive questions and turns the table on the typical parent/child relationship in which children do all the asking and parents become numb to their young one's questions.

It takes a while to get the hang of using the workbook. To avoid making the same mistakes I made, consider the following five suggestions. If you don't plan to use the book, read this section anyway. You'll pick up pointers on asking interest-related questions, including the kinds of questions to ask, how to phrase them to suit your child, and the best time to ask them.

1. Use the approach that's right for your child. I approached my son with the workbook after lunch one day. We sat at the kitchen table and got through exactly two questions before he wanted absolutely nothing to do with it. That night, I brought it out and suggested we go through it instead of reading books. Nothing doing. By the next day, the mere sight of the book turned him off.

"Don't sit down and try to do the workbook at one time," says Susan Griggs, talent development coordinator and enrichment specialist for Westerly Public Schools, in Westerly, Rhode Island.

Griggs, who has administered the workbook to students and trains teachers to use it, also recommends discussing the book with your child. "Children should know why you're using the book," she says. "Tell them it's not a test, but something to find out about their uniqueness."

Even if you don't use the workbook, it's important to approach the topic of interests slowly and gradually. You won't learn all there is to know about your child's interests in one sitting, and your child probably won't sit still long enough to listen. At first you might explain what interests are and why they're important. Later you might describe your own interests.

Reasoning that my son would probably continue to resist sitting down with the workbook even after I explained to him the value of doing so, I took a different approach. I began taking the book with me when I picked him up from preschool. On the way home I'd ask him about his day, then weave a workbook question into the conversation.

One day his school hosted a visitor from Africa who discussed his country and culture. On the way home from school I said, "That was very special, having someone come to your school. If you could invite anyone to your school to be a teacher for one day, who would you invite?" "Someone who could talk about insects," he replied. Now we were getting somewhere.

2. Move beyond the usual line of questioning. Because the workbook is geared toward teachers, some of the questions need to be rephrased to make them relevant to parents. For example, instead of "Do you collect anything?" ask, "What would you like to collect?" Instead of "Are you a member of any special group, club, or team?" ask, "What special group, club, or team would you like to join?"

Also, build on the questions. For example, ask the workbook question "Pretend you could invite any person you wanted to be a teacher in your class for one day. Who would you invite? Why?" Then offer a modified version of the question: "Pretend you could invite someone you never met before for a play date. Who would you invite, and what could that person teach you?" Likewise, ask the workbook question "Pretend that you are in charge of a class field trip. Where would you go?" Then ask your own version of that question: "If you could go anywhere for a day with Mom or Dad, where would we go? Why?"

As you work your way through the book, you'll move beyond the questioning rut in which parents often find themselves. Instead of "What did you learn in school today?"—a question so many parents automatically ask their youngsters—you might follow it up with "What would you like to study at school?" or "What was the best thing you learned at school today?" Perhaps Paulina studied caves, but what she'd really like to learn about is how crystals are formed inside those caves.

In the car, at bedtime, meal times, putting on shoes, ask your child an interest-related question: "What's your favorite color? Why?" "Do you know how birds fly? Do you care?" One morning I asked my son, if he could be any animal, what would it be? "A bat, a black panther, or a red panda," he replied. Though not an obvious insight into a specific interest, his answer provided interesting food for thought.

3. Roll with the conversation. Trying to keep a five- or six-year-old's conversation on track is like trying to make a beeline with your child to the restroom in a toy store. But that's fine, because using the workbook is not about giving concrete answers to questions but about opening up a conversation.

You might ask the question "Do you like doing science experiments?" But the conversation stemming from that question might end with a discussion about your child's desire to perform in a play—maybe in the role of a scientist.

4. Make the questions age-appropriate. The workbook gets children to think outside their usual thought processes. But some of the questions are over their heads. This would explain my son's response to several of the questions: "I don't know."

In some cases, he couldn't respond because he had never before pondered the questions—he'd never considered the best thing that ever happened to him or the kinds of games he enjoys. (All the more reason to ask these kinds of questions.) In other instances, he didn't understand time frames that involved his entire—albeit short—life or questions dealing with different "types" of books. "What's a type of book?" he asked.

The realization that my son wasn't prepared to answer some of the questions prompted me to phrase them in more age-appropriate ways. Instead of asking him to describe the best thing that *ever* happened to him, I asked, "What was the best thing that happened to you *today?*" Instead of asking him to describe the kinds of books he enjoys, I asked him to select his favorite book from five types—one describing animal habitats, another chronicling a boy's adventure, and others focusing on poetry, artists, and insects.

5. *Look for general interest patterns.* By the time I'd completed the workbook, I had a lot of leads but had not uncovered any specific interests. It was then that I realized I had only touched the tip of the interest iceberg.

It's possible to find specific interests by using the workbook. However, I didn't. So I did what interest-development experts recommend. I looked for general patterns of interest that fall into basic educational categories, such as performing arts, creative writing, math, business, athletics, history, social action, fine arts and crafts, science, and technology.

General patterns are a good guide for parents whose children profess to have no interests. If you can squeeze no more out of Nathan than that he might possibly like to pursue science as an interest, then you've accomplished something. Or perhaps Maria has so many interests that organizing them into categories would enable you both to determine which area holds her greatest interest.

Once you've established general interest patterns, move to specific ones. If there's an interest in science, try narrowing it down to a specific area, such as biology, astronomy, or geology. The focus might spark an interest in an even more specialized area, such as the science of the natural world, which in turn might lead to a focus on frogs. An interest in geography might unlock an interest in travel, which might lead to a desire to collect stamps with a focus on Australia. An interest in drawing might lead to a focus on colorful pastel drawings depicting local scenes.

From the workbook, I discovered that my son's interests fell into four categories slightly more specific than the previously mentioned general categories: animals, music, drawing, and photography. He loved learning about animals, specifically insects, reptiles, and dogs; listening to a variety of music; drawing "monsters" that possessed special powers; and taking photographs.

Once you have an idea of your child's interests, consider ways to pursue them. Some of the ways to pursue my son's interests include visiting farms, the zoo, and the Museum of Natural History; growing butterflies from caterpillars; attending free concerts held every summer in a nearby park; allowing him to shoot his own roll of film; and creating books about his imaginary monsters.

QUESTIONNAIRES FOR OLDER CHILDREN

Though "My Book of Things and Stuff" is said to be appropriate for children age six to eleven, older children in that range may do better with an interest questionnaire designed more specifically for them. Developed by gifted-child educator Joseph S. Renzulli, the "Interest-a-Lyzer" is geared toward students in grades four through eight. For high school students, there's the "Secondary Interest-a-Lyzer." Here are some of the questions:

> "Imagine you have the time and the money to collect anything you wanted. What would you collect?"
> —from the "Interest-a-Lyzer" for students in grades four through eight

> "Imagine that you have become a famous author of a well-known book. What is the general subject of your book?"
> —from the "Interest-a-Lyzer" for students in grades four through eight

> "You are a photographer and you have one picture left to take on your roll of film. What will it be of? Why?"
> —from the "Secondary Interest-a-Lyzer" for students in grades nine through twelve

> "You have written your first book, which you are ready to submit for publication. What is the title? What is the book about?"
> —from the "Secondary Interest-a-Lyzer" for students in grades nine through twelve

For students in grades K through three, there's the "Primary Interest-a-Lyzer," which is slightly more advanced than "My Book of Things and Stuff." For children with an artistic bent, check out the "Art Interest-a-Lyzer" for elementary and middle school students and the "Primary Art Interest-a-Lyzer" for younger children. Both explore painting, drawing, photography, sculpture, printmaking, commercial art, and art history.

Like "My Book of Things and Stuff," these products are targeted to teachers; unlike "My Book of Things and Stuff," they are not sold individually but in sets of thirty. For young children, I'd recommend "My Book of Things and Stuff," which is half the price of one set of "Interest-a-Lyzers." For older children, consider paying the thirty dollars for the product if you feel you need something to get started. You can always donate the unused questionnaires to your child's teacher for use in the classroom.*

A Little Interest Goes a Long Way

Susan Irvine, the enrichment teacher at Southeast Elementary School, has been administering the "Interest-a-Lyzer" to third- and fourth-grade students for six years. She also uses the "Primary Interest-a-Lyzer," allowing her fourth-graders to pair up with kindergarten students to complete them. A fourth-grader reads the question to the kindergarten student, explains it, then writes in the answer. Parents can adopt this method, allowing their older children to administer the questionnaire to younger siblings.

Acknowledging that the tool reveals interests that parents may already know about, Irvine says she does, however, occasionally find something that surprises even parents. "Sometimes a student has never heard of a particular topic, then hears about it in the 'Interest-a-Lyzer,' " she says. "In the same way that we're finding out interests students may only show at home, the opposite is true—that parents find interests only explored at school or interests that nobody had considered before. One student found an interest in drama and started a drama club."

She adds: "Even if you find a little interest, it can go a long way."

*See the Resources section for ordering information.

Asking interest-related questions and documenting the responses also plants the interest bug, and shows your child that you value interests. Maybe you'll hear nothing about it for weeks. Then, out of the blue, your daughter will say, "Remember when you asked me what I'd like to do with you? I know now. I want to fly a kite and learn how it stays up in the air."

Irvine notes that parents who complete a workbook should show it (with the child's permission) to their child's teacher if the school doesn't use these books. "If a parent were to bring in a completed 'Interest-a-Lyzer,' that would be great," she says. "It would change how the teacher first approaches a child—knowing she takes horseback riding lessons and has won awards, or that he is a scout. It would get them off to a good start."

As your child begins to realize what interests are, why they're important, and that he is master of selecting his own (or at least he should be), you'll start to focus on specific interests. Once my five-year-old could absorb the notion that his father and mother were once children, he became curious about what we did as kids. As he realized that he, too, could have interests, a light bulb went off in his head. Not only were interests now on the table for discussion, they were ready to be acted upon.

What You Need to Know About Awakening Your Child's Interests

- Expose your child to new experiences.
- Observe how your child plays, selects, and uses materials, relates with adults, comments on her world, and modifies routines to accommodate her interests.
- Make a joint project out of recording your child's interests, using something as simple as folders or as elaborate as an artist's portfolio.
- Professionally designed interest questionnaires enable children and parents to discover interests they may never have considered. The questionnaires are available for children in preschool through high school.
- Explain to your child what interests are, why they're impor-

tant, and what interests *you*. Then gradually work your way into discussing interests your child would like to pursue.

- Without overwhelming your child, make asking interest-related questions part of your everyday conversation. Think of ways to rephrase typical questions—such as "How was school today?"—to give them interest-related slants; for example, "What was the most interesting thing you learned in school today?"

- When discussing interests, roll with the conversation. Your child will naturally lead you to areas of interest.

- If your interest-related questions draw blank stares, rephrase what you asked in terms your child can understand.

- If no specific interests emerge from your efforts, look for patterns of interest that fall into general categories, such as performing arts, creative writing, math, business, athletics, history, social action, fine arts and crafts, science, and technology.

- Whether you and your child record interests using a portfolio or an interest questionnaire, or both, share your findings with your child's teacher—but first get your child's permission.

• *Birds of a Feather* •

It's six o'clock on a fall Saturday morning in northern California. Ken is behind the wheel of his truck. Fast asleep in the backseat is his young daughter Meghan.

"She'd wake up, and I'd have a roll or something and she'd have breakfast," says Ken. "Then she'd fly hawks with me and my friends."

These excursions, which took place from October through the end of February over some ten years, were instrumental in developing Meghan's interest in falconry, a medieval sport in which falcons are trained to hunt small game.

Beyond that, however, was a genuine passion for the sport. "The falcons have always been a part of her life, but she's also al-

ways had a great interest in them," says Ken. "I have a friend who's into horses, and has horses, and his daughter could not care less about horses."

For Meghan, the best thing about falconry is "the fact that you get to do something that most people can't," she says. "Not everyone can have a falcon, and even if they could, they wouldn't know what to do with it."

Flying High in School

By the time Meghan was in first grade, she was giving falconry demonstrations in grammar schools. "She's had this falcon, Chaz, since she was six," says her father, who officially owns the bird. "She'll fly him in gymnasiums and outside."

(In California, a person may not own a falcon until the age of fourteen, at which point she can apply for an apprenticeship by taking a written test administered by the California Fish and Game Department. Upon passing the test, she may study with a licensed falconer for two years, at which point she becomes a licensed falconer.)

By the time Meghan was ten, she was lecturing with her father and flying her bird before a class of ornithology students at the University of California, Davis. "They knew me," says Ken. "I showed up with Meghan, and she had her bird. Now we go twice a year."

In addition, father and daughter have given demonstrations during a raptor identification class at a community college where her father teaches in the theater arts department.

At the age of eight, Meghan competed in the state's falconry club competition in which her bird was the only falcon to catch a pigeon—an accomplishment that didn't go over well with her competitors.

"They allowed her to do it, and after she and her bird did so well, they were very upset about it," says Ken. "We're talking about big boys serious about their toys. They said, 'She's not a legal falconer . . . and therefore, she cannot be awarded a prize.'"

Two weeks later, Meghan received a framed line drawing of a peregrine falcon in flight from the man who had organized the meet. "He recognized that what they had done was wrong," says Ken. "But he had gotten so much pressure from the other adult men [that he couldn't award her a plaque]."

Though the experience dampened Meghan's enthusiasm for competing, she still occasionally participates in events sponsored by the California Hawking Club. "I flew Chaz at the mini-meet we had a couple months ago," she says. "We got second place in one event and third place in another."

Other Interests

Today, foureen-year-old Meghan still flies her bird and occasionally competes. However, other interests are taking up her attention.

"It's just being in eighth grade—boys, school work, gymnastics, volleyball, the orchestra," says Ken.

In the past couple of years, too, the social aspect of the sport has lost its aura. "Her friends used to come out and fly with us, but getting up early and going out in the field and hunting is an unfeminine thing," says Ken. "So when the girls got older, they kind of go, 'Well, that's Meghan, and she does that with her dad. Yeah, Meghan's the bird girl.' "

Still, according to Meghan, falconry is something she will always practice in one way or another. "I don't think I'll ever not want to do it," she says. "There'll probably be times when I won't be able to, like if I can't have a bird if I'm living at college. But whenever I can, I probably will."

Still Enthusiastic

While the social aspect of her interest may have slowed down, Meghan's enthusiasm for the sport has not. She remains "excited" about taking her apprentice test, which assesses falconers' ability to recognize different types of raptors, as well as their knowledge of regulations, training, and medical requirements.

She's also incorporated her interest into her school work. She wrote a report on her sport and keeps a jar of feathers her falcon *has shed. "One year I did a science project with them to see if he lost the same feathers at the same time every year," she says.*

As an offshoot to falconry, Meghan and her father raise pheasants, and have been given permission to release them on property where they can fly their birds. "She does ninety percent of the raising of those pheasants," says Ken. "She collects eggs every morning and puts them in the incubators and handles all the babies when they hatch."

And while her school friends may not find her interest as exciting as they once did, through her father's participation in the sport Meghan has found others who do.

As a master falconer, Ken assists two apprentices. One is fifteen and lives a five-hour drive away with her parents and their horses. "Laurel comes down for three or four days, and we do falconry," says Ken. "Then I take Meghan to Laurel's house for a week or so, and they ride horses."

Aside from the demonstrations, competitions and the state apprentice test are the essential day-to-day responsibilities associated with caring for a living creature. "We have to feed him every day, and I try to fly him at least three times a week," says Meghan. "Sometimes we let him fly around the house downstairs.

"It's something you do every day, like walking your dog," she adds. "It's just a normal thing to do."

3

Choosing an Interest

Dan loves to play guitar, and he and his wife Jennifer often have music playing in the house. So it was only natural when their son Tyler was born that they would continue their musical routines.

Beyond being surrounded by music, young Tyler seemed to truly enjoy it. Music made him stop crying, and at as young as five months he was content to sit by his father and watch him play guitar.

At sixteen months, Tyler got his own guitar—a four-stringer the same color as his father's Martin. "You should have seen the look on Tyler's face," says Jennifer. "He takes that thing everywhere."

Tyler especially enjoyed using the instrument the way his father does, copying how Dan props his against the wall and trying to play like his father. "Dan was sitting on the couch playing something," says Jennifer. "Tyler got his guitar, sat in his little chair opposite of where his dad was, and was trying to play exactly how his dad was playing."

Now two, Tyler's interest is still strong. "I understand that pretty much all children, especially his age, love music and most of them dance every time they hear music," says his mother. "But not very many of them have a blast in a guitar shop, going around to every guitar and saying, 'Gar!' "

In addition to visiting guitar stores, Tyler tries to tune his guitar with his father's electronic tuner, stores his guitar in its case, and gets frustrated because his guitar doesn't have a cord to plug into the amp. His continued interest has earned him a larger, six-string guitar.

"We don't have to make an extra effort to encourage Tyler because music is always around him," says Jennifer. "For him, I think, it is just a natural part of life."

Nevertheless, Jennifer and Dan are taking steps to ensure that Tyler's interest continues. "In a few months, Dan will start trying to teach Tyler specifics on the guitar," says Jennifer. "He is a very independent boy, though, and he likes to figure things out for himself, so it will be interesting to see how he progresses."

JUST DO IT!

For Jennifer and Dan, nurturing their child's interest felt natural. It wasn't forced. There were no pressures. Tyler will grow up with music a natural part of his life. He'll think it odd when he visits a friend's house where music isn't playing and musical instruments aren't visible.

Jennifer and Dan took the bull by the horns and began the process. They weren't afraid of making a wrong decision. They didn't wait until their son could verbally tell them whether he wanted to pursue the guitar. They saw an opportunity and seized it.

Perhaps Tyler will develop a lifelong love of the guitar. Maybe he'll focus on classical playing or blues. Then again, perhaps he'll develop an interest in a nonmusical area. Such a switch will require flexibility and understanding on the part of his parents. Nevertheless, the experience of sharing an interest together as a family gives everyone something special to remember from that period of their lives.

INTEREST-RELATED FACT

Choosing an interest is like driving a car with no particular destination. You continually shift gears. There are lots of twists and turns in the road. You try different places, and you leave them for new destinations. It's a journey with no pressures and lots of pit stops.

THREE WAYS TO CHOOSE AN INTEREST

Jennifer and Dan are typical of many parents who want to pass along their own interest to their child. In fact, about half the children I interviewed adopted their parents' interest in one form or another.

Other children I interviewed gravitated toward an interest unrelated to anything their parents do. In some cases, it is almost like a calling. In others, it's the result of exposure to a particular event or activity.

For some children, however, finding an interest isn't so straightforward. Just remember that it's there nonetheless. Lurking beneath these children is an interest waiting to captivate their young minds. Helping them find their interests requires time and effort, but the undertaking is immensely rewarding. What's more, starting with a so-called clean slate has its advantages.

Let's explore three means of choosing an interest. Doing so will provide ideas for helping your child find an interest.

THE PASSION STEMS FROM THE PARENTS

Parents who introduce their children to their own interests often do so for two reasons: They enjoy the interest so much they want to pass that joy along to their child; and they can't imagine not pursuing the interest, or pursuing it less, because they have children.

"Gardening is such a passion for us I can't see how our kids can ever be completely removed from it," says Kris, who gardens with her husband Peter and two children, Cole, eleven, and Lily, eight, on seven acres of land.

Cindy Ross and her husband Todd Gladfelter are so passionate about backpacking they have involved their two children, Sierra, twelve, and Bryce, ten, since they were infants. "We're doing it because we love it and it makes us happy and we can't live any other way," says Cindy. "But it turned into something that we don't want to do without them now because they bring so much more joy into it and a different perspective."

She adds: "Plus, they have come to realize that they need it to be happy too, on some level."

In both instances it would have been easier, on physical and mental levels, to exclude the youngsters. Kris could have sat her young children in front of the television while she and her husband gardened. Or perhaps they could have taken shifts, one gardening while the other watched the children. Cindy Ross could have arranged for her children to stay with relatives or friends while she and her husband enjoyed a week of quiet, uninterrupted backpacking.

But neither did. And there are lots of other parents who take it upon themselves to coach their children in their interests—a massive undertaking that requires countless hours, plenty of patience, hard-to-find resources, and creativity.

Ross spent so much time nurturing her children's interest in backpacking that she compiled her experiences, as well as those of other parents who pursue the outdoors with their children, into a book, *Kids in the Wild: A Family Guide to Outdoor Recreation* (The Mountaineers Books, 1995).

"You wonder if the work involved will be daunting and, frankly, worth it," she writes in the book. "But you love it out there, you don't want to abandon your outdoor sports that you participated in before parenthood, and you really would like to know ways to share it with your children and have them come to love the outdoors too."

Going to Great Lengths

To backpack successfully with their young ones, Ross and her husband planned trips around Sierra and Bryce. Their philosophy: Make sure the children associate backpacking with pleasure, not discomfort and unhappiness.

That means singing songs when you're tired, allowing the children to play in the dirt, and ensuring they're well rested, fed, and comfortable. It means lugging their favorite toys (and surprise ones, too) into the woods and keeping the children from getting on each other's nerves. It also means seeing to their needs first, before setting up camp, and allowing them to "help" break camp when you'd rather they let you do it more quickly and more efficiently.

Ross's hard work paid off. "When our first child was three months old and the spring caused the sap to rise in our blood, we decided to just try it," she writes. "It was a great first experience and we just kept on building on it until it was second nature to bring them along. The older they become, the easier they are to deal with in the wilds, and the more they contribute."

Second Nature

A child who adopts one parent's or both parents' interest grows up with a natural affinity for it. In fact, such a child might even feel somewhat lost without it.

A parent's interest doesn't have to be as big as the great outdoors or as all-consuming as Ken and his daughter Meghan's interest in falconry. It can be as small as a poem or a song.

Susan always had a fondness for Mercutio's Queen Mab speech from Shakespeare's *Romeo and Juliet,* so for her it was only natural to recite it often as her baby grew into toddler-hood. "I think that speech is utterly enchanting for all ages," says Susan. "In fact, my daughter Julie loves it as much as I do."

HANDS-ON IDEA

The nice thing about helping your child pursue your interest is that *you* know lots about it. You can answer your daughter's questions. You can give your son hands-on help. You can also weave it into your family's routine.

Early on in the process, however, look for opportunities for your child to shine. Note when she observes something you've never noticed or teaches you something new pertaining to the interest. Also, insert chances for her to demonstrate her mastery. Then heap on the praise and encouragement.

In Another Direction

Don't be surprised if your child takes your interest and runs in a different direction with it. Though Julie, now thirteen, grew to love Shakespeare's poems and plays, she eventually transitioned into acting. "She's very clear about wanting to differentiate herself from her mom," says Susan.

It's common for children exposed to their parents' interests to adopt a related, albeit different, one—whether out of a need to distinguish themselves from their parents or because it just better matches their personalities. Taking tangents allows parents to remain involved, yet lets children be independent.

Like their parents, Cole and his sister Lilly love to garden. But both children have developed additional, related passions. Cole studies birds; Lily writes poems based on her observations of the natural world.

And though Sierra likes to backpack, she has gravitated toward other outdoor activities, including horseback riding and fly-fishing. "Anytime we were near water, she was out there with a net or a cup trying to catch minnows," says Ross. "We went canoeing, and she was out there with her net as soon as we stopped. It didn't matter if she was starving—she was out there catching these minnows. I said, 'All right, we're going to learn to fish.' "

Practice What You Once Preached

If you no longer practice your interest, revive it to see if your child has a passion for it.

My husband majored in music and once made a living as a musician. Although he's given it up except for playing the piano once in a while, he uses his experience to see what aspect of music would interest our son. He checks listings for musical events, and purchases a variety of CD titles to play at home and in the car. When our son was five, my husband encouraged him to write words to a song that my husband put to music.

THE INTEREST IS APPARENT

When Linda was starting a new business, she attended a trade show designed to help entrepreneurs advertise their products and services to the public. While there, her five-year-old daughter, Hillary, wandered off and was eventually found playing on a potter's wheel at a booth featuring a ceramics teacher who had opened a studio for children.

That auspicious event sparked an eleven-year passion. Sixteen-year-old Hillary continues to study with the same teacher she met at the trade show, and has never grown tired of working with clay on a potter's wheel. "I love to do it," she says simply.

Fortunately, Linda was in the right place at the right time. Though Hillary fell into her interest by accident, the situation vividly illustrates that interests lurk in odd places and awaken our children's curiosity when we least expect it.

Worth mentioning, too, is the fact that Linda didn't dismiss her child's interest. All too often, despite an obvious interest, parents doubt their children's ability to know what they want or what is good for them. Ten-year-old Bryan loved to act, but his parents felt he would be better off participating in an activity with neighborhood children. "We live in an area that's into sports," says his mother, Judy. "We made him join a baseball team."

The experience had Bryan "pleading not to do it again," says Judy. "We said, 'This is sad. He needs something to reinforce his self-esteem.' So we put him in acting because that's what interested him."

Hillary's inkling of an interest could have been squashed on the spot. But her mother acted on her daughter's enthusiasm. She followed up. She took the logical and correct step of enrolling Hillary in the teacher's school.

HANDS-ON IDEA

It's natural to think of hobbies in broad terms such as gardening, model railroading, kite flying. But within these and most other hobbies lie many sub-hobbies. Finding these niches allows parents to zero in on the aspect of the interest that most appeals to their child.

Within kite flying, for example, there's single-, dual- and quad-line kites; miniature kites; flat kites; bowed kites; and box kites. There's kite surfing and kite buggying, in which a kite is used for propulsion and the driver steers the buggy with her feet. The history of kites and artwork found on them are yet other areas that appeal to enthusiasts.

Photography is incredibly versatile, says Neil Johnson, author of *National Geographic Photography Guide for Kids.* "You can go in any direction with it—as art, as travel, to help you remember or to communicate to a friend," he says. "There's a million things you can do with photography that kids are going to take whatever they are interested in and use."

Subtle Signs

Not every interest is as obvious as Hillary's. Some are subtle and require sensitive, perceptive parents to bring out.

Kris and Peter noticed that their seven-year-old son Cole enjoyed watching the birds in the backyard as well as those at the feeders at his grandmother's house. "We thought, 'He likes birds,' " says Kris. "But he never at that early age came out and said, 'Hey, I love birds.' "

Kris and Peter recognized a subtle interest and went to work on bringing it out. How they and other parents help their children pursue interests is detailed in chapters 6 and 7.

For now, remember that there are no mistakes in the interest-development process. If something doesn't work, you simply move on. The trick is to know you can take any broad interest in a hundred directions. With any luck, the two of you will make enough twists and turns that you'll find something your child loves.

Eight-year-old Sean used to pick up pieces of bark that molted from the large sycamore tree in his yard. He'd use the pieces to dig, hold small rocks. He'd also float them in his sister's kiddie pool, pretending they were a fleet of boats.

One day, his father took Sean on a guided canoe tour. During the ride, the guide noted how Native Americans in the area would make canoes, containers, fans, utensils, and archer's armguards from birchbark. That comment sparked Sean's passion for studying the art and history behind these artifacts.

HANDS-ON IDEA

When choosing interests, consider your child's favorite activities, then brainstorm interests related to them.

Ever since he was young enough to splash in the bathtub, seven-year-old Matthew loved water. His mother will fill the kitchen sink with it, add bubble bath and allow him to play in it with his action figures. He washes them, imagines them swimming in the ocean, and fills cups with the liquid, then pours it over them.

Perhaps Matthew would like to build a water rocket with a parent or a model sailboat he could float in a pond. Maybe he'd like to collect pond water and analyze it under a microscope for microorganisms, start a water garden, go canoeing, collect rainwater for the garden, or study life that exists in and around water. The possibilities are endless.

THE INTEREST ISN'T OBVIOUS

Oh, sure, easy for those parents, you say. What about me? I did the Interest-a-Lyzer with my child, and I still can't find an interest.

What makes it even more frustrating is that it's probably true that inside every child lies an interest waiting to be released. Not being able to bring it out can be hard, but that shouldn't deter you from continually trying. It won't be time wasted.

Take the bold and beautiful step and choose the interest yourself. Pursue something that overlaps an area you enjoy and that coincides with your child's natural abilities and preferences.

Even an interest that you wouldn't think would appeal to your child can be made appealing. For example, you like to garden, but imagine your son never would. The trick is to incorporate activities into the interest that appeal to your son. Perhaps he'd like to make compost from a worm box or grow produce to sell.

In her book *Sunflower Houses: A Book for Children and Their Grown-Ups* (Workman Publishing, 1991), author Sharon Lovejoy offers numerous ways to make gardening enjoyable to children, including how to make an enclosure out of giant sunflowers and morning glories with an opening for a doorway. "The kids have a natural play area, and it is a magical space for them," she says. "They may go in and lie there with their friends and giggle and dig in the soil."

Never hesitate to pursue an interest, because every interest is worth pursuing. The interest may evaporate in a week. That's okay. Then it's on to the next one, and the next and the next. Finding an interest may take years because it's a slow process. But, again, it's time well spent.

As you search for your child's interest, continue to expose her to different experiences. A cooking class at your local supermarket, an art education class at the community center, the opening of the children's plot at a botanical garden, a family hike sponsored by a local club. These one-shot experiences widen your child's horizons, and enable you to see hints of an interest.

Your child may balk at your efforts, but keep suggesting that she try something new. My son complained about having to see a play. Once he was seated and the performance had begun, however, he didn't want it to end.

Grab any opportunity to remove your child from her environment. Removing a child from his routines and surroundings allows interests to surface. Five-year-old Parthiv's fascination with flags from around the world stemmed in part from his exposure to them when his father's job brought the family to France for a year. "It was entirely accidental," says his mother Kalpana of her son's interest.

"On an average day in Paris, you see flags all over the place, especially on, say, Bastille Day," she says. "You'd see flags at the Arc de Triomphe and in our neighborhood, which was a diplomatic enclave. Flags were coming out of everywhere."

HANDS-ON IDEA

One of the best things to come out of children's publishing is the vast array of biographies and autobiographies. Read these books with your child. Then discuss the early interests those profiled in the books had as children. Doing so may coax your young one to consider adopting an interest.

Forget Age-Appropriate

Parents who share their own interests with their children often do so without thought to whether their children will be able to tackle the challenge.

Most children are capable of a lot more than parents give them credit for. Give them something to sink their teeth into, and they'll astound you with where they take it.

With that in mind, don't avoid interests considered beyond your child's age level. You'll be there to ensure your child's safety. Ken exposed his daughter to falconry when she was two, despite the fact that most states don't allow children to fly falcons alone until they are into their teen years. Hillary started wheel-throwing at the age of five, when most ceramics teachers wouldn't let such a young child near a potter's wheel. Eight-year-old Chris marched as a drummer in historic reenactments, although for reasons of safety and historical accuracy, such an honor is generally reserved for teenagers and adults.

The parents of these children didn't advise their young ones to wait until they were a little older to pursue their interest. They never said, "You're too young" (or "too small" or "too clumsy" or "too whatever"). These adults saw an opportunity to pursue an interest, and they ran with it.

HANDS-ON IDEA

An extracurricular activity can be a great starting point for developing an interest. If your child enjoys a particular activity, explore it in all its detail. Bring it into your home. Get involved. And research offshoots of it. If your child takes ballet, research other forms of dance, go to shows featuring dance, and read together about the history of dance, the costumes, and the music. Her interest may lie in one of these areas.

EXTRACURRICULAR ACTIVITIES

One of the challenges in writing this book was differentiating between interests and extracurricular activities. Is softball an interest or an extracurricular activity? What about dance lessons? Boy Scouts? Girl Scouts? While interests and extracurricular activities share many similarities, they differ in several important ways:

- Interests stem from an inner need to pursue them, and thus are intensely personal; for example, a child may like to play softball but *needs* to learn how some rocks become gems. In that sense, softball is an extracurricular activity; studying gems is an interest.

- Interests require greater one-on-one involvement from parents than extracurricular activities in which a parent's role is limited to cheerleader, observer, or coach to a team of children.

- Interests know no time frame. A child with a passion for gardening pursues it when the ground outside is frozen. She pores over seed catalogs, designs next year's garden, reads about famous gardens, and experiments with coaxing seeds to sprout indoors. A child interested in soccer studies the sport off-season, reading about its origins, contemplating the eye–foot coordination required to play, and collecting soccer memorabilia.

- Interests are typically (though not always) less structured than extracurricular activities, and thus give children greater freedom to choose when, and often where, to pursue them. The majority of extracurricular activities involve being at a particular place at a certain time.

   In some cases, extracurricular activities get in the way of the interest. "My daughter stopped dancing and Girl Scouts because she didn't have enough time to do what she wanted," says Cindy Ross, whose daughter's interest hinges on the natural world. "If that meant just walking outside or sitting on the hammock and reading a book, that's what she wanted to do."

- Interests involve a good deal of quiet downtime. A child may take weekly horseback riding lessons. But she may have crossed the threshold from extracurricular activity to interest when she devotes her free time to pursuing the activity— lying on her bed daydreaming about how a horse's mane ripples in the wind, sketching horses and reading about them.

- Interests tend to be explored in-depth. This requires a fair amount of time and resources, which consequently limits the number of interests to one or two. On the other hand, a child can easily pursue several extracurricular activities concurrently. The difference lies in the *depth* of knowledge and skills acquired with an interest versus the *breadth* of knowl-

edge and skills acquired pursuing several extracurricular activities. It's the difference between knowing a little about a
lot of things versus knowing a lot about one or two things.

Interestingly, this difference is something college admissions
officers take quite seriously. In fact, an April 1999 *Newsweek* article illustrates just how seriously some colleges value applicants
with deep-seated passions versus applicants with long lists of extracurricular activities.

When considering applicants, the University of Chicago looks
at the student's academic record *and* "range of experiences and
interests," according to the article. A student who begins high
school with low grades but shows consistent improvement and
also exhibits strong interests is more desirable than a student
with straight A's and no interests, or too many of them.

In fact, big city kids and their counterparts from small towns
are often more desirable to college and university admissions officers, according to the article. Children from large metropolitan
areas, it seems, are exposed to more, and aren't criticized by their
peers for cultivating interests. Small-town children may have less
to choose from, but choose they do, resulting in a smaller range
of interests, but greater focus within those interests.

In our effort to expose our children to many things, we often
lose sight of what interests them. Ask parents to list the activities
in which their children are involved, and they rattle them off with
no problem. Ask a parent what her child's interests are, and you
may get a blank stare in return.

Maybe Tim plays softball, but he cherishes the cactuses he
keeps in his room—a gift from a trip to Arizona. Perhaps he'd
like to learn more about succulents and desert life, but he's so
busy with other activities there's no time to explore that aspect of
his interests.

Certainly, an extracurricular activity can spark a long-term
passion. From the age of three, Katie took dance lessons. "She
taps sitting down," says her mother, Pat. "We've known for
a long time that this is her thing." What Pat didn't know early

on was that her daughter would sidestep mainstream forms of dance, including tap and jazz, in favor of a fast, precise form of dance with roots in Irish step dancing, known as clogging.

INTEREST-RELATED FACT

Many parents I spoke with indicated that their children's interests were things the youngsters have always done—although not to the degree they do now.

Cole always watched birds. Chris always loved playing a toy drum and marching. Katie always loved dancing. Their parents saw a glimmer of an interest and nurtured it into a passion.

Is there anything your child "always does"?

YOU'RE NOT CHOOSING A PROFESSION

The *Newsweek* article raises the issue: If colleges prefer applicants with strong interests, then it follows that I should choose an interest that will get my child into an elite college, earn her a scholarship, and perhaps even secure her financial future.

A child's interest can become such a big part of a family's life that the tendency is to put it on a pedestal and expect the world from it. That pressure is felt by children. So be extremely careful before suggesting your child's interest may one day earn her a scholarship or fame and fortune.

In fact, interests often have little to do with the path children's adult lives take. "I have had students who now have Ph.D.'s, are doctors and lawyers, and they all had early interests that were not related to their professions," says Sally Reis, president of the National Association for Gifted Children, Washington, D.C., and professor of educational psychology at the University of Connecticut, Storrs, Connecticut.

"To me, within a gifted population, early sustained interests is the single best predictor of success in life," she adds.

Though Reis's experience is limited to the gifted population, I believe her statement applies equally to all children. It's not the interest itself that matters; it's the act of pursuing it.

Certainly, it's natural for parents to ponder the possibility that their children will weave their interests into future plans. But in most cases, parents I spoke with are careful not to push that notion onto their children.

"We always thought, 'What's he going to be?' which is a dangerous thing," says one mother. "You don't want to set this course for them because they're so talented in this he's going to grow up to be X. It limits them in terms of what they want to do."

Adds the mother of two children, ages eight and eleven, with interests: "Who knows? Someday we may have two truck drivers. If that's what they want to do and can earn a living to support themselves, that's okay."

HANDS-ON IDEA

Interests often surface when parents diverge from routines. Instead of reading your child's favorite book over and over again, encourage her to memorize parts of it, pretend to be one of the characters in the story, or dream up a new ending.

POPULAR INTERESTS

If you're at a loss as to choosing an interest, consider a popular broad-based interest, such as gardening, fishing, bird watching, stamp collecting, genealogy, astronomy, or quilting. You'll use these as starting points, then research offshoots that even better suit your youngster.

Popular interests offer children lots of resources and the opportunity for social interaction. Indeed, some children are more comfortable pursuing an interest they know others in their age group are pursuing. That's where local stamp, cycling, science, theater, golf, and other clubs come in handy.

But perhaps there isn't a club in your area that caters to your child's interest. Or perhaps your child prefers to pursue the interest in the privacy of his own home, or is too young to join. (And you've already asked the club's adult leader if he'd consider waiving the age requirement to allow your child to participate.)

You may still be able to capture that club atmosphere by having your child join a junior division of an interest-related organization. In an effort to boost membership rosters, many organizations have added junior groups to their list of offerings. Young members benefit from pursuing their interest with like-minded peers; the organization benefits by grooming young members for adult membership. Among the junior divisions I came across:

- The Junior Philatelists of America is run by and for young stamp collectors under the age of seventeen. Members operate services; write for its publication, "The Philatelic Observer"; participate in study groups; serve on committees; and elect their own officers. Even if you don't join, check out the site to learn how to get started and avoid mistakes made by beginning stamp collectors.
  www.jpastampsl.org
- The American Numismatic Association is dedicated to the study and collection of money, including coins, tokens, medals, and paper currency. Its junior division offers young collectors a weekly e-mail newsletter on youth projects, upcoming events and activities, games and quizzes.
  www.money.org
- The National Wildlife Federation has three junior clubs—for elementary, middle, and high school students. Members receive a magazine or newsletter targeted to their age group, as well as opportunities to network and participate in environmental-related activities.
  www.nwf.org/kids
- The American Kennel Club offers children ages ten through eighteen the opportunity to compete with others of their own age in various club events—from junior showmanship

classes, where they are judged on how to present their dogs, to training and exhibiting their dogs in obedience, agility, and performance events. Junior members also receive a newsletter three times a year.
www.akc.org/dic/juniors/index.cfm

EMBRACE THE UNFAMILIAR

Many of us have a tendency to avoid those things with which we are unfamiliar. But don't steer your children away from interests you know nothing about. Stretch yourself, and embrace what you don't know.

The nice thing about interests is that they carry with them the opportunity to take us outside our often small worlds. "We didn't know anything about clogging before she started," says Pat of her twelve-year-old daughter Katie, who discovered clogging when a new dance instructor began giving lessons at the school she had been attending for six years.

Now Pat finds herself educating others. "There is a tremendous lack of knowledge about clogging in the general public, so I'm constantly explaining what it is that takes up so much of her time," she says.

Clark went from marching throughout the house with his young son Chris who'd bang on a toy drum, to marching together at live historical reenactments while he played fife and his son played the drum. Prior to that, "We'd never heard of reenactments," says Clark. "I had no interest or musical background. I taught myself to play the fife. I never knew these things existed."

QUIRKY IS OKAY

Your son has taken to painting rocks. Now that his bedroom is filled with them, he wants to display them throughout the house—on the kitchen windowsill, next to your Waterford crystal in your china cabinet. The interest you once labeled "cute" is now overwhelming you.

First, set rules as to where his rocks may be placed. Next to the crystal is unacceptable, but the kitchen windowsill is a possibility. Then get creative.

Find related activities that will expand his interest while limiting the growth of his collection. Would he like to paint a rock garden outside? Learn about cave painting at a museum? Read about artists who paint on such surfaces? What other natural surfaces might he like to use as a canvas?

Just as the adage goes, There are no dumb questions, so, too, there are no dumb interests. A fascination with mobiles, curiosity about how ponds function, and a desire to learn all there is to know about earthworms are all legitimate interests. The interest doesn't have to fit neatly into a familiar category stamped with society's seal of approval

Take your child's quirky interest and do a little research. You'll probably discover that it's not as quirky as you thought. Your research on mobiles reveals the name of the late artist Alexander Calder, world renowned for his mobiles. Maybe your daughter is on to something. You purchase books on Calder, and you research museums containing his works with the intention of taking your daughter to see them.

As you encourage your child's quirky interest, be sensitive to the fact that it may elicit wide eyes and "Oh, really's?" from less sensitive adults. To protect your child from unwanted comments, share the interest with carefully selected adults and children. Home-schooled children can pursue their interests without fear of their classmates criticizing them; most children cannot.

Quirky interests also have a way of becoming less acceptable as children mature. Pursuing falconry with her father was a novelty for Meghan throughout her elementary school years. "When she was young, they were curious and she was held special," says her father Ken, whose daughter is now fourteen.

"Seventh- and eighth-grade girls, and hawks and falcons—I don't see how it works in our world," he continues. "It's not fingernails and hair. I think she's had to deal with it as a freakish sort of thing. The last couple of years she's backed away from it socially."

Even young children can find it difficult to share their interest with peers. Four-year-old Kyle's love of history was something of little interest to most children his age. "I would take him to the park, and he would be playing on the toy train with another kid," says his mother, Terry. "I'd hear him saying to the kid, 'Do you like history?' The kid would look at him and say, 'What's that?' or 'Oh, sure,' obviously having no idea what it was. This was Kyle's way of finding out if he'd made a real friend. That was kind of sad."

It's even more difficult when children's interests are deemed inappropriate for their gender. Bryan loved to collect lots of items—toy trains, stamps, records. But it was his collection of dollhouse furniture that caused heads to turn. "He'd say the dollhouse collection was his sister's," says his mother Judy.

What's important, here, however, is that snide comments and rolling eyes didn't prevent these children from pursuing their interests. In some cases, the interest became a private passion shared only within the family.

In a way, these children are interest pioneers. By pursuing what they love despite criticism, they are breaking down barriers. The day cannot come too soon when people won't raise their eyebrows if a boy loves to quilt and a girl is passionate about rocketry.

Encourage your child's interest no matter how offbeat. After all, it's the act of having an interest, not the interest itself, that builds self-esteem.

A FAD AIN'T BAD

Despite your best efforts, your child's favorite interest is the latest fad. Don't worry. It's not necessarily bad.

My five-year-old son's interest in Pokemon had me concerned. Then I read about the fad's creator, Satoshi Tajiri. As a child, he collected insects and later used them as the basis for creating Pokemon characters.

When I told my son this his eyes widened. He started drawing his own creatures, which not surprisingly had insect appendages and characteristics. He'd ask me to draw my own creatures, and we would battle them on paper—just like Pokemon characters battle among each other.

Eventually, his interest in Pokemon lessened. But his interest in drawing didn't. Today he collects metal insects and continues to draw creatures with insectlike features.

HANDS-ON IDEA

Combining interests is a great way to funnel more time and energy into one pursuit. If Emily loves cats and enjoys watching her mother sew, why not combine the two? It's not as odd as you'd think. In fact, there are lots of people out there who love to create quilts featuring cats. You can find them at *www.catswhoquilt.com.*

HOW MANY?

Eight-year-old Lily gardens, writes poetry, and expresses a desire to become a veterinarian someday. She has her own twenty-by-twenty-foot garden plot, has had her poems published, and tries to diagnose her dog's illnesses using guides her parents purchased for her.

For now, that's fine. As she gets older, school work and extracurricular activities may start to invade on her free time, pushing her to make choices about the number of interests she can reasonably pursue.

Some children will pursue an additional interest related to the one they're already pursuing. In effect, they're maximizing the amount of time they can devote to interests. Lily writes poetry based on her observations of the natural world, which she experiences firsthand in her garden. Meghan hunts small game with her falcon, and also raises pheasants she releases in the wild for her bird to catch.

Julie has loved to act since she was a toddler. Her interest in writing was evident since second grade. Says her mother Susan "I think her interest in drama has led to her interest in creative writing: stories, plays and, just recently, a very funny stand-up comedy routine that she and a friend performed as emcees of the school's annual variety show."

HANDS-ON IDEA

Explore possible interests by reading with your child books you wouldn't typically read together, including reference and coffee-table books. These types of publications draw in young readers with eye-popping artwork and cover in detail narrow topics, which, after all, are what interests are all about. Better yet, they can be found at tremendous discount from such online booksellers as Daedalus Books (www.daedalus-books.com), BookcloseOuts (www.bookcloseouts.com), and On Art Bookstore (www.onart.com), to name just a few.

READ ALL ABOUT IT

Following a visit to a museum to view a collection of Egyptian artifacts, Terry and her three-and-a-half-year-old son Kyle strolled into the gift shop. "He spotted a book on ancient Egypt that he insisted on having," she says. "I said no. It was way too advanced for him—it was dense with lots of text and small pictures.

"Finally, I thought, 'He's always been interested in books. What the heck, he'll grow into it.' So I bought it," she continues. "He wanted us to read more and more from it all the time and never grew tired of it. He would play games pretending he was discovering King Tut's tomb."

Kyle's interest eventually branched out to encompass ancient Greece. "He wanted to read about Alexander the Great," says Terry. "I found myself reading a lot of biographies to him. I'd take him to the library when he was three and four, and he would head straight for the children's bio section. He'd say, 'Who's this?' and 'Who's this?' I'd keep stopping and saying, 'You want to go out and play?' He'd say, 'No, more, more, more.' "

Kyle's interest in history was fueled by books. Like many children with interests, he read books considered beyond his age level. "It was around when he was three and four, he wasn't interested in typical children's books," says Terry. "He liked books that had a lot going on on one page."

HANDS-ON IDEA

Just hecause children are proficient at something doesn't mean they want to pursue it. In selecting interests, base choices on your child's preferences rather than her abilities. Children are generally drawn to interests because they love them, not because they're good at them. The proficiency comes later.

SOMETHING MOST PEOPLE CAN'T DO

The children interviewed in this book have interests that couldn't be more different. What the children share in common in many cases is the reason they like their interests. Oftentimes, they're drawn to an interest because it's something others aren't able to do, or wouldn't be allowed to do.

What Meghan likes about falconry is the "fact that you can do something that most people can't do."

Chris had marched as a drummer in historical reenactments years before he was technically allowed to. His involvement has also given him the opportunity to camp at sites off limits to the general public.

Hillary has been "wheel-throwing" since she was five.

When Sierra was three and her brother Bryce was one, they backpacked with their parents the entire Continental Divide Trail—on llamas!

Eleven-year-old Cole has banded owls, and got the thrill of his young life when an ornithologist invited him to see a golden eagle that had been wounded by a hunter. "We were all jumping out of our skins with excitement," says his mother Kris. "This sort of opportunity keeps the fire of Cole's interest in birds strong."

These youngsters have developed passions within fields that have historically been off limits to people their age. So whether it's fencing, rocketry, or rock climbing, if your child shows a passion for it, pursue it. You'll be present to keep it slow and safe.

What You Need to Know About Choosing an Interest

- Some children adopt the interests of one or both parents, while other youngsters gravitate toward an interest on their own. Still others require more time and energy to draw it out.
- Parents who introduce their children to their own interests often do so for two reasons: They enjoy the interest so much they want to pass that joy along to their children; and they can't imagine not pursuing the interest, or pursuing it less, because they have children.
- Don't avoid interests considered beyond your child's age level. You'll be there to ensure her safety.
- Interests differ from extracurricular activities in that they are intensely personal, require greater one-on-one involvement from parents, are pursued year round, and are typically less structured.
- Do not choose an interest based on its ability to get your child into a top college, earn a scholarship, or secure a future of fame and fortune. It puts undue pressure on the child.

What's more, interests often have little to do with the path children's adult lives take.

- Popular interests offer children lots of resources and the opportunity for social interaction through participation in local clubs, as well as junior divisions of adult-based interest organizations.
- The nice thing about interests is that they carry with them the opportunity to take us outside our often small worlds. With that in mind, don't steer your children away from interests you know nothing about. Stretch yourself, and embrace what you don't know.
- Encourage your child's quirky interest. Upon closer inspection, you may find it's not so peculiar after all. However, be sensitive to the fact that it may raise some adult eyebrows and attract snide comments from like-age peers.
- Interests based on fads aren't necessarily bad. Fads can introduce young children to the idea of interests and often segue into non-fad-based interests.
- It's common for young children to have more than one interest. As schoolwork and extracurricular activities become a bigger part of their lives, they will cut back on some or figure out how to combine them.
- Books are ideal vehicles for sparking an interest. But don't limit yourself to children's books. Expand both your reading horizons with reference and coffee-table books.
- When asked what they like about their interests, children often point to the fact that what they do is something most children their age can't do. Keep this in mind when choosing an interest with your child.

• Marching to the Beat of His Own Drum •

The music of John Philip Sousa isn't the kind you listen to sitting down. So when Chris's grandfather would play it, marching seemed the natural thing to do.

"When Chris was four or five, he would march around the house with his grandfather and myself," says Chris's father Clark. "He had a toy drum, and we'd be marching around banging things."

In addition to marching, Chris was drawn to eighteenth-century-style soldiers, including toy soldiers resembling Continental and British troops, as well as the classic movie March of the Wooden Soldiers.

"He liked the rescue scene at the end when the soldiers come in," says Clark, who would tell his son bedtime stories in which Chris was a soldier in the movie. "You could see where his imagination was going."

Then Chris's grandfather came across a newspaper article describing historical reenactments, and they attended several. "The reenacting was interesting to him," Clark says. "He saw all these soldiers in true life marching around shooting muskets."

A Father in Tune

On a whim, Clark purchased a fife at one of the reenactments. "I figured, he likes playing the drum, so I got used to playing some notes on the fife," he says. "I let him drum, and I would just improvise."

One day, Chris asked his father if he would accompany him with his fife on a march. "I said, 'Sure, I'll do that with you,' " he says. "I didn't realize he wanted to do it outside!"

So father and son marched throughout the neighborhood. "People would come to their doors, and they couldn't believe what they were seeing," says Clark, who decided it was high time to join a reenactment group.

To make it more of a family affair, Clark's wife Susan and younger daughter Ashleigh joined. Chris was outfitted with a child-size reproduction of an eighteenth-century drum, and the entire clan donned appropriate historical clothing, including a green regimental coat Chris's mother sewed for him.

The family has also participated in two militia-sponsored

camping trips in which families sleep in eighteenth-century-style tents and cook their food over an open fire. "It can be uncomfortable," says Clark.

Chris, now twelve, agrees. "It was not too fun because each time there were too many mosquitoes around and in our tent," he says.

Bending the Rules

Clearly, Chris's fascination with historical reenactments involved drumming and marching. "Drummers are important because they tell the troops what to do using drum signals," he says. "They also played songs during battle to keep the men marching and keep up the spirits."

However, safety rules and a passion for historical accuracy prevented Chris from participating with the militia group. "Muskets were being fired," says Clark. "You wouldn't normally find a seven- or eight-year-old carrying a drum—it was usually a man or a teenager."

However, Chris's dedication to learning the field music, commands, and signals used to communicate with the troops impressed members of the militia enough that "they bent the rules a little bit, within reason," says Clark.

By the time Chris was nine, he played well, was eager to participate, and was always accompanied by his father. Still, Chris had to work hard to keep up with the adults.

"My legs were small, and I couldn't take big steps, so I never could keep up with the men," says Chris, adding, "They treated me well, and they were always glad I was there drumming."

In addition to studying field music books and tapes provided by fife and drum members, and taking lessons from an instructor with experience in eighteenth-century drumming, Chris received one-on-one guidance from several reenactment drummers. "They gave him little individual lessons every time he went to an event," says Clark.

The lessons paid off. Chris passed his fifth level of drumming proficiency as awarded by a historical association dedicated to authentically recreating the life and times of the soldiers of the American War for Independence.

In fact, Chris is the only person to have passed such a level, and is determined to memorize the thirty or so new tunes required to pass the sixth, and final, level. "It was easy, but it took almost a year," he says of his fifth-level test.

Just as Chris received, so, too, does he give. Every few months, he mentors an eleven-year-old up-and-coming drummer who accompanies Clark and Chris on marches. "I teach him beginner drum signals and rudiments," says Chris.

In Demand

In addition to taking part in reenactments, father and son perform at Chris's school as well as at a local summer day camp in which children learn about different historical periods.

"Once we were at his school doing a demonstration, and he was so good at the drum that they were just amazed," says Clark. "So even though he was dressed up in this unusual clothing, when they're in third, fourth, and fifth grades, they think, Hey, this is really cool."

The "unusual clothing" concerns Clark, who worries that Chris may someday decide he doesn't want to dress as an eighteenth-century drummer. "I would assume some of the other drummers in these groups, when they get into later teenage years, they start thinking, I don't look cool anymore wearing these clothes," says Clark. "I'd like to keep him going, he has such a talent."

Toward that end, Clark has cut back on the number of reenactments in which they participate, indulges Chris in his interest in basketball by taking him to live games, and has purchased a drum set so Chris "can branch out."

Chris maintains a comfortable balance between the past and present, practicing revolutionary war drumming and taking modern drum lessons. "During these lessons, I do some revolutionary war drumming, but mostly modern drumming," he says, explain-

ing, "In modern drumming the rolls are closed, and in Revolutionary War drumming they are open."

With the oncoming teen years, Clark maintains a realistic attitude toward his son's interest. "Kids can go in any direction when they get older," he says. "We just keep trying to expose him to different things."

4

Collections: The Heart and Soul of Interests

Like many families, the Bradshaws of California wanted their children to learn firsthand about state government. And like many families, they sought to accomplish that via a trip to their state capital, Sacramento.

Unlike most families, though, the Bradshaws didn't unpack upon arriving in their hotel room. Their ten-year-old son Bryan made a bee line for the Yellow Pages, where he located a more important must-see destination: a used-record store near the state capitol building.

"He pleaded with us, 'Just an hour,' " says his mother Judy. "My husband and I ended up seeing the state capital in shifts, because he wouldn't leave the store."

That was just the beginning.

"He and I went through scenarios like that with movie cards and posters from the time he was eleven till college," she says.

"We didn't have to nurture his interest in collections," she adds. "It grew exponentially."

"There is a distinction to be drawn between true collectors and accumulators. Collectors are discriminating; accumulators act at random."—Russell Lynes (1910–1991), American editor, critic

An Early Passion

Bryan's passion for collections started at the age of two when he absconded with a clear plastic tube filled with miniatures—a gift from his parents to his younger sister.

"We didn't have to worry about him putting them in his mouth," says Judy. "He'd lay them on the floor and group them."

A love of all things miniature led to a fascination with doll-houses and their accessories, small cars, and stamps.

Bryan later developed a passion for big-band recordings, which were introduced to him by a friend at camp. "He was in junior high, and he'd pester me to take him to hear the big bands," says Judy. "He would get autographs, and knew all about the music."

In case you think his interests were passing fads, Bryan, who today is in his thirties, meticulously maintains all his collections, which are stored in his boyhood bedroom, as well as his two-bedroom apartment. "They still mean so much to me," he says.

Collecting Facts

Don't roll your eyes the next time your child marvels yet again over the rich colors and intricate shapes of his collection of dinosaur figures. It's that childlike fascination over the minute details of their collectibles that defines many renowned adult collectors.

British collector Robert Opie is one such person. Well known for his enormous collection of advertising and packaging products, he recalled in a 1993 interview how as a child he would spend his savings on the latest Matchbox car, which to him was nothing less than a work of art. "[I would] think, 'Gosh, what a marvelous piece of engineering. How clever for all that detail to be put into one tiny little box.' "

A LITTLE HEART AND SOUL

A sock filled with marbles, an envelope with a colorful stamp affixed to it, a gray rock with white crystals growing from it. To collectors of these items, such objects elicit a feeling of euphoria incomprehensible to noncollectors.

It's no wonder collections have been called the "heart and soul" of interests. Collections can spark a new interest, reinforce an existing interest, or make up the interest itself. In many cases, collections are a tangible representation of people's passions.

Some children's passions over their collections run so deep as to influence and define their later lives. A well-known book dealer got started as a result of collecting *Wizard of Oz* books as a child. Charles Darwin collected (not surprisingly) shells, flowers, beetles, and birds' eggs.

What's impressive about collectors who choose careers based on their collections is that the fulfillment they reaped from their childhood collections preceded the success they found in adulthood. No pressure was exerted on them to collect, no one tied it to their vocations, and the desire to collect sprang from the child.

HANDS-ON IDEA

Introduce a child to collecting by visiting a museum. Explain that museums hold many of the best collections in the world, whether they're amassed by the museums' curators or donated in order that they be shared with the public and preserved.

SOME THINGS NEVER CHANGE

Collecting as a hobby for young children hasn't changed much in more than a hundred years. In fact, children today collect many of the same items children did at the turn of the century.

Consider the following lists. The first two record the most popular collectibles by boys and girls in 1900. The findings were gathered from some 1,200 elementary schoolchildren in California by child and educational psychologist G. Stanley Hall (1844–1924).

Most Popular Collectibles, 1900

Girls
1. Stamps
2. Shells
3. Picture cards
4. Cigar tags
5. Buttons
6. Marbles
7. Pieces of cloth
8. Paper dolls

Boys
1. Cigar tags
2. Stamps
3. Birds' eggs
4. Marbles
5. Shells
6. Buttons
7. Rocks
8. Picture cards

Fast-forward eighty-eight years to a study of 275 children, ages seven to twelve, conducted by Dr. Ann McGreevy, enrichment coordinator with the Pentucket Regional Schools, West New-

bury, Massachusetts, and professor of education at the former
Notre Dame College, in Manchester, New Hampshire.

Although McGreevy found that a smaller percentage of children collected in her study than in the earlier study, several of her
findings were similar to Hall's. For example, those who did collect had an average of three collections, and children around the
age of ten were the most avid collectors.

Both sets of students also collected similar items: shells, marbles, rocks and stickers. (Let's assume that "picture cards" are anal-
ogous to today's stickers.)

Most Popular Collectibles, 1988

Girls
1. Stuffed animals
2. Stickers
3. Rocks
4. Shells
5. Books
6. Posters
7. Dolls

Boys
1. Sports cards
2. Small cars and trucks
3. Coins and foreign money
4. Rocks
5. He-Man figures
6. Marbles
7. Stuffed animals

COLLECTIBLES GET COMMERCIAL

While it's comforting to know that children today collect many of
the same objects their counterparts did in 1900, less comforting is
the finding that today young people's collectibles are more likely

to require an outlay of cash. (I assume that children in 1900 didn't purchase cigars and that stamps were removed from envelopes containing the family's mail.)

One reason for the shift is the inroads marketing has made into the collectibles market. (If you have any doubt about this trend, just think eBay or visit a search engine and type in "kids collectibles.")

"It [the collectibles market] used to be a clearly defined line that has become totally blurred," says Pam Danziger, president, founder, and CEO of Unity Marketing, Stevens, Pennsylvania, which specializes in the collectibles market.

That blurry line is a result of a generational shift in the collectibles market. Not only are young adult collectors replacing older adult collectors; more important, Baby Boomer and Generation X collectors have children. In fact, the presence of children in collecting households rose almost twofold in just two years, from 21 percent in 1998 to 43 percent in 2000, according to Unity Marketing.

These Baby Boomers and GenXers represent a new generation of collectors who want "new products for their tastes, certainly not the collectibles of their mothers' and grandmothers' generation," according to a Unity Marketing report. Young adult collectors also recognize that collecting is an enjoyable way to spend quality time with their children.

The trend has spawned what marketers refer to as "family collecting." Here, toys and collectibles merge to create product lines of classic toys targeting adult collectors and their children. For example, what were once just toys are now "collectibles": Barbie dolls, American Girl dolls, and Hot Wheels and Matchbox cars.

In many cases, new products tie into a nostalgia influenced by the mass media. Reflecting our fondness for television and film, today's popular collectibles feature characters from Sesame Street, Looney Tunes cartoons, Disney films, *Star Wars* movies and *Star Trek* films and TV episodes. It's no wonder companies that manufacture toys and stuffed animals hold licenses to such well-known names as Coca-Cola, Mickey Mouse, Scooby Doo, Rolie Polie Olie, Curious George, and Babe.

Family collecting can be a terrific way to get families to interact and learn from each other. But the collection should be the child's, not the parent's. Collect something together, but also have your child establish her own collection, and allow her to make many of her own decisions related to it.

My idea of family collecting is when each member of the family collects something that interests him or her. Ten-year-old Noah collects tin toys, Beatle memorabilia, rocks, and colorful wall hangings called arpilleras. His mother collects Fiesta ware and other vintage kitchen products; his father, old comics and rubber stamps.

Certainly, many of the young collectors I came across share a common trait: Their parents collect and have a high tolerance for filling their homes with collectibles.

"A parent who has a clean, spare house is not likely to have a kid who collects," says Barbara H. Jacksier, editor of *Country Collectibles,* a quarterly magazine that occasionally profiles child collectors. "We have photographed thousands of homes, and I've never seen one of those clean, spare people."

SO MANY COLLECTIONS, SO LITTLE TIME

In both Hall's and McGreevy's study on young collectors, participants had an average of three collections each.

Managing more than one collection is easy for some children, but that doesn't mean you should give in to your child every time he wants to start a new one. And certainly don't fall for the line "I'm collecting collections."

You are the best judge of your child's ability to manage her collections—whether it's one or six. If she wants to start a second, third, or fourth collection, take into consideration the time she has available, expense factors, and her ability to juggle homework and other responsibilities.

Base your decision, too, on how your child treats his collections. Whether or not they're active, collections should be valued. That means they should be organized and stored carefully. If your child manhandles his collection of sports cards, it may be time to stop collecting them or to start collecting something less fragile, or something that requires little or no cash outlay.

Start with one collection and see how it progresses. If your child wants to start another, ask her if she wants to continue the old one. Add that she'll have to spread over two collections the same budget she has for one.

If she wants to cease the first collection, suggest that the two of you pack it away carefully and store it in a special place where it's still accessible. Such a step reinforces to your child that you value the work and energy that went into the original collection.

Ten-year-old Noah's collection of arpilleras hangs on his bedroom walls. His collection of tin toys is kept on a shelf there, and his collection of dreidels is stored in a box and brought out in December. "Pretty much everything is kept in my room," he says of his collections.

Don't dwell on the money spent on the collection. Don't reprimand your child for her decision to stop collecting. And whatever you do, don't throw it away! Cherish the experience and resulting happy memories, and someday she may just pull it out, dust it off, and pick up where she left off.

GOING DOTTY

To some, collections are all about numbers—big numbers. To prove the point, a fourth-grade class from Falls Church, Virginia, collected one million paper dots from hole punchers. The collection is exhibited in a large pretzel jar and several small pickle jars.

Of course, the exercise had more to do with mathematics than with a fondness for small circular pieces of paper. But to a young child, one million pieces of an object they love may seem just about right.

To keep your child's collection in perspective, explain that it's quality, not quantity, that makes a collection—and quality is, of course, in the eye of your little beholder. But that may not be a strong enough argument to sway your young audience.

Better yet, to reduce the number of potential objects in any one collection, narrow down the topic area. If it's rocks, how about white and pink ones only? If it's candles, how about those depicting frogs? If it's plants, how about miniature roses?

"Parents line up in two categories: Those who want the collection to be easy to find and those who don't," says *Country Collectibles* editor Jacksier.

"I was of the 'those who don't' category," says Jacksier, whose sixteen-year-old son Frederic started collecting glass insulators at the age of six. His stuffed foxes collection began when he received one as a gift at the age of one. "I didn't want the house to be overrun, and I wanted the hunt to be a meaningful, time-consuming effort."

When it comes to narrowing down a collectible, it seems the French excel. In the book *The Cultures of Collecting*, Duke University literature professor Naomi Schor writes: "Some French collectors, especially of Parisian postcards, are even said to push their sense of the local so far as to specialize in a single street, no doubt their own."

SPENDING LIMITS

With the exception of sticks and leaves, just about anything that can be collected can be bought in a store. Thus, a simple trip to a mall becomes an opportunity for your child to add to her collection.

Jacksier found a way to nurture her son's desire to collect and simultaneously keep shopping trips from becoming collecting free-for-alls. "I discovered early on that when you go shopping, if your child has something he's collecting, it's a wonderful way to buy yourself time," she says.

"My son had found a glass insulator in the woods when we moved to Virginia," she adds. "A couple weeks later, I was shopping and he was getting whiny, and I said, 'Look, there's an insulator just like the one you found in the woods.' And he went, 'They want five dollars for it.' So when he saw one for fifty cents, he said, 'Oh, maybe I should buy it. That one's much cheaper.' "

Key to keeping the collection in perspective, according to Jacksier, is sticking to predetermined rules and budgets. "I've heard from collectors that if you start off a collection going gung-ho, it sets a bad precedent," she says. "When you go shopping, give them a budget that is below what most of what is collected costs. So if most insulators cost in the five- to six-dollar range, give him three."

Apply the same budgetary rules to your own collecting. "I collect Fiesta ware dishes in a fruit and flower pattern, and he certainly watched me look at the perfect soup bowls and go, 'Nope, twenty dollars a bowl is above what I spend," says Jacksier "You have to set examples."

COLLECTING AS AN INVESTMENT OPPORTUNITY

There's a *New Yorker* cartoon in which two girls, about the age of six and wearing party dresses, are surrounded by balloons, gifts, and a birthday cake. The birthday girl is holding in her lap a present she has just unwrapped—a doll packaged inside a clear plastic box. The other girl says, "Don't take her out of the box—she'll depreciate."

An amusing comment coming from such a young child. But hardly an improbable one, given today's emphasis on collecting for profit.

Among the young adult collectors in the Unity Marketing survey, many showed an interest in collecting as an investment opportunity. Browse through the "collectibles" section of a large bookstore and you'll notice that the bulk of the books there consist of price guides.

The trend has trickled down to children and their collectibles—Beanie Babies destined to remain in their clear plastic boxes, die-cast metal cars rarely taken out of their packaging.

Even the lexicon of young collectors has taken on that of investors. Some Pokemon cards are "rare," Barbie dolls come in "collector's editions," and not only are Beanie Babies packaged in clear plastic boxes, so are the identification tags attached to them.

Ideally, a child's collection should transcend monetary value. And, indeed, the passion many young collectors feel for their objects usually surpasses the worth of those objects. Jessica's collection of pencils may look like a pile of wood to one person. But to her, each is a one-of-a-kind piece with its own special history.

John wouldn't part with his collection of marbles for all the other collections in the world—unless perhaps they're other marble collections. And still the time and thought that went into his collection mean more to him than the beauty of anyone else's collection of marbles.

If your young collector's interest in the value of her collection makes you uneasy, explain to her that collecting as an investment opportunity is just one aspect of her hobby. It shouldn't overshadow other features, such as collecting as a learning experience, as a family activity, and for the sheer enjoyment of it.

While parents perceive a range of benefits from their children's collections, including strong self-esteem and responsibility, children collect for simpler reasons.

In a survey of 1,600 collecting families by collectibles manufacturer Enesco Group Inc., Itasca, Illinois, the majority of children (46 percent) said they like adding to their collections because they enjoy playing with or looking at them.

CHOOSING COLLECTIBLES

For some children, choosing a collectible is a lot like selecting a puppy—you don't choose it, it chooses you. For the majority of children, choosing a collectible requires a thoughtful, caring adult—

someone who takes into consideration budgets, interests, and educational opportunities afforded by the collectible. Not doing so can lead to lots of pitfalls.

Take seven-year-old Jeremy, who was so excited about finding his first toy inside a cereal box that his mother suggested collecting them—a suggestion she soon came to regret as each trip to the supermarket became an argument over how many boxes of sugar-laden cereal Jeremy could fit in the cart.

Good intentions, but little foresight. Perhaps if Jeremy were given a budget and adhered to it, or if he showed more restraint over the kinds of toys he collected, the collection might actually work.

Work with your child to choose a collectible. After all, you may both be living with it for years to come. Do you have room to display it properly? Can it help expand your child's horizons? Is it something you can pursue together? Can it lead to the pursuit of a related interest?

Childhood collections can conjure up memories that last a lifetime. With any luck, those memories will be fond ones. Following are ways to help you achieve that goal.

IT'S NEVER TOO EARLY

Some children aren't even aware they're collecting. That's because their parents start their collections before they're born.

Anne received two baby rattles as gifts before her daughter Iris was born. Today, eleven-year-old Iris has more than forty rattles in her collection.

Prior to her son's birth, Saarin purchased two arpilleras, three-dimensional wall hangings made by South American women from pieces of colored cloth. "We live in earthquake country, and I didn't want anything on the wall to fall and hurt him," she says. "Coincidentally, an aunt of mine sent him one. What's the saying? Three makes a collection?"

HANDS-ON IDEA

If you decide to start a collection for your soon-to-be-born child or very young child, choose collectibles that are suitable for little hands.

Avoid objects that are breakable or could be swallowed. Unless you're willing to hide them until she's old enough to handle the items properly, you may inadvertently turn off your child from collecting altogether.

INSPIRING GIFTS

Ashley began her collection of horse figurines at the age of four when her mother gave her one. Neal's father bought him a pewter dragon figurine for having a good report card.

Ted's mother thought a model car would help her son's concentration, so she bought him one as a gift. Today, Ted has seventeen models.

Sean's father bought him his first toy train after telling his son how much fun he had collecting trains as a child. Michael began collecting coins after his grandmother brought him some from Europe.

A small gift is often all that's needed to start a passion for collecting. Almost half (45 percent) of some 2,000 adult collectors surveyed by Unity Marketing said they began their collections with items received as gifts.

Think about that the next time you need to purchase a birthday or holiday gift for your child, niece, nephew, godchild, or grandchild. Then build on the collectible item with the next gift. Such a thoughtful gesture will not be lost on its young recipient.

STRENGTHEN AN INTEREST

Paulina, ten, loves to garden, and particularly loves the colorful seed packets she sees her father bring home from the nursery. She was thrilled when he suggested she collect packets featuring her favorite plants.

Twelve-year-old Julie's love of Shakespearean poems, plays, and acting prodded her to collect movie-ticket stubs from every movie she's seen since 1997.

For a child with a general interest, a collection can help strengthen and sharpen it. If Jeffrey likes art, consider collecting business or store cards with eye-catching graphics. If it's animals, focus on coins depicting wildlife. If it's history, try stamps depicting important historical dates.

If it's a family interest you're intent on sparking, consider helping your child start a collection related to it. Cindy Ross and her family hike and backpack together. Her daughter's interest in the great outdoors is strengthened by collecting items from nature, such as rocks, seashells, and feathers.

HANDS-ON IDEA

Everyday comments often reveal tremendous insights into the kinds of things your child might enjoy collecting. Ten-year-old Joel always liked "stuff I can fit into my pocket." He recently started collecting yo-yos. Listen to your child's comments and see what they reveal.

SEARCH THE ATTIC

Chances are, at least one collection lurks in your house. Maybe it's in the family junk drawer, the spare change bottle, boxes in the attic containing your and your husband's childhood mementos.

Among the possible collectibles in my house are foreign coins and bills, teapots from Asia, and musical instruments, and from my childhood, stamps, charms from gumball machines, spools of thread, and pop-up books.

Look, too, at items that come into your house every day. Some mail still contains stamps. (And if it doesn't, ask a friend or relative to write your child and affix a special stamp to the envelope.)

Your change purse contains statehood quarters. Collectibles are even hiding in the newspaper that arrives on your driveway each morning. Thirteen-year-old Kelsey collects newspaper cuttings of topics that interest her, including earth science, planetary science, archaeology, and mythology.

Hands-on Idea

Your child's room may hold the beginnings of a collection. Children often amass objects they love and keep them in special places. Isabel keeps her wood puzzles stacked neatly beside her bed. Look in your child's room and see what she values.

Grab Hold of Opportunities

When a postal clerk offered five-year-old Peter tickets to an international stamp exposition, his mother accepted. That was the beginning of a collection passion that spanned twelve years.

One eleven-year-old Sydney, Australia, native started her pin collection when the Olympics were held near her home. She gathered almost a hundred pins from athletes and officials at the event.

In 1996 the Smithsonian Institution provided a veritable breeding ground for young collectors. As part of its 150th birthday celebration, it invited sixty young people to display their collections, which included antique rulers, chopstick rests, lunch boxes, magnets, cowboy hats, snow globes, and fossils. (You can hear several young attendees describing their collections on the Smithsonian's site at kids.si.edu/collecting.)

Keep track of events that might trigger your child's desire to collect. County fairs routinely feature young collectors' tents. Subscribe to publications from museums and facilities near your home, or bookmark their web sites. Living near New York's American Museum of Natural History has enabled me to expose my son to collections of dinosaur bones, insects preserved in amber, and Egyptian mummies.

Local newspapers are a treasure trove of activities related to collections. Look for listings of collections on display at libraries and schools, and check for notices advertising meeting times for stamp, rock, and other collectibles clubs.

Your Collection Connections

Consider how your life lends itself to a particular collectible, and form a collection around that. My husband frequently travels to Asia and Europe. He brings back coins and stamps with animals on them

One father drove with his young son cross country one summer. He bought his son a hat, which they decorated with pins collected from museums and other tourist sites along the way. Today, his son collects other pins but cherishes his summer pin hat.

Also consider acquaintances who have collections. Invite them to dinner. Instead of the usual bottle of wine, ask them to bring samples from their collection to share with your child.

Hands-on Idea

Collections offer the opportunity to learn the terminology associated with a specific collectible—"commemorative" coins, a record's "first pressing," for example.

And the next time your child doesn't put away her collection of movie-ticket stubs, disposable pens, seed packets, holiday cards, daily menus or playbills, state firmly, "Put away this ephemera right now, or no dessert." Then explain that "ephemera" refers to anything produced that was not meant to last—just like his television rights.

Cheap Is Good, Free Is Better

If you and your child are unsure what to collect, consider choosing something that won't put a big dent in your wallet.

Objects found in nature make ideal collectibles—they are free and uniquely beautiful. However, avoid removing from nature objects that are rare, alive, or dangerous in young hands. (Rocks are an ideal collectible for young children unless they're into throwing them.)

If your child isn't impressed with collectibles found in nature, consider free or inexpensive collectibles: pins, business cards, holiday cards, statehood quarters, letters from pen pals and relatives, disposable menus, newspaper articles on a particular topic, pencils, postcards, and sea glass.

Keep an eye out, too, for offers of free or inexpensive collectibles. The owner of a gardening center charges children visiting her nursery just twenty-five cents for miniature rose plants, which are attractive to children because they're small and come in different colors. U.S. government agencies, such as the Environmental Protection Agency and the Coast Guard, offer free coloring and activity books geared toward children.

Popular Collectibles

Marya has collected some of her best stickers via chain letters. Henry attends a monthly stamp club meeting after school at his local library. Trish visits a kid-friendly web site to view the latest finds of young coin collectors.

Popular collectibles are ideal for children who like lots of bells and whistles. Whether it's rocks, stamps, pins, or coins, popular collectibles have established infrastructures featuring recently published books; eye-appealing, kid-friendly websites; and age-appropriate clubs.

Also, popular collectibles encompass so many topics that it's relatively easy to narrow them down. Instead of collecting animal pins, focus on pins depicting ducks; if it's transportation pins, select only those with motorcycles; and if it's special events pins, choose those highlighting parades. A useful site dedicated to helping children start pin collections is www.pinfever.com/kidszone.html.

The same applies to stamp collecting. In fact, "thematic," or topical, stamp collecting is the fastest-growing segment of stamp collecting. Here, collectors can focus on such specific topics as birds, bridges, flowers, fish, plants, holograms, and a host of other subjects. For a list of topics covered by the American Topical Association, see www.philately.com/philately/ata.htm.

FAD COLLECTIBLES

When it comes to fad collectibles, you'll find the good, the bad, and the ugly.

The good is that if all your child wants to collect is the latest fad, at least she's collecting. Whether it's Pokemon cards, Crazy Bones, or Beanie Babies, the fad will expose her to the process of collecting—and eventually the fad will fade away.

Fad collectibles can also make insecure children feel confident. Collecting the same items peers collect makes children feel part of the crowd. And even though they're collecting the same items, the collections are unique, which makes the collectors feel special.

The bad is that the possibilities for adult involvement are limited. "If you can get them hooked on something that isn't a child's collectible, I think it opens them up and they can take it further," says Jacksier, whose son collected insulators and stuffed, wooden, and metal foxes.

"When people we knew traveled, they would send my son books about foxes in foreign languages," she continues. "If you're collecting Beanie Babies, it's harder to get that adult input."

The ugly is that you can easily become oversaturated by the constant barrage of commercials, television shows, movies, clothing, and other accessories tied to the fad. "I always prayed there would be no major fox cartoon developed," says Jacksier.

HANDS-ON IDEA

Outdoor flea markets and consignment shops offer lots of opportunities to find collectible items. "There is no kid I have ever met who on a twenty-minute shopping tour through one of those consignment malls won't be attracted to something," says Barbara H. Jacksier, editor of *Country Collectibles* magazine. "Your only hope is that it's not a two-hundred-dollar something."

OTHER COLLECTIBLES

Collectibles aren't limited to rocks, stamps, and dolls. When it comes to collectibles, you're limited only by your imagination. Consider these collectibles, which range from the wearable to the intangible:

- *Wearable collectibles:* Most children are proud of their collections, so why not select a collectible they can model for others?

  Scarves, socks, gloves, handkerchiefs, hats and pins (avoid underwear) are items your child can wear to school. And maybe, just maybe, she'll be excited about getting dressed in the morning.
- *Functional collectibles:* Wearable collectibles fit into this category, too, as well as mugs, thimbles, calculators, and pencil sharpeners.
- *Theme collectibles:* Maybe your child loves the beach because his grandparents live there. Start a collection with a beach theme. Sea glass, shells, sand toys, sailboats, sea gulls, a life preserver are all items that would fit well into this collection.

  Lots of kids seem drawn to all things miniature. "I love animals, and I love tiny things, so it just seemed natural to start collecting miniature animal figures," says Diedre, who has about sixty pieces that she displays in a shadow box in her bedroom.

- *"Slice-of-life" collectibles:* Once children are old enough to grasp history, they often become interested in a particular period. Colonial, Viking, Native American, and the 1960s are all periods around which to form a collection.
- *Intangible collectibles:* On hiking across the polar ice cap in 1985, adventurer Michael McGuire stated: "I like to collect experiences the way other people like to collect coins and stamps."

Collecting intangible objects is an easy way to introduce children to collecting. Names of birds seen on walks, poems, hand-game rhymes, and songs for jumping rope are just a few.

SHORT-TERM COLLECTIONS

Some young children may not have the attention span necessary to maintain a collection. Other children may need to have a collection or two under their belts before they catch on to the idea of collecting.

In these cases, consider a short-term collection. Although most collections revolve around a lifetime of collecting, you can introduce your child to collecting by creating a collection based on a vacation. If you visit a ranch, for example, collect mementos from the trip, including disposable menus, rocks, pieces of hay, a strand of horse hair, ticket stubs, postcards, and brochures.

Seasonal collections also teach children lots about collecting, without the long-term commitment. In autumn, collect pine cones, dried flower blossoms, and acorns.

Sea glass and shells are great summertime collectibles. If you live along the coast, make it a habit one summer to visit different beaches and collect beach-themed postcards from your destinations.

In spring, collect flowers. Press them in heavy books and identify them. Animals are out and the ground is often muddy, so consider making molds of those prints.

In winter, take hikes in the woods and photograph animal tracks. Take paper and crayons on your hikes and make rubbings of different tree bark.

COLLECTIBLES THAT RAISE EYEBROWS

Twelve-year-old Melissa has been collecting shot glasses since she was ten years old. She saw her first one at a county fair and was drawn to the small size and Ferris wheel design printed on it. Today, the young collector has more than twenty-five glasses in her collection.

Whether your child collects shot glasses, comic books, or professional wrestling memorabilia, be prepared for the onslaught of snide comments from adults who question your child's choice—and your judgment in allowing her to collect the items.

As a parent, you know when an activity is negatively influencing your child, and when that activity is nothing more than an innocent interest. Often what's needed is nothing more than some additional supervision and discussion.

Certainly, if you find the collectible unacceptable, pull the plug on it immediately. However, if you're okay with your child's choice, support it. But explain why some adults might find her decision questionable (and why her friends might find it really cool).

You may also want to steer your child toward more appropriate items within her collection. If it's comic books, focus on superhero books. If your child balks at such childish material, consider more challenging titles, subject to your approval.

Your child's choice of collectible may also come under scrutiny if it's deemed inappropriate for the child's gender or age. A love of all things miniature led Bryan to collect dollhouse accessories. His love of collecting big band music as a teenager also brought on unwanted criticism. "I was at sleep-away camp, and the counselor suggested playing some of my music for everyone to hear," says Bryan. "I begged her not to, but she did, and the kids hated it. My face turned bright red."

It's your duty to protect your child from unwanted criticism and ridicule. If it means keeping the collection a secret from peers, do it. Do whatever is necessary to encourage your child's love of the collectible and to protect him from criticism.

Use the situation as a learning opportunity. Explain that adults collect lots of things that other adults consider strange, such as airsickness bags, printed toilet paper, plastic frogs, and all things purple. Take your child to an antique store and explain that at one time people considered the items in the store junk. Now the items are not only bought and sold but featured in museums.

RESPECT THE CHOICE

While many adults are the main influence on their child's choice of collectible, not all children share their parents' tastes when it comes to items to collect. Respect your child's choice.

"If your child happens to be interested in Nancy Drew books and you pooh-pooh it, it doesn't build a lot of self-esteem," says Jacksier.

The fact that your child wants to collect anything is a clear sign she's interested in something. Perhaps it will lead to other interests, and perhaps it will be the interest itself.

Tips on Choosing Collectibles

- Collections have been called the "heart and soul" of interests. Collections can spark a new interest, reinforce an existing interest, or make up the interest itself.
- Children today collect many of the same objects their counterparts did in 1900. However, today young people's collectibles are more likely to require an outlay of cash.
- It's not unusual for a child to want more than one collection. If she wants to start a second, third, or fourth collection,

take into consideration the time she has available, expense factors, and her ability to juggle homework and other responsibilities.

- To reduce the number of potential objects in any one collection, narrow down the topic area. If it's rocks, how about white and pink ones? If it's candles, how about those depicting frogs? If it's plants, how about miniature roses?

- Given today's emphasis on collecting for profit, it's not unusual for a child to become overly concerned with the value of his collection. If your young collector's interest in the value of her collection makes you uneasy, explain to her that collecting as an investment opportunity is just one aspect of her hobby. It shouldn't overshadow other features, such as collecting as a learning experience, as a family activity, and for the sheer enjoyment of it.

- A small gift is often all that's needed to start a passion for collecting. Think about that the next time you need to purchase a birthday or holiday gift for your child, niece, nephew, godchild, or grandchild.

- For a child whose interest is just starting, a collection can help strengthen it.

- Chances are, at least one collection lurks in your house. Maybe it's in the family junk drawer, the spare change bottle, or boxes in the attic containing your and your husband's childhood mementos.

- Keep track of events that might trigger your child's desire to collect. County fairs routinely feature young collectors' tents. Subscribe to publications from museums and facilities near your home, or bookmark their web sites. Look for local newspaper listings of collections on display at libraries and schools, and check for notices advertising meeting times for stamp, rock, and other collectibles clubs.

- If your child is unsure of what to collect, consider free or inexpensive collectibles, such as objects found in nature, pins, business cards, holiday cards, statehood quarters, letters from pen pals and relatives, disposable menus, newspaper articles on a particular topic, pencils, postcards, and sea glass.

- Popular collectibles are ideal for children who like lots of bells and whistles. Such collectibles have established infrastructures featuring recently published books; eye-appealing, kid-friendly web sites; and age-appropriate clubs.
- To keep a collection from overrunning your home, choose a theme for your child's collection. If he collects pins, consider pins depicting a particular animal.
- Fad collectibles expose children to the idea of collecting and can make insecure children feel confident. However, they can limit the possibility for adult involvement, and the hype associated with them can become annoying.
- Collectibles aren't limited to rocks, stamps, and dolls. Other possibilities include wearable, functional, theme, and slice-of-life collectibles.
- Short-term collections focusing on a trip or season are ideal for young children who may not have the attention span necessary to maintain a long-term collection.

• Kid-Friendly Collectibles •

Collections have been called the "heart and soul" of interests. They can reinforce an existing interest or spark an entirely new interest. A collection can even be the interest itself.

Below are more than 150 collectibles well suited to children. I specifically chose items that are safe and inexpensive. To avoid being inundated with a collectible, suggest specializing within a category; for example, focusing on bells from different countries as opposed to all bells.

Action figures	Awards
All things of a certain color	Baby rattles
Angels	Balls
Animal figures or pictures	Banks
Aprons	Banners
Autographs from friends,	Baseball cards
family members, relatives	Bells

Beads
Bears
Birthday candles, cards,
   hats, invitations, noise-
   makers
Board games
Books
Bookmarks
Bottles
Bottle caps
Boy Scout items
Business cards
Buttons (clothing)
Buttons (pins)
Candles
Cereal box toys or other
   premiums
Charms
Coins
Coloring/activity books
Comic books
Costume jewelry
Costumes
Cowboy items
Cups
Dice
Die-cast cars
Dinosaurs
Dolls
Egg cups
Ethnic or cultural collectibles
Eyeglasses
Facts
Fast-food toys
Feathers
Figurines

First letter of your child's
   first name
Fishing gear
Flags
Flashlights
Flowerpots
Flowers (dried, pressed)
Fossils
Frisbees
Games
Gardening tools
Girl Scout items
Gloves
Greeting cards
Handkerchiefs
Hats
Hat pins
Historical documents
Holiday ornaments
Holiday cards
Ice cream scoopers
Insects (metal or plastic)
Jigsaw puzzles
Jump ropes
Kaleidoscopes
Keys
Key chains
Kitchen items
Kites
Letters from pen pals
   or relatives
Lunch boxes
Magazines aimed at children
Magic tricks
Maps (topical, bus routes,
   subway)

Marbles
Medals
Memorabilia from a particular
   decade
Menus
Miniatures
Model cars
Mouse pads
Mugs
Music boxes
Native American items
Necklaces
Neckties
Newspaper clippings
Old radios
Packaging
Paint brushes
Paintings
Paper
Paper weights
Party hats
Patches (embroidered or
   printed)
Pencils
Pens
Pencil sharpeners
Photographs
Picture frames
Piggy banks
Pins
Plants
Plates
Playbills
Playing cards
Political memorabilia
Pop-up books
Porcelain figures

Postcards
Posters
Pottery
Pull toys
Quilts
Refrigerator magnets
Ribbons
Rocks
Rubber ducks
Rubber stamps
Salt and pepper shaker
   sets
Sand toys
Scarves
Scrapbooks
Sea glass
Seashells
Seed packets
Sheet music
Shoestrings
Snow globes
Soap
Socks
Spoons
Stamps
Star-shaped items
State quarters
Stationery
Stickers
Store cards
Stuffed toys
Teacups
Telephone insulators
Thimbles
Ticket stubs
Titanic items
Trains

T-shirts
Tools
Toy dishes
Toy trains
Transportation toys

Unicorns
Vacation souvenirs
Walking sticks
Watches
Yo-yos

5

Avoid Collecting Dust

Judith Pellettieri understands the power of collections. As an educator, she has broken the ice with visitors, occupied small hands, and engaged the minds of her students with her own collection of some twenty nesting dolls—those smooth, round wooden figures that open in half to reveal a slightly smaller doll, and so on, until the last one in the set is exposed.

She has brought the dolls to a third-grade class working on estimating, and to a kindergarten class doing a math lesson on patterns. Doing so, she says, has made her in her students' eyes a person first and a principal second.

Today, as principal of Simonds Elementary School, in Warner, New Hampshire, Pellettieri encourages her 180 kindergarten through fifth-grade students to display their collections in a case outside her office. To date, the case has held collections of dolls, marbles, baseball cards, rocks, cars, nutcrackers, and seashells.

"Some collections are formal, like coins displayed in holders, while others are personal, like the DO NOT DISTURB signs a boy collected from his travels," says Pellettieri. "The size and worth of the collection pale in importance compared to the knowledge the collector receives. It feels good for a child to speak knowledgeably about an item to an adult or to other children. Everyone can be an expert about something."

Regardless of what children collect, they derive positive benefits. A majority of adults (83 percent) said collecting has allowed their child to learn responsibility, according to a 1996 survey of more than 1,600 households containing at least one child collector by collectibles manufacturer Enesco Group Inc., Itasca, Illinois.

The survey also found that 78 percent believe collecting has been a good activity for the family; 72 percent said collecting has helped to teach the child the value of money; and 68 percent said collecting enhances the child's self-esteem.

BEYOND AN ARRAY OF OBJECTS

Brendan collects Crazy Bones to feel part of the crowd. Suzanne collects postcards because they remind her of places she's visited. Rose believes her collection of miniature kites looks awesome on her bedroom wall. Timothy considers his collection of die-cast metal cars a good investment.

Though these children are drawn to their collectibles for different reasons, they share similar benefits from collecting. Among them:

Comfort Food

Family life can be chaotic for a child. As parents, we try to shield our children from tragic news, but aren't always successful.

But a collection is always there to reassure. It's a way to exercise control over the outer world by laying things out, grouping them and handling them. One collector, whose son and husband also collect, said, "I feel like our collections feather our nest."

It also represents stability and safety, not unlike a security blanket. "My son's collections were, and still are, a great source of comfort to him," says Judy of her son Bryan, who collected as a child and still cherishes his collection in adulthood.

Escapism

"A phenomenon often associated with the passion of collecting is the loss of all sense of the present," writes French author Maurice Rheims in *The Strange Life of Objects: 35 Centuries of Art Collecting and Collectors* (Atheneum Publishers, 1961).

Naomi Schor, professor of romance studies and literature at Duke University, North Carolina, and a collector of postcards depicting Paris, calls this loss of the present a "sort of collector's time, a time out of time."

By transcending time, collections offer a much needed respite from school and after-school activities. Youngsters can enjoy their collections at their own pace and without being told what to do. In fact, you know when your child is passionate about her collection when she sits for extended periods sorting, comparing, and arranging her possessions.

Sense of Accomplishment

Children's self-esteem soars when they set out to collect something and accomplish that feat despite setbacks. They beam when they find an item that falls within their budget, and when they see items similar to the ones they collect in a book or on display at an antiques fair.

Such positive feelings come only to children who aren't handed a collection on a silver platter. Pursue the collection slowly. As it grows, so too will your child's sense of accomplishment.

Child and educational psychologist G. Stanley Hall (1844–1924) called collections a "natural power in the soul. They [collections] build self-esteem and contribute to one's creative self."

The Desire to Want to Learn

Collections inject children with a desire to think, explore, and learn beyond textbooks and classrooms.

Home-schoolers routinely use their children's collections as teaching aids. Anne home-schools her two children and uses stamps to teach her kids about almost every subject. Her son Chris, fifteen, collects stamps about aviation and rain forests. Rose, nine, favors stamps featuring underwater life.

Adults who collected as children will many times credit their collections with influencing them academically. Paul credits model-train collecting with helping him learn to read because he would review all the model-train magazines.

Hannibal Tabu began collecting comic books and action figures at the age of five. "I've learned so much from comics—Dr. Solar taught me that the speed of light is 186,000 miles per second, Iron Man taught me the first French phrases I ever knew," says Tabu, who is in his late twenties. "It was such a leg up to me in so many ways that I make my ten-year-old brother call from home and we discuss the week's comics. Despite the harder edge some of today's books and figures have, they're great ways to expand your mind."

Social Skills

The social aspect of collecting is the main draw for many collectors. In a survey of 2,000 adult collectors, the youngest group of participants, the "Generation Xers," indicated they collected because they enjoy the opportunities collecting affords for socializing and making new friends, according to Unity Marketing, Stevens, Pennsylvania, which specializes in the collectibles market.

Children who collect are no different. Their desire to share what they've learned about collecting, as well as the items they've collected, is so strong that they'll interact with people and groups outside their immediate social circles.

"It gives them something to discuss with adults other than how school is going," says Barbara H. Jacksier, editor of *Country*

Collectibles, who has interviewed some sixty young collectors for the magazine. "It can't hurt for a child to get more verbal practice and skills."

In their book *Hidden Treasures: Searching for Masterpieces of American Furniture* (Warner Books 2000), authors and twin sisters Leigh and Leslie Keno describe how, as twelve-year-olds, they conducted a "lecture" at the upstate New York home of a collector of stoneware to an audience of antiques dealers. And they would attend flea markets where they'd routinely discuss price and condition with adult dealers.

Collecting also encourages interaction across generational lines. The Morgans' collection of model trains spans three generations. Thomas Sr. began collecting when he worked at Grand Central Station in New York City. His son followed suit at the age of four, and continues to collect trains from New York and New Jersey spanning the early 1800s through the 1970s. Thomas Jr.'s teenage son, Thomas III, carries on the love of model-train collecting.

NATURAL COLLECTORS

Young children are natural collectors. French author Maurice Rheims has described collecting as an innate desire. Even from an early age, he states, children can become attached to an object. They select their favorite objects and surround themselves with them, which Rheims describes as "reflex actions of the collector."

But parents being parents, they often unintentionally squash the collecting bug. One mother wrote on a parenting site: "My four-year-old daughter has become highly interested in bringing me home every rock she finds now. Any ideas on how to 'let her down easy' instead of saying no, thank you?"

Another parent wrote: "My six-year-old tends to collect kind of odd things—sticks being his current fave[sic]. I'm constantly finding sticks all over the house, but he gets upset when I try to get rid of them. Should I just humor him?"

This parent needs to do more than just humor her son. She

should help him pursue collecting at a level he enjoys, which may mean helping him organize his sticks, asking where he found each one, comparing different bark types, playing a game with them, and talking about collecting in general.

Collecting is from the Latin *colligere*—to select and assemble.

A CHILD'S-EYE VIEW

When four-year-old Shelly covered her collection of small plastic farm animals with Play-doh, her mother scolded her for not keeping them clean and organizing them in the box bought expressly for that purpose. You could almost *hear* the joy of collecting seeping from Shelly.

Collecting becomes rewarding and enjoyable when adults refrain from putting high expectations on young collectors. Understanding and accepting the kinds of activities children are capable of at certain points in their lives are key elements to successful collecting.

Children as young as two or three can sort their collections according to size or color. In fact, realizing that objects can be sorted in different ways is an important higher-level thinking skill.

Your youngster may not want to organize his collection. Or he may organize it according to an attribute of his own choosing—an attribute you don't really "get," but one that makes your child happy.

If Adam wants to organize his seashells in a way that has meaning only to him, let him. Bite your nails, grit your teeth, but do not tell him it would make more sense to group them by color or size—or to group them at all if he prefers not to.

In his autobiography, Charles Darwin, who as a child collected shells, flowers, rocks, and birds' eggs, admitted that he had his own, unscientific way of collecting. He wrote, "With respect to science, I continued collecting minerals with much zeal, but quite unscientifically—all that I cared for was a new named mineral and I hardly ever attempted to classify them."

Regardless of how your young child plays with his collection, he'll probably move on to something else in five or ten minutes. But in that time you'll have laid important groundwork, showing your child what collecting is and that it's fun.

Five- and six-year-olds can begin to learn facts about their collections—how to care for the items, how they're used, how each was acquired. At this age, a child is capable of using the correct terminology associated with his collection. If my five-year-old can say pachycephalosaurus without missing a beat, your stamp-collecting five-year-old can learn philatelic terms.

The ages between seven and twelve have been termed the active phase of collecting by education experts G. Stanley Hall and Dr. Ann McGreevy. Social philosopher Jean Baudrillard describes this time as the "period of latency prior to puberty." With the onset of puberty, he writes, "the collecting impulse tends to disappear."

Between the ages of seven and twelve, children seek greater independence. A collection enables them to assert their autonomy as they seek items they deem appropriate to the collection and exercise authority over it.

Teenagers are quick learners of the basics of their collectibles, so whatever you do, don't treat them like preteens. Take the collection to a higher level, and lead your teen to information. But don't decipher it for him.

Consider a subscription to a periodical related to the collection. Allow teens to earn and spend their money on the collectibles. They'll be able to mix with older collectors and may even find a mentor.

A teenager's collection is his parents' ticket to spending time with their teen. "Oh, there's a fossil show coming to town next week. Want to go?" "Did I tell you a co-worker of mine collects fossils? Should I invite him to dinner and ask him to bring his collection?" "I was thinking of taking a weekend trip. Want to go to New York and visit the American Museum of Natural History?"

Social and educational priorities often crowd out collecting.

Teens who once collected may decide to stop. In this case, display some of the collectibles where your teen can see them, or store them where they're easily accessible. Who knows when the collecting bug will bite again? And even if it doesn't, chances are, your teen will pick up the collection later in life.

On the other hand, it's common for children who start collecting in their teen years to become so enamored they find it difficult to focus on anything else. "We found that teenagers who pick up a collection tend to get really caught up in it," says Jacksier. "There's a teen collector we met who is so gung-ho on Coca-Cola items, he spends every penny he earns on it."

KEEP GIRLS COLLECTING

While it's common for children to lose the collecting bug at some point in their lives, girls seem to lose it earlier and for longer periods. "Girls stop once they find out about boys, around fourteen to sixteen years of age," says Pam Danziger, president of Unity Marketing, Stevens, Pennsylvania. "They generally don't start again until about thirty-five."

Danziger attributes the collecting defection of females in their mid-teens to the discovery of boys and cars. (She adds that women often pick up their collections after establishing careers and families.)

On the other hand, "boys keep collecting," she says. Danziger adds that boys tend to carry their collecting passion through their twenties and into adulthood.

Parents of girls may want to implement some precautionary measures to maintain an interest in collecting throughout the teen years. Consider starting a collection together. Fourteen-year-old Stacy and her mom both collected trolls when they were little, and still do today.

Also, consider collectibles she won't outgrow. While your young daughter may want to collect Beanie Babies now, she may not want to do that in her teens. Why not collect Beanie Babies and something else, such as postcards, key chains, or antique hair clips—objects that may retain not only her interest but that of her teen peers as well.

Items that elicit a feeling of nostalgia are popular among young adult collectors. Why not start your daughter collecting games or candy bar wrappers? They'll make for fun conversation pieces when her friends come over. Who knows, her friends may actually consider them cool.

DUST OFF AN OLD COLLECTION

My first after-school job was as a cashier at a supermarket where to alleviate the boredom I began seeking out old coins. If I came across an old wheat penny, I'd replace it with a newer one and keep the old one. I gradually sought out coins from other sources, including mail order, through which I bought some buffalo nickels.

I hadn't thought about those coins until I purchased a coin collecting book for my six-year-old. The book, *Coin Collecting for Kids* (Innovative Kids, 2000), by Steve Otfinoski, contains slots for inserting birth coins, statehood quarters, pennies from 1960 to 2000, millennium coins, and coins minted in the early part of the twentieth century.

As we wound our way through the book, we discussed the idea behind collecting and my earlier involvement in it. Then I showed him my coin collection. It's an understatement to say he was thrilled when I gave him for his collection a bicentennial quarter, an Eisenhower dollar, and a buffalo nickel. After that, he would continually ask me if we could go through my collection together. I happily obliged.

If you have a collection from your childhood, show it to your son or daughter. If you stopped collecting, explain why, then suggest dusting it off and pursuing it together. Perhaps later your child will earn the privilege to own the collection. That is, if you're willing to give it up.

If your child isn't interested in your collection, restart it yourself or start a new one. The idea is for your child to observe you taking delight in the act of collecting. With any luck, he'll get it in his head to take one up too.

HANDS-ON IDEA

Introduce the idea of collecting into your child's school by organizing a Collection Night.

A Collection Night brings together students, parents, siblings, relatives, and community members who exhibit their collectibles on tables. The setting up, sorting through, labeling, and subsequent dialogue make for a stimulating evening.

AVOID CONFLICT

Key to collecting with children is keeping it fun and free of conflict—not an easy task when parents are thrown into the mix.

Too often parents can't resist contributing their two cents even when it's neither requested nor needed. So think before you speak, and back off when your child doesn't implement your suggestion. But, certainly, drop your magazine or put aside your bill paying and join your child when he requests your help.

Here are additional ways to avoid conflict:

"It's Mine, Not Yours!"

Reflecting on her collection of dollhouse accessories, Ann's strongest memory is of her father's obsession with "helping" her. "He bought way too much too quickly, and didn't let me choose what I wanted," she says.

Though rules on purchases and maintenance of the collection are a must, the collection is the child's. Therefore, it should be based upon her preferences and ideas. Make suggestions, certainly, but be flexible.

The Thrill of the Hunt

Of the many aspects of collecting, the one that often overpowers all the others is the act of adding to it. But collections are not initiated to be completed. As many longtime collectors note, one of the most pleasurable aspects about their hobbies is the thrill of the hunt. To many, it's a letdown to complete a collection.

Collecting teaches patience—a trait too often overshadowed by the desire for, and expectation of, instant gratification. It's okay for a child to get frustrated trying to seek out a particularly elusive item. Help your child add to her collection, but do it slowly. "An ideal collection is something that's not too easy to find and not too hard," says the mother of one young collector.

That's not always easy given the fact that most collectibles can be bought in a store or over the Internet. (Remember the survey of children collectors in 1900 compared to a similar study done in 1988? One of the biggest differences between the two was that in the earlier survey, more children had found or hunted for objects than the children in the later study, most of whom bought objects or collected items that were bought for them.)

Many young collectors are keenly aware that adding another object to their collection is as easy as pestering mom or dad to drive them to a nearby store or sit with them as they traverse the web. Retailers have embraced the trend by increasing young collectors' ability to socialize with club meetings, online chat rooms, artist signings, collectors' shows, and store-based special events. Though the activities add to the social aspect of collecting, their goal is to get collectors and their parents to part with their money.

It's a parent's job to set limits on when objects may be added and the amount of money to be spent. Noah had good reason to collect two of every animal. Your child doesn't need to collect every item eligible for membership in his collection.

Keep track of the amount you spend by taping receipts in a notebook. Show older children where to find pricing information and how to work within a budget.

Oftentimes, too, parents set the purchasing bar high. See how little you can get away with spending. Kalpana limited her son's collection of flags in terms of quantity and quality. "I didn't buy him too many flags," she says. "I bought him the kind of flags you buy at party stores and come with a stand. He has maybe fifteen on his table."

Tie purchases to chores, good deeds, and special occasions. Tell friends and family that your child collects. Birthdays and holidays then become opportunities to add to the collection.

By limiting the amount of money spent and the number of items that may be accrued, unexpected purchases become more meaningful. Though Jacksier generally limited new additions to her son's collection of foxes to one a year, she did make exceptions. "He found one once on summer vacation that was a puppet and we bought it," she says, "and one in Italy and we bought it."

Finally, convey to your child that you expect the collection to transcend purchases. Then seek ways to pursue the collection that don't involve purchases. I'll explore those ways later in this chapter.

Beware Negative Nincompoops

No matter how cool your child considers her collection, there are those out there who will belittle it. Whether they've never had a collection or consider their own far superior, the reasons are not important. What is important is that you avoid these people just as you would avoid anyone who would disparage your child's interest.

Beware, too, collection snobs, who come in two varieties: adults who have never had a collection, and children who resent what others cherish. A collection snob will chuckle at your child's pencil collection. They'll scratch their heads over why anyone, even a child, would want to collect bottle caps. Whether their comments are meant to sting is irrelevant. Often all that's needed is a gentle but firm reminder that you don't appreciate such comments. If that doesn't work, scratch Uncle Ken from future functions at your home.

If someone does direct a negative comment your child's way,

assure the youngster that it's only one person's opinion. Then consider how your child reacts to it. A child who is passionate about her collection won't be swayed by a negative comment. In fact, it'll test her devotion to it.

Different Reasons for Collecting

The obvious oftentimes eludes us. That's why it's important to ask your child why she likes to collect, even if you think you know the answer. Chances are, her response will differ from the one you expected.

Indeed, when asked why they collect rocks, three children, ages ten to thirteen, gave three different answers:

- "They're interesting to look at and they make great paper-weights, doorstops, centerpieces, and bookends."
- "Collecting rocks gets me outdoors and helps me learn more about Earth's history."
- "I find it pleasing to look at a rock and know not only what it is but where it came from and all about its location in geology."

Knowing what drives your child to collect will help you pursue the activity from a perspective that interests your child. The quote from the first rock collector indicates she would probably enjoy displaying her collection for others to view. The second collector might enjoy combining rock collecting with hiking where she could find specimens. The third might enjoy beefing up his collection with a selection of rock-related books.

If You Can't Say Something Nice . . .

It's absolutely amazing, but given the chance parents can, and often will, say or do something negative regarding their child's collection.

A comment meant to amuse friends—"Can you believe my kid actually collects this stuff?" An act such as cleaning your paint brush in a mug from your daughter's mug collection. These are the kinds of things that destroy in minutes the self-esteem that grew from the collection and took months to nurture.

Treat your child's collection with respect, and don't under any circumstances toss the collection if your child loses interest in it. Certainly, many of us have painful memories of similar experiences, including Bryan, who as an adult still remembers vividly the day his mother threw away ephemera he collected as a youngster. "My mother threw out a box that contained magazines and other things," he recalls. "I was furious."

READY, SET, COLLECT!

"The taste for collecting is like a game played with utter passion," says Rheims. To keep that passion alive, consider the following ways to pursue collecting with your child:

Center Activities Around It

Incorporate the collection into your child's favorite activities. If Brian collects model airplanes and loves to draw, have him sketch his favorite ones.

Create craft projects around the collection. At a stamp collecting club, members glue everyday stamps on paper to create unique artwork. One child pasted to a sheet of paper flag stamps in the shape of a tree. Have your child decorate his school notebook with stickers from his collection. Build a tiny forest of twigs and rocks for your child's collection of miniature animal figurines.

When your child has a friend over, whip out the collection. Have them spend a few minutes with it. Allow your child to demonstrate his knowledge of the collection by explaining its various intricacies. If the friend shows interest in it, suggest they collect together.

Encourage your child to organize her collection in unique ways. Instead of color, size, shape, and texture, organize it by when the items were acquired, by value as measured by your child—most sentimental, most attractive.

Instead of reading a book at night, or in addition to it, study the collection. Discuss aspects of it you like best. What you'd like to learn about it. How to overcome obstacles related to it. One fifteen-year-old stamp collector put his problem-solving skills to the test when he figured out that he could reduce the time it takes to soak off self-adhesive stamps from envelopes by using his fish tank heater.

Data Collectors

Collecting goes beyond gathering objects. It also involves assembling information.

Encourage your child to check out library books on his collectible. If your daughter has earned the honor of purchasing an ancient Greek or Roman coin (they're not uncommon and cost only a few dollars), research it and discuss the stories behind it, the history, the drama.

Reference books offer information on where a collectible was manufactured, how it was advertised, who used it, and how it was used. Such a search often leads youngsters out of the children's section of their local libraries and into the grown-up world of the adult section.

Jacksier credits her son's interest in collecting insulators with getting him to want to read and learn the history behind them. "I do a lot of book reviews," she says, "and one day he asked, 'Are there any books on glass insulators?' I said, 'I don't know. Why don't you look it up online.' That was when he was twelve or thirteen, and he found a book for nineteen dollars. I said, 'Okay, we'll get it for you the next time we have a gift-giving occasion.' "

Young collectors can also take their passion beyond books. Jacksier has met children who collect butter pats, small individual plates for butter popular during the Victorian era. As a result, she says, "They got interested in butter making and made their own butter."

Look for books that feature characters and topics related to your child's collectibles. If four-year-old Shelly collects cat figurines, locate books featuring cat characters or fiction about cats written in foreign languages.

Become a Fun Fact Master

Make a habit of searching out facts related to your child's collection.

If your son collects coins featuring animals, tell him the model for the buffalo nickel was a real bison named Black Diamond who lived in New York City's Central Park Zoo at the turn of the century. Whether he has a buffalo nickel is irrelevant. Such trivia adds a new dimension to collecting and injects children with the learning bug.

If your daughter collects statehood quarters, show her how to locate on each coin the letter "P," "D" or "S." Tell her each represents one of the three mints—Philadelphia, Denver, and San Francisco—that produce state quarters.

Read (and Write) All About It

Young collectors often don't need much prodding to incorporate their collectibles into school work. "Foxes appeared in lots of essays, art projects, and science reports," says Jacksier of her son Frederic.

Collections can also be used to physically illustrate homework problems. Use Carolyn's collection of horse figurines to illustrate addition and subtraction problems. Whip out the shell collection for a geology lesson. Use Kevin's collection of rulers to study measurement.

In addition to incorporating the collection into homework, bring the collection to school. Allow Kelly to bring in her collection of party hats to show-and-tell. If the collectible is large (or, God forbid, alive), photograph it and have your child bring in a snapshot.

Discuss with the school's principal ways to encourage students to display their collectibles. Simonds Elementary School principal Judith Pellettieri set up a case outside her office for the sole purpose of displaying her students' collections. Other schools exhibit their students' collections on tables, shelves, and cases in their lobbies and libraries.

Ask your child if she'd like to display her collection in her local public library. Children's sections in these facilities often feature cases for such purposes. However, waiting time can be as long as six months, so you may want to book it but wait till your slot comes up before notifying your young one.

When the library staff at ten-year-old Noah's school discovered he collected colorful wall hangings, they offered to display them on a bulletin board in the library. The staff also turned them into a teaching tool.

"I volunteer at the school library, and we do art projects at lunchtime," says Noah's mother. "The librarian designed a project around the display, and the kids made collages with bits of fabric glued to them."

HANDS-ON IDEA

If your child enjoys the social aspects of collecting, order business cards for her or print a batch on your home computer. Give her the title "Collector," include lots of color, and if you can, scan onto it a photo of her favorite collectible.

Take a Little Trip

Incorporate the collection into a vacation or day trip. If Alison collects lighthouses, visit a real one. If Holly collects seeds, take her on a hike to collect specimens. (In fact, many hiking clubs feature family hikes on which you may run into children interested in collecting with your child.)

If your child has exhausted the local library's selections dealing with her collectibles, consider visiting a larger library in a nearby city, or visiting bookstores that specialize in the collectible.

Keep an eye out for temporary exhibits at nearby museums. Terry collects shells. When a nearby museum featured an exhibit on pearls, her parents took her to it. Or plan family vacations around special-interest museums. If Timothy collects fire trucks, visit The Firehouse Museum in San Diego, California. If Melissa collects horse figurines, visit the American Saddlebred Museum in Lexington, Kentucky.

Members Only

Join a club related to your child's collection, and if you can't find a club, start one.

Paul Krell is a longtime stamp collector who decided to share his interest with children. "I thought, Wouldn't it be exciting to introduce the kids to this most popular hobby?" His first club went so well he started clubs in two more towns. "In one town, we started with four kids," he says. "At the second meeting, seven attended. We're now up to fifteen."

The groups meet once a month, except in July and August, and are limited to children ages nine to thirteen. "I figure at that age, they have some understanding and appreciation for the importance of collecting stamps," says Krell. "I make exceptions if I see an eight-year-old who's bright and sharp and interested."

If the idea of starting a club isn't in the cards, consider forming a sort of quasi-club of collectors consisting of your child's cousins. Family gatherings then become occasions to discuss the collections, play with them and add to them. To avoid quarrels and hurt feelings (among the children, that is), get everyone's agreement that they'll adhere to preestablished rules and budgets.

HANDS-ON IDEA

Consider bringing the joy of collecting into another child's life. If your niece or nephew likes sharks, find stamps or stickers featuring sharks and attach them to a birthday gift.

Start a Journal

In their book *Hidden Treasures,* antique experts Leigh and Leslie Keno describe how at the age of twelve they started a joint diary to keep track of their stoneware purchases. "Happy News!! Just now our mother (mom) told us that she had a birthday present picked. And better than that, the present is stoneware," reads one of the entries.

The Keno twins used an ordinary spiral-bound notebook. Today, you can go all out and purchase fancy notebooks, stencils, and special pens. If it entices your child to keep a journal, perhaps it's worth the extra cash outlay.

If your child bristles at the idea of keeping any sort of journal, at least maintain a ledger of how the item was acquired, its cost, and the date received. Such information gives a collection a whole new dimension. If the ledger is too much work, jot the information on a label and place it on the collectible or on the packaging in which it came.

Love on Display

Nothing says love like parents who allow their home to be overtaken by their child's collection.

Amy allows her fifteen-year-old son to keep his collection of some 300 antique appliances in several rooms in their house. Dina's mother cleared off enough tabletop space in her living room to display her daughter's collection of some 25 pottery pieces. Nine-year-old Elisabeth is allowed to display her collection of more than 400 stickers on her bedroom door.

Find a place in your home specifically for your child's collection. Put it where visitors will see it, in the family room perhaps, where it can serve double duty as a distraction from the television.

Keep the display visually and physically accessible to your child. If it's on a shelf, hang it so your child can reach it. If your child's statehood quarter collection is kept in a foldable cardboard book, prop it open on a shelf for all to see. A pin collection can be easily mounted on felt-covered cardboard and hung on the wall.

Even with budgets and limitations on the scope of the collection, it may outgrow the space allotted to it. "My house came close to becoming inundated with foxes," says Jacksier. "[My son's] room was definitely overrun, so we started rotating the stock in and out of the closet."

Collections don't end when your child loses interest in, or outgrows, them. When Frederic started high school, he decided to redecorate his room, whose theme was clearly one of forests and foxes. "He didn't want his friends coming in and seeing four hundred foxes," says Jacksier.

Today all but a handful of foxes have been removed from his room. "Most of them are sitting in large bins in a spare room, and some he talked me into 'adopting,' " says Jacksier, who displays several in the living room and porch. "I figure it's his house, and part of who he is as a collector."

HANDS-ON IDEA

A shadow box is a display case for collectibles. It can consist of a box with a glass cover hung on the wall to hold one or more items. It can also have compartments within it to hold several collectibles. Those without a glass front enable children to remove and add items, and to organize the collectibles in different ways.

Validate the Effort

Whether or not they'll admit it—and many older children won't—young collectors appreciate their parents' efforts to validate their collections. Certainly, displaying the collection is an effective way to endorse your child's efforts. Other ways include having a display shelf or case specially made for the collection, or having a sign made—"Jennifer's party hat collection."

When Frederic and his family moved to Virginia, he went with his mother to register the family's two cars, which included a station wagon. "Unlike New York State, it was only like ten dollars to get a vanity plate," says Jacksier, who agreed to purchase license plates that read FOXWAGON and FOXWOOD—the latter named after the place of residence of a fox in one of Frederic's books.

Upgrading the collection is another way to validate it. "I bought an Australian purple insulator when all of his were white and green," says Jacksier, referring to her son's collection of glass insulators. "I spent twenty-five dollars on it as a special gift. It took the collection to a new level."

She adds that her move was a one-time act that wasn't repeated. "It was nice to have that special one, but now he still looks for bargains," she says.

The Web That Binds

The thrill of the hunt used to be the main reason for collecting. Today, combing through flea markets, riffling through "junk," and haggling face-to-face have been replaced by a computer screen and a keyboard. Are children destined to become couch-potato collectors?

The Internet makes it easy to collect, "which is why we avoid it," says Jacksier, who adds that it can teach children valuable lessons about the many so-called bargains that can be found online. "Having a child spend his own money and get bad merchandise is a great lesson," she adds.

Because the Internet looms large over children's collectibles, it's important to use it sparingly. Parents of young children can avoid it altogether. Parents can use it as they would a reference book to learn more about the collectible and pass along the information verbally to their child.

For older children, reading entries from other young people is a way to socialize with their collecting counterparts. But the time spent doing so should be limited and supervised.

For technically advanced parents, the web is a computerized display case for the world to see. One parent designed a web site to display his daughter's collection of rubber ducks. It can be found at www.hand-family.org/Claire/Duckies.

Trading Pieces

Children have been trading collectibles since Hall did his study in 1900. For young children, oversee their trades. Children often get caught up in trading, only later to realize they've swapped their favorite or most valuable card for an inferior one.

To avoid tears and hurt feelings, impose trading rules: The collection stays in the house, no trading unless an adult is present, and trades are subject to a one-day waiting period during which the tradee may reconsider the transaction.

START NOW

Pursuing a collection is like pursuing an interest—on a smaller scale. Like interests, collections are a source of pride. They involve the child at a higher level than most everything else she does. She decides what to collect, how to organize it, and what to add to it (within reason).

A collection of rabbit-themed thimbles could initiate an interest in sewing stuffed rabbits. A child interested in writing might start collecting pens. Or a collection of paperweights could be the interest itself.

The important thing is to start collecting. Don't agonize over what to collect. Choose something your child likes and slowly—very slowly—add to it and enjoy it together. You'll collect some very fond memories.

What You Need to Know About Pursuing a Collection

- Collections offer children reassurance, escapism, a sense of accomplishment, and a desire to want to learn.
- The social aspect of collecting is what draws many adults to collect. But children, too, enjoy the social aspect of collecting, especially sharing their collections with people and groups outside their immediate social circles.

- Young children are natural collectors. They often become attached to objects, selecting their favorites and surrounding themselves with them.
- Collecting becomes rewarding and enjoyable when adults refrain from putting high expectations on young collectors. A two-year-old may want to sort her collection by color, or she may not want to organize her collection at all.
- The ages between seven and twelve have been termed the active phase of collecting. During this time, children seek greater independence. A collection enables them to assert their autonomy as they seek out items they deem appropriate to the collection and exercise authority over it.
- Teenagers are quick learners of the basics of their collectibles, so whatever you do, don't treat them like preteens. Lead your teen to information on the collectibles, but don't decipher it for him.
- While it's common for children to lose the collecting bug at some point in their lives, girls seem to lose it earlier and for longer periods. To retain the passion for collecting, consider starting a collection together with your daughter. Collect objects she's less likely to outgrow, such as postcards, key chains, or nostalgia-based items.
- Though rules on purchases and maintenance of the collection are a must, the collection should be based on your child's preferences and ideas.
- Collections are not initiated to be completed. Help your child add to her collection, but set limits on when objects may be added and the amount of money to be spent.
- Avoid people who belittle your child's collection.
- Knowing what drives your child to collect will help you pursue the activity from a perspective that interests him—whether it's reading books on the collectible, displaying them for all to see, or cataloging the items in a ledger.
- Treat your child's collection with respect. If your child loses interest in the collection, store it away carefully in a place your child can access—in case she decides to revive it. But don't under any circumstances throw it away.

- Incorporate the collection into your child's favorite activities. If Brian collects model airplanes and likes to draw, have him sketch his favorite ones.
- Encourage your child to read reference and historical books as well as fiction related to her collectibles, and to incorporate the collection into school essays, art projects, and science reports.
- Search for facts related to the collection, then share them with your child.
- Libraries and schools often have display cases in which children may display their collections. Ask your child if she would like to participate in such an activity.
- Encourage your child to maintain a journal related to his collection. If he bristles at the idea, suggest keeping a ledger listing such information as how the item was acquired, its cost, and the date received. Such information gives a collection a whole new dimension.
- Set aside a special place in your home for your child's collection. Put it where visitors will see it and where it is visually and physically accessible to your child.
- Validate your child's collection by having a display shelf or case specially made for it, or having a sign made—"Bobby's boat collection."

• The Birth of a Young Collector •

Many people collect something. Some others, like Noah, are born collectors.

"When I was waiting for Noah to be born, I was preparing a room for his nursery—we live in earthquake country, so I didn't want anything on the wall to fall and hurt him. I thought it would be nice to have cloth wall hangings. I saw them at a store and bought two," says Noah's mother Saarin.

"Coincidentally, an aunt of mine sent him one," she continues. "What's the saying? Three makes a collection?"

The wall hangings are called "arpilleras" and are made by

women's collectives in South America. A typical arpillera consists of a large piece of fabric on which colorful smaller pieces of cloth are hand-stitched to create a background of sky, mountains, and fields. Onto this background are sewn small three-dimensional cloth dolls, vegetables, and farm animals.

Wall Art

Ten-year-old Noah's collection graces his bedroom walls and depicts farms as well as less common designs, including a zoo, a Maypole festival, and Noah's ark. Having been surrounded by his arpilleras since infancy, the ten-year-old has no intention of replacing them with anything else.

However, he was persuaded to take them down temporarily to display them on a bulletin board in his school library. "I volunteer at the school library, and we do art projects at lunchtime," says Saarin. "The librarian designed a project around the display, and the kids made collages with bits of fabric glued onto them."

Though proud of the notoriety he received, Noah admits he missed his wall hangings. "When the arpilleras were taken down to go to the library and I walked into the room, it felt enormous," he says. "I missed them at first and was very glad when they were hung up back in their places."

Still, Noah harbors an interest in exhibiting his arpilleras yet again—in the young collector's tent at the annual county fair, which awards prizes to the best collections. "We always intended to enter my arpilleras in the contest," he says. "I would definitely love to do that. I always love to look around there."

A Family Affair

It's no surprise that Noah appreciates collections. "It's hard to escape being a collector in our family," says Saarin, who collects Fiesta ware and other vintage kitchenware, as well as moose figurines. Her husband collects old comics and rubber stamps.

"My interest in brightly colored Fiesta ware has probably piqued Noah's interest in arpilleras," adds Saarin.

In addition to arpilleras, Noah collects tin toys, dreidels, Beatles memorabilia, rocks, and most recently, penguins. But his main passion is for his arpilleras. "They're beautiful to look at," he says simply.

Interestingly, you would think that a boy who loves collecting would be awash in the collectible. But not Noah. Though he has been collecting arpilleras all his life, he has just eleven of the wall hangings.

"It grows very slowly, normally around birthdays and holidays," he says. "Each year I seem to gain one or two more."

The pace at which his collection grows suits Noah fine. "Noah enjoys having the collection, but he's not so into the process of seeking them," says Saarin. "I, too, would rather do it slowly, and enjoy going to antique stores and flea markets rather than eBay.

"The ideal collection is one that is not too easy to find and not too hard," she adds.

A Neat Ten-Year-Old?

Noah's respect for his collections is evident in the way in which he organizes and maintains them. "Pretty much everything is in my room," says Noah of his collectibles. "My tin toys are kept on a shelf; the dreidels are in a box I take out in December."

Like his arpilleras, Noah's other collections expand at an unhurried pace. "Some [collections] grow slowly because I'm not into them anymore, and some grow faster by accident, and some grow deliberately," he says.

Such a laid-back approach helps to keep collecting fresh. "Every once in a while he takes the tin toys or rocks out and plays with them," says Saarin. "It's like getting something new."

Perhaps Noah's appreciation for his collections stems from the fact that all the items he collects fascinate him, whether it's the intricate handwork that goes into his arpilleras or the natural beauty inherent in a rock. This would explain his advice to other young collectors: "Collect something that runs parallel to your interests and pleasures."

6

In Pursuit of Interests—Part I

Passionate about gardening, Kris and Peter wanted to ensure that their children loved it as much as they did. "I think Cole was two years old when we decided that the best way for him to develop a love of gardening was to give him his own garden," says Kris.

Today, each of their two children, ages eleven and eight, has a twenty-square-foot garden—small when compared to the seven acres of property their parents tend. Yet within that space, each child decides what to plant. "Their gardens are small, but fanciful," says Kris.

"This year we took Latin classes, and Cole made a Mount Vesuvius garden," she says. "He made a huge conical mound of soil and had marigolds coming down like lava, and white verbena and black pansies for the ash."

A SENSE OF ACCOMPLISHMENT

Giving children a sense of responsibility gives them the opportunity to feel accomplished. Accomplishments come in many sizes—

from huge successes to tiny triumphs. All should be praised. Here are ways to do that:

- Sprinkle your conversation with positive comments, without going overboard in either direction.

Disparaging remarks will make the time you spend together sound like a criticizing fest. Also unproductive are over-the-top remarks such as "You're better than anyone else in the world!" Not only do both of you know it's not true, it won't accomplish its intended purpose: making your child feel good about pursuing her interest. Rather, stick with comments that mirror the truth: "You're really getting good at that," "I'm so proud of you," and "You're teaching me."

You also want to avoid becoming a nonstop mouthpiece for your child's interest. If someone asks a question pertaining to your child's interest, answer it in a straightforward, matter-of-fact manner. Stick to the interest itself, and don't go overboard detailing how fantastic, magnificent, and just plain superb your child is at it. Such a move may embarrass your child or create in her a feeling of having to live up to your grandiose descriptions.

- Instill a sense of accomplishment the first time you pursue the interest with your child.

Praise your child for reading a book on the interest. Commend her for suggesting a unique way to pursue her interest. "Every true effort is good, and you need to tell them that," says Richard Starr, a woodworking teacher in Hanover, New Hampshire, and author of *Woodworking With Your Kids* (Taunton Press, 1990).

Learn to find joy in your mistakes. Cole and his family built an earthworm box to produce castings to use as fertilizer in the garden. "We didn't have the shocking results where we had a seething mass of worms," says Kris. "But we still loved to do it."

- Make your child feel in charge when it comes to pursuing the interest. "Find out what they like and then do that with them," says Cindy Ross, who instilled in her two children a love of the great outdoors.

"There are so many outdoor sports that it doesn't have to be hiking," she says. "It can be anything. And then, where do they want to go? What do they want to see? Do they like animals? Do they like the weather better? Would they like to see Florida instead of New England? That lets them be the boss."

Kevin Nierman, who teaches children ceramics at his Kids 'N' Clay Pottery Studio in West Berkeley, California, says his mother was instrumental in encouraging him to take charge. "If I was having a problem with something, she'd say, 'Well, what if . . . ?' That's the way we worked it, and that's the way she structured my life," he says.

"It allowed me to be more creative about finding my way," he continues, "thereby staying with what I loved and finding a way to keep doing what I loved, which was working with clay."

HANDS-ON IDEA

When parents see the glimmer of an interest, they often seek to enroll their child in a class or program related to it. Before making such an investment, consider activities you and your child can pursue together.

MAKE IT A SOCIAL AFFAIR

Children with passions benefit when their parents commit themselves to nurturing those interests. But an interest can really take off when others are involved, including siblings, grandparents, your child's friends, your acquaintances, and mentors.

Siblings

When Steve was five years old, he was head over heels about dinosaurs. But as he got older, his passion faded. "My love for fossils seemed to disappear as soon as I discovered my passion for baseball," says the now seventeen-year-old.

Chris, Steve's younger brother by four years, never outgrew the dinosaur phase. Starting at the age of four, he put on dinosaur puppet shows for his friends and transformed his room into a dinosaur museum. Aptly named Dino Land, it is filled with dinosaur figures, fossils, posters, magazines, news clippings, and hundreds of books.

When he was ten, Chris asked his brother for help with a report he was writing on dinosaurs. "I began looking through his books and became hooked," says Steve. "Paleontology grew on me so quickly that I began to read voraciously, started to communicate with those who shared my interest, and decided on a career in paleontology."

Together, the brothers maintain Dino Land, and plan to continue doing so "until we go our separate ways in college," says Steve, who has even designed a website around Dino Land: www.geocities.com/CapeCanaveral/Galaxy/8152/dinoland.html.

Leigh and Leslie Keno are another set of siblings, albeit identical twins, who have thrived on nurturing each other's passion for antiques. Well known for their appearances on public television's "Antiques Roadshow," the Kenos spent their childhood in upstate New York, where they would search the land, finding such artifacts as nineteenth century U.S. military-issue bullets and antique wrought iron hinges and door handles. They write in their book, *Hidden Treasures: Searching for Masterpieces of American Furniture* (Warner Books 2000): "We always worked and bought objects as a team. Honestly, I don't think it even occurred to us to go it alone. We just took so much pleasure in our partnership and dialogue, it would have been unnatural, if not boring, to have competed for things."

Though Steve and Chris were willing to maintain one "museum" and the Keno twins worked as a team, your children may need more of a separate but equal set up. Kris allocated a separate garden plot to each of her children and encouraged them to develop their own interests outside gardening.

Another way to encourage your children to pursue the same interest is by choosing one with a broad theme. Gardening covers lots of territory. It allowed Cole and Lily to create their own fanciful gardens—in fact, except for the dirt, their gardens have little in common. Gardening also gave them the foundation to develop additional interests, including bird watching and writing poetry containing nature themes.

Outdoor recreation is such a broad interest that it enables each member of the Ross family to pursue his or her own interests simultaneously. When her daughter expressed an interest in fishing, Cindy Ross chose fly-fishing, because it would enable other family members who preferred not to fish to enjoy the outdoors in their own way.

Hands-on Interest

Given that cars are beginning to resemble family rooms, more parents are warming to the idea of installing a television or DVD player in their vehicle. Don't do it.

Instead, stock your car with items geared toward your children's interests. Promote creativity, not passivity, by stocking your car with colored pencils, paper, an audiocassette player and tapes, books, binoculars, field guides, and magnifying glasses. Rotate the items so things stay fresh. Now a car trip becomes an opportunity for siblings to pursue an interest together.

Grandparents

Grandparents bring to the interest-development process unique qualities. They are likely to appreciate interests, especially having one to fall back on later in life. They may compare the slow pursuit of interests with the simpler days of their own childhoods. They also tend to have more time than parents, minus parental pressures.

As a girl growing up in California, Lovejoy was mentored by her grandmother. Their relationship was so strong that when her grandmother passed away, it took years before Lovejoy began gardening again. "When my grandma died, I played outside all the time," she says. "I roamed around the hills and climbed trees, but it took a while for it to come back. Then when I was a teen-ager, I started gardening again."

HANDS-ON IDEA

Respect your child's preference with regard to sharing her interest. That means getting her permission before sharing the interest with another adult or child. The last thing you want is for your child's interest to alienate her from her friends.

If your child chooses to share her interest with no one other than yourself, consider yourself lucky. Pursuing an interest alone with your child is one of life's little pleasures. Cherish it. And protect it from outside influences that may hinder or even squash it.

Friends

Boys who garden might be a recipe for social ostracizing from like-aged peers. But take an eleven-year-old male who grows enormous pumpkins for his friends and creates sunflower mazes for them to cavort through, and you suddenly have a hero.

"Cole's friends think his garden is so cool," says Kris. "They're always interested in it and are wowed by it and express an interest in doing it at their houses."

Children might very well be drawn to sunflower mazes and "power" veggies. They might marvel at your son's ability to fly a two-handed kite or your daughter's knowledge of folk art produced by children her own age during the eighteenth century. But if the interest doesn't pique their curiosity, they will very quickly let it be known they'd rather discuss and do something else.

Children with interests learn fairly quickly when to back away from sharing them with peers. Respect their decision, because they understand better than you the social etiquette requirements among their own set.

Thirteen-year-old Julie's love of Shakespearean acting is a passion not easily shared with most children. "She's very careful about who she shares that interest with," says her mother Susan.

Children who are passionate about their interest will find ways to pursue it while at the same time being accepted by peers. Julie uses her talent as a social ice-breaker. "Her ability to do impressions and accents wins her a lot of fans," says Susan.

Children with interests often have two sets of friends, differentiated by whether they're involved in the interest. Meghan's friends once accompanied her and her father on falconry outings. But as she got older, her friends' interest diminished. It's now something Meghan does with her father as well as with a female teenager who apprentices with her father and has become a friend.

Certainly, it pays to keep an eye open for events, activities, and other opportunities that involve your child with youngsters interested in the same things. In these forums, children are free to pursue their passions without the fear of social ostracism.

Lovejoy has long recognized the importance of get-togethers to strengthen passions. To that end, she helped organize two annual festivals, a Rosemary Festival and a Children's Faerie Festival. "I found that festivals and traditions outside were important for kids," she says.

"Bring them together and establish traditions," Lovejoy continues. "They love it! They absolutely love celebrations. I'm not talking about celebrations where you get a pile of birthday gifts. But they're hearing music. We have a man who dresses up like a tree and plays the guitar and sings nature songs. We have speakers who bring bugs, and the kids love it."

INTEREST-RELATED FACT

Being the human sponges that they are, many children with interests move quickly from amateur to junior expert status.

But that doesn't apply to all children, and just because a child pursues an interest doesn't mean he has to be good at it. The idea behind interests is to build self-esteem, which comes from infusing children with a sense of mastery—regardless of their level of expertise.

Adult Acquaintances

Siblings and like-aged peers may not always give your child the kind of attention that encourages her interest. A sensitive adult can often fill that void.

If your child enjoys sharing her interest with others, involve them. "The first thing we do is, if the kids don't suggest it, we suggest, 'Hey, why don't we take Uncle Bill down to see your garden,' " says Kris. "They're enormously proud of their gardens. It's one of the first things they want to show people when they come."

Amanda prefers to keep her interest a "private passion," according to her mother Rachel. However, she has found encouragement from adults, including her mother's friend, who gave a journal and pen to Amanda for her eighth birthday. "My friend knew that my daughter enjoyed writing because it was something my friend and I also enjoyed," says Rachel. "She was anxious to encourage that talent in my daughter also and knew that my daughter was showing an interest in it."

As your child learns more about his interest, keep an eye out for opportunities to involve him with adults. As teenagers, Leigh and Leslie Keno gave informal lectures on their collection of stoneware to adult audiences. Cole has given talks on birds at senior centers. Meghan demonstrates falconry before an audience of college students.

If you practice the interest with your child, you may want to assist your child in giving a talk on her interest. Meghan's father accompanies her on her demonstrations. Clark and Chris demonstrate historic drum and fife playing at an elementary school and a summer camp. Such an activity introduces your child to the concept of lecturing without the fear of going it alone.

HANDS-ON IDEA

Chances are, someone in your community shares the same interest as your child. It might be a 4-H leader, a teacher, or someone in your book group. Read the local newspaper, talk to parents, and keep an eye and an ear out for the name of someone who can help your child further her interest.

Mentors

Mentors do not necessarily have to be experts in a particular field. They can simply be caring people who can fill voids that you cannot.

A mentor can be someone in your community. When nine-year-old Kathryn expressed an interest in agility training for her new border collie, her father joined a local collie club. One member has spent a good deal of time with them advising them on trainers and agility events in their area.

A mentor can be a teacher. Twelve-year-old Julie's teachers alerted her parents to their daughter's writing and acting abilities. "Her sixth-grade teacher asked at the first parent-teacher conference last year if we'd considered getting Julie into community theater, and strongly suggested that we look for acting opportunities for her," says Julie's mother.

If your child's interest centers around the arts, find an art teacher who appreciates your child's passion. "Teachers in the arts sometimes see a completely different child," says Richard Starr, who has taught woodworking for thirty years in the Dresden School District of Hanover, New Hampshire, and Norwich, Vermont. "My role is to be supportive. I don't compare one kid's work to another kid's work."

Mentors are all around us. The problem is that few people take advantage of all they have to offer, says Neil Johnson, author of National Geographic's *Photography Guide for Kids* (2001). "As a photographer, I've been in this one community for over twenty years, and people every once in a while will come to me and say, 'I really love photography. Help me with this,' " he says. "I grab hold of these people, because they're fairly rare, and say, 'I'm open. Call me anytime.'

"It's so rare that people do that," he continues. "It's surprisingly rare. It's disappointing. You know everyone out there is taking pictures. But [of] the people who call me, and I'm talking about out of the blue, [one] might be the child of a friend, but it's very rare."

The people who do call him tend to be teenagers or college

students. "Somebody from the college down the highway called me and wanted to buy me lunch," he says. "I said, 'Absolutely, let's go. You name the time and I'll drop what I'm doing.' "

His advice? "Not just photography but in any field, people are out there willing to help you. All you have to do is ask. There are people who say, 'No, I don't have time.' But there are plenty of people out there who are totally willing to say, 'Call me anytime.' Don't be afraid to ask. Explain what you're doing, and I guarantee there's a lot of help out there in whatever field."

In fact, that person may be sitting next to you in the dentist's office. While waiting for a cleaning, Peter and his nine-year-old son Cole struck up a conversation with a gentleman who turned out to be George V. Van Deventer, of the Live Poets Society, Maine.

Sensing an opportunity, Peter asked George if he would teach a poetry class to some home-schoolers, including Cole and his six-year-old daughter Lily. Though George considered Lily too young, he obliged.

"We have enormous faith in our children's ability to learn and never feel that they are too young to tackle a subject they are interested in," says Kris. "If they are interested, we figure they're ready."

Lily turned out to be a natural. So much so, in fact, that Van Deventer submitted three of her poems to *Off the Coast*, the publication of the Live Poets Society. All were accepted and published.

"We were unaware that he had submitted these on her behalf," says Kris. "We were thrilled, though, after he e-mailed us and told us they were accepted and would be published."

Some children are lucky enough to fall upon a group of mentors. When he realized the degree to which his son Chris loved participating in historical reenactments, Clark decided it was time to join such a group. Though Chris was young, and technically not supposed to participate in the reenactments, members admired his passion. They not only allowed him to march with them (as long as his father marched alongside) but provided him with field-music books and tapes and helped him learn to play the drum.

It's important to note that Clark was able to get his son into the group in a capacity generally reserved for teenagers and adults. He didn't wait until Chris was of age to march with the other participants.

Likewise, Kris wasn't deterred when local Audubon members told her that her son was too young to participate in a seminar on owls followed by a banding expedition. Not only did Cole eventually attend the seminar, he wowed the audience with his knowledge of birds. Today, he counts as a mentor and friend an ornithologist from a local nonprofit educational institution.

Lovejoy has seen firsthand what mentoring can do. "What has been happening in a lot of cities [is that] the kids are raising small plots of tomatoes and hot peppers and stuff," she says. "They sell it at a farmer's market or they make something from it, with mentors, and they sell it through school or through various organizations."

She warns against limiting mentors to just adults. "Older kids are good mentors too," she says. "You still have to have sort of an overseer because it can get pretty wild sometimes with kids throwing weeds and tossing tomatoes at each other. It gives older kids a sense of importance. They're almost like docents."

HANDS-ON IDEA

As you and your child become absorbed in a particular interest, you may want to consider becoming a mentor to another child. Meghan's father, a lifelong falconer, has two teenage apprentices under his wing.

Your child may even become a mentor. As a twelve-year-old drummer proficient in eighteenth century field music, Chris remembers what it was like to start out with a militia group. Today, Chris mentors a ten-year-old up-and-coming drummer in his reenactment group.

Make It Manageable

Eager to immerse their children in an interest, parents often overwhelm them. Here are ways to avoid that:

Start Small

If you want children to grow passionate about an interest, start small, says Lovejoy. "It has to be the sort of manageable thing that isn't hanging like a big lead weight over their heads," she says. "I love to have small plots of ground or little container gardens."

Starting small also avoids overwhelming or overprogramming your child. Says one mother: "Give her time to lie on her bed, stare at the ceiling, listen to music, and otherwise just 'be.' "

Hands-on Idea

Children love unusual-sounding words. So why not find those terms within a child's interest that make him giggle or spur him to explore the interest further? In basketball there's the "slam-dunk," in ceramics there's "wheel-throwing," in gardening there's "deadheading," and in coin collecting there's "cherrypicking," in which hobbyists look for rare coins still in circulation. Finding unusual words and phrases that coincide with an interest is like music to a child's ears.

Keep It Simple but Interesting

Simple and interesting *are* compatible. Think Shaker furniture. Chocolate cake. The little black dress.

"I have this poem I wrote," says Lovejoy. " 'Long straight rows are such a bore, gardens shouldn't be a chore.' " What kid is going to be enchanted by a long straight row of corn? What I did in my book was, I did a three sisters' garden of corn, beans, and squash, and I made a teepee that kids could crawl into. I did everything pretty much around themes."

As Kris's two children's interests branch out from gardening, she keeps the gardening interest strong by changing the theme of the children's gardens every year, and incorporating new elements into it, including chickens. "We discovered our chickens love cherry tomatoes," she says. "So now we're looking at the garden as a vehicle for producing healthy food for them as well as for us."

Make It Routine

Unless formal lessons are involved, throw away any idea of scheduling a specific time for the interest. Rather, weave activities related to it into your routines.

Read books about the interest at bedtime. Look for television shows related to the interest and watch them as a family. Or tape them and save them for a Friday TV night.

Parthiv's father helped his son pursue his interest in flags while watching the World Cup soccer matches on television. His father would quiz his son on matching flags with their corresponding countries. "Every time a team played, a flag would appear," says Parthiv's mother, Kalpana. "When he was five, he could recognize some one hundred flags."

HANDS-ON IDEA

Though you want to weave the pursuit of your child's interest into your routine, now and then you also want to add spontaneity.

On the way to an Audubon meeting, Cole spotted a "big, fat lump" in a tree. Recognizing an opportunity, his father pulled over and played an owl tape to see if the owl would respond. "It was a barred owl," says Cole, "and it was really amazing that we were able to see that."

Another father, who flies falcons with his two sons, will occasionally (depending on their grades) skip a day of school to fly falcons. He considers the time with them well spent. "We could skip a few days of math for what we gained in those outings," he says.

Slow It Down, Speedy

Obsessive is a word that comes to mind when dealing with interests. But often it's not children, but parents, who become consumed with pursuing the interest.

"What I found over the years is that some parents will say, 'My child loves this so much. Can we do three classes a week?' Sometimes I'll say yes," says ceramics teacher Kevin Nierman. "But depending on how the child is in the class, how interested, sometimes I'll say, 'I don't think it's such a great idea.' "

Cramming six months worth of activities into one month can be a big turn-off to a youngster. It's tempting, but remember, you're in this for the long haul. What's more, children are quite capable of committing themselves to a long-term project—a concept some parents seem to have trouble accepting, says woodworking teacher Richard Starr.

"In my class, one of the things that parents are amazed at is that a kid can work on a project that takes an extended amount of time," he says. "From the parents' point of view, they've never seen their kids carry through on a commitment. It has to do with being in a situation where the kids believe it's going to work and have a positive outcome."

HANDS-ON IDEA

Your daughter is fascinated by shells, so you take her to a museum featuring an exhibit on pearls.

Get the most out of the trip by prepping yourself beforehand. Read about the exhibit online and check out library books on the topic. Spend a few nights beforehand reading about pearls with your daughter. When you get there, you won't waste time deciphering the text by each display as your daughter bounces from one exhibit to another.

Behind the Scenes

Actively pursuing the interest with your child is only half the job; the other half involves your working behind the scenes, considering subsets of her interest that may be more appealing, scouting out opportunities to pursue the interest, and prepping yourself to get the most from your interest-related excursions.

To encourage her son's interest in flags and the countries they represent, Kalpana looks for opportunities to travel with her children. But before leaving for a destination, she performs a good deal of research. "Whenever we travel anywhere, we get books beforehand," she says.

Check your calendar and note days off from school, winter and spring recesses, and when summer vacation begins and ends. Then plan ways to use that time—even if it's just a half-day excursion.

Kalpana plans to use her summer to expose her two children to the history of their home state, California, by taking short trips to various sites. "I've listed out a bunch of landmarks, county by county," she says.

When the U.S. history bug bit her son Kyle at the age of three, Terry and her family began incorporating into their East Coast trips visits to battle sites like Bull Run, Antietam, and Gettysburg. "We probably wouldn't have thought of going to those places if not for Kyle," says Terry.

Don't forget, too, that even errands are trips—albeit short ones. But with the right planning they can be large learning experiences. "When you go to the nursery, have an idea of what you want," says Lovejoy. "Maybe you've gone to a botanical garden or a nursery and gotten an idea of what interested the kids."

What You Need to Know About Pursuing Interests— Part I

- A sense of responsibility and accomplishment is essential in developing interests. Give your child responsibility, then allow her to achieve something with it.
- Make the child feel in charge when it comes to choosing how to pursue the interest. Once you find out what they like, zero in on how they want to approach it.
- You don't have to go it alone. Involve siblings, grandparents, friends, and mentors.

• Start small, go slowly, make the interest part of your routine, and most important, keep it simple but interesting.

• A Work of Art in Progress •

As a new business owner, Linda decided to participate in a local workshop featuring entrepreneurs who wanted to advertise their products and services to the community. Accompanying her was her five-year-old daughter Hillary.

It wasn't long before the youngster grew bored and wandered off. "I went looking for her, and she was at Kevin's booth playing on the [potter's] wheel," says Linda, referring to Kevin Nierman, a ceramics artist who was at the show promoting his Kids 'N' Clay Pottery Studio, in Berkeley, California.

"I said, 'Oh, I'm sorry that she's over here,' " says Linda. "And he said, 'That's fine. Leave her. She's okay.' "

At the end of the day, Linda went to retrieve her daughter. "I said to him, 'You practically babysat her all day, so I feel like I should have her take your class,' " she says. "That's how it started."

From "Blob" to "Beautiful"

Today, Hillary is sixteen years old and has been regularly attending Nierman's school for the past eleven years. "The best thing about ceramics is the fact that you can take a blob of mud and make it into something beautiful," she says.

In addition to studying with Nierman, Hillary works for him as a summer counselor with his young students. "I once helped a three-year-old," says Hillary. "She did pretty well. She made a bowl."

Hillary can appreciate these small, early works because she was barely out of toddler-hood herself when she first sat at the wheel. "If you look at the things I made when I was little, it was stuff I was proud of at the time," she says. "But it was small and not that attractive."

As Hillary has grown, so too has her work. "It's gotten bigger and looks a little bit more professional," she says.

Among the bowls and vases she's made is one of her latest creations: a two-foot-tall, double-handled urn. "It's beautiful," says Linda. "People see her art and want to buy it."

Beyond mere size, Hillary's work has grown in complexity. "I'm trying to find out how the glazes work and how to get what I want out of them," she says. "I've switched from using the regular glazes that are just colors to Raku." (Raku is a Japanese method for firing clay that involves controlling a variety of factors.)

Spinning Presents

Hillary's more immediate concerns pertain to getting back to her own work after completing several pieces she gave as Christmas presents. "They were very late Christmas presents," she adds.

Perhaps she'll turn her attention to correcting glitches in some earlier pieces. "I like creating new things," she says, "and trying to improve on some of the things I've done."

One of those works includes a small table fountain. "I might make another fountain because the one I made didn't work very well," she says. "You buy the water pump from Home Depot and construct it so the water goes up and flows down."

On which table the finished piece will end up is anyone's guess. "I don't think there's any room that doesn't have a piece of my ceramics in it," she says, laughing. "It's everywhere."

How do her friends react to her interest? "My friends know that I do it," she says. "Not a lot of them have seen my work. But if they come to my house, they see it and say, 'That's cool.'"

Not Too Young to Know

Hillary's immediate attraction to the potter's wheel proves that children as young as preschoolers are capable not only of knowing what they want but sticking with it. It's enough to make any parent think twice before saying, "You have the attention span of a five-year-old."

In fact, sometimes it takes the unbiased eye of an outsider to detect the interest. "I didn't think it was something that could hold her interest," says Linda. "But Kevin says it was like she saw it and knew there was something there for her."

In Hillary's case, having the right teacher was paramount. While many ceramics teachers would direct youngsters into less complicated ceramic techniques such as hand-building or sculpture, Nierman has perfected the art of teaching children "wheel-throwing" techniques, and Hillary has proven an able student.

"It's difficult," says Linda. "But she did it."

Where Hillary will take her passion—or where it will take her—is anyone's guess, even Hillary's. "I'm probably going to continue doing it through high school," she says. "But I don't know later on. I might go to art school. I'm not sure."

Certainly, schoolwork has already begun to eat into her time at the wheel.

"She's slowing down now because she has high school and a lot of work," says Linda. "But she still goes down there [to Nierman's studio]."

No matter what turn Hillary's passion takes, she knows she can count on her mother for support. "When I was little, she would stay [at the studio] and help me even though she didn't know how to do it," says Hillary. "Now she is supportive on the side, telling me I do good. She likes all the things I make."

7

In Pursuit of Interests—Part II

When Terry found herself huddling beneath her big oak desk with her two young children during California's 1989 Loma Prieta earthquake, the last thing she expected was her four-year-old son Kyle's unexpected, but under the circumstances, relevant statement.

"We had all these redwood trees around us, and they were just snapping," says Terry. "The house twisted off its foundation. Kyle screamed, 'Give me liberty from this earthquake or give me death.' "

She adds: "We had read a bio on Patrick Henry at the library."

THE LOWDOWN ON HIGHBROW READING

As you and your child pursue an interest, consider all types of reading materials related to it, even—and perhaps especially—those outside your child's age level. All printed matter that may captivate your child's imagination is appropriate, as long as you find it acceptable.

Starting out, you may naturally gravitate toward reading material targeted to your child's age. But if the interest is strong, you may find yourself quickly depleting all the publishing world has to offer. "One thing that was frustrating was that for a kid interested in history, we exhausted the books quickly," says Terry of her son Kyle.

When Kyle was three years old, he would note the cover of the latest issue of *Newsweek* magazine lying around the house. In fact, he became incensed upon learning that when his mother went to vote in the primaries she didn't cast her ballot for Jesse Jackson, who had been featured on the cover of the newsweekly. "He was just furious," says Terry.

You'll know when your child is ready to sink his baby teeth into more substantial reading material. Coffee-table books and consumer magazines are fine on the condition that a parent is there to edit out inappropriate content. My six-year-old bellows with laughter over cartoons in *The New Yorker* magazine that I've dog-eared beforehand. In fact, he's so fond of the drawings, we cut them out and tack them to his bulletin board.

Consider a magazine subscription purchased in your child's name. While you may naturally gravitate toward children's magazines, they are usually limited to broad categories such as poetry, nature, and science. Niche magazines targeted to adults may be more appropriate. Not only will the publication cover topics in depth, it is something the two of you can learn from and share together.

In recent years, coloring books have matured to the point that they now fill the void between broad-based children's magazines and adult niche magazines. Today's coloring books delve into tightly focused topics, are targeted to specific age groups, and offer informative facts as well as what you'd expect from such a product—pictures to color.

When Kris noticed her seven-year-old son Cole continually watching the birds outside, she purchased *Peterson Field Guide Coloring Book—Birds*. "The Peterson coloring books are actually extremely sophisticated—very fine, small and informational," she says. "You learn a lot about different types of feathers and wings."

HANDS-ON IDEA

Coloring books have come a long way since I was a kid. They cover many niche subjects and contain a lot of information. Some are printed on heavy white paper rather than standard newsprint. The following web sites offer a variety of reasonably priced high-end coloring books:

Clare's Coloring Cottage offers coloring books for ages two through fourteen, starting at a couple of dollars, on topics ranging from farm life to great paintings to Vikings.
www.coloringcottage.com

ColoringBookDepot.com offers more than 1,500 coloring books on such topics as homes of American presidents and Victorian fashions.
www.colorbooks.com

SLIM PICKINGS

Children's interests often fall into offbeat categories not generally acknowledged by mainstream toy manufacturers and book publishers (which, I might add, is a good thing). Consequently, it can be challenging for parents to find resources that relate to their children's interests.

"You just kind of have your radar out for things," says Terry, who adds that she and her young son would go to four different libraries in her area to find history books. That was thirteen years ago. As for outside activities, Terry says, "I don't remember taking him to any lectures because I don't remember seeing any lectures."

Lacking readily available materials forces parents to be creative. When Cole exhausted his coloring books featuring birds, as well as field guides and tapes, Kris picked up the phone and called her local Audubon chapter.

"We just try to look for any opportunity," says Kris. "We always have our eyes peeled when we read the paper."

Kris's eight-year-old daughter, Lily, has indicated an interest in becoming a veterinarian. Her mother has already inquired about having her daughter volunteer at the local veterinary hospital, but was told she's too young.

"At some point, if the interest is still keen, we'll pursue that," says Kris. "Meanwhile, we bought her vet guides, and when our dogs don't feel well, she does research and tries to figure out what's wrong with them."

To build on her two children's love of the outdoors, Cindy Ross took them to a star party held every new moon in a Pennsylvania state park known for its dark night sky. Astronomers set up telescopes there and describe to attendees the sites above.

"They were so blown away," says Ross. "Now Sierra wants a telescope for Christmas, and it's my responsibility to get her something like that. . . . She wants me to find a gem club that goes out digging for stuff. I have to find that for her. If I'm going to be a good parent and I want her to turn into who she's supposed to be, then that's my next step."

Because interests have a way of changing direction, seek opportunities that allow your child to explore different areas within her interest. Although Susan suspected her elementary-school-age daughter was more interested in being a movie star than in acting, she nevertheless searched out opportunities for her daughter to play small roles in high school renditions of dramas that called for children. It was these roles that Susan believes sparked Julie's interest in acting.

The upside to the scarcity of interest-related materials is that it tests your child's desire to pursue the interest. Pat's daughter Katie fell in love with competitive clogging at the age of nine. Unfortunately, the start of her interest coincided with her family's move to another state.

Katie's interest was so strong, however, that her parents were persuaded to find a clogging team for their daughter—a search that took two years. It was at a regional competition where they "saw one team perform that seemed very exciting," says Pat. "I tracked down a parent to find out where they were based. It was about thirty miles away—not a long distance for this area—so I talked to the director and Katie started with the team right away."

Be Enthusiastic

As difficult as it may sometimes be to muster up enthusiasm for your child's passion, it's essential. "I always tell people, if there's just one person, one grownup, to go out and enjoy the garden, to experience it, that's all it takes," says gardening author Sharon Lovejoy.

It also takes a parent willing to go along with his child's whims. Probably the last thing Clark imagined himself doing was marching throughout his neighborhood playing a fife while his six-year-old son Chris rat-a-tat-tatted on a toy drum. But he did it, because his son asked him to.

Young children with burgeoning interests can at times bring a parent to the brink of frustration. For a child, any fun activity worth doing once is worth doing over and over. Such was the case with Cole, who in the early stages of his interest in birds wanted nothing more than to color them in his coloring book.

"For a while it was painful," says his mother. "Every day for hours he'd want mom and dad to color birds with him in the book. At first it's fun. But as an adult you color three or four birds in the book with your child, and they still want to do it for several more hours. You want to make dinner or have a conversation with your spouse."

Though you acquiesce, you also begin considering ways to move the interest forward. Three-year-old Julie loved to hear her favorite fairy tale, "Rapunzel," read over and over again. Instead of pushing for different bedtime books, her father encouraged her to memorize the text. Later, she began to play the part of the witch, cackle and all.

Rather than marching throughout their neighborhood, Clark and his family joined a militia group. Now father and son could

march side by side as part of an organized historical reenactment. Chris's mother and younger sister also participate,
marching in parades and participating in nonviolent aspects of
reenactments.

Clark stuck to his son's side. He was with his son on reenactments. He even used his vacation time to accompany his son
to schools and summer camps to demonstrate the tunes, commands, and signals used by drummers during the American
Revolution.

You want to be with your child as much as possible as she pursues her interest. Pat can often be found at her daughter's clogging competitions. You'll recognize her by the T-shirt she wears.
It reads "My daughter is a Doll," which refers to the name of
Katie's clogging team, the Dynamite Dolls. Katie's sister wears a
shirt that reads "My sister is a Doll."

While it may sometimes feel more like work than play, remember that your good deeds will probably not be forgotten.
Cole never forgot his parents' patience and guidance. "My parents encourage me a lot," says Cole. "I was very interested in the
owl survey, and dad signed me up at once."

Remember that the next time you feel like you'll explode if
your daughter asks you for the umpteenth time to help her draw
gargoyles. Remember, too, that sometimes it's all right for your
child to know you've had enough. Sometimes it might even lead
to something profound.

Amanda has loved writing since she was a first-grader. When
she was twelve, she became so taken by the process her mother
went through publishing a homemaking newsletter that she asked
to be involved. "I finally told her that if she wanted to help with
the newsletter so much she should go start her own," says
Rachel, her mother. "So she did."

Amanda combined her love of writing with her love of animals and published a newsletter to raise money for the local humane society. Rachel's comment may have been made in a
moment of frustration, but she knew her daughter was capable of
publishing her own newsletter and helped her do it.

There are literally hundreds of children's activity books on the market—everything from *1001 Things to Do With Your Kids* (Galahad Books, 1999) to *365 Afterschool Activities* (Gramercy, 2003).

Unfortunately, there are relatively few children's activity books devoted to one particular interest. The handful I located cover such interests as photography, woodworking, gardening, ceramics, backpacking, quilting, cooking, fishing, climbing, and scrapbooking. The advice in these books is indispensable to parents seeking to help a child pursue an interest.

With any luck, as more parents seek to nurture their children's interests, publishers will fill the void.

REMEMBER WHAT FUN IS?

If you find yourself pursuing an interest with your child and neither of you is smiling or laughing, it's time to reevaluate what you're doing.

It's not easy to clown around when you're backpacking with two young children in the wilds. But Cindy Ross has found that it's necessary if you're serious about instilling an interest in children. "I don't think that parents know how to have fun anymore," she says. "It's always, 'This is what we're going to do' or 'This is what the schedule is' or 'We're going to go here, that wasn't in the plan.'

"My husband and I are big planners and big dreamers, and we always have a schedule and things like that, but we try to go out and have fun," she continues. "We'll ride bikes across Missouri for 250 miles, and [the children] might get bored sometimes, but we'll work with them. We'll sing, we'll play games, we'll take a break every hour. We give them as much freedom as possible to do what they need to do so we can do what we want to do.

"But when they're little, they're in charge. If they can't walk, you don't make them. One other thing that makes them miserable is when parents aren't prepared. I see parents, and their kids are hungry and they're tired and they're cold. We bend over backward to make sure all those things are covered."

People who have helped children pursue interests understand the importance of having fun. "My grandmother never said, 'I'm going to teach you about separating the irises and how to plant bulbs,' " says Lovejoy. "We just did it! And it was fun."

Ross takes a similar approach. "I introduce my kids to many different experiences, mostly outdoor experiences, but I let them go," she says. "I don't try to have my son draw a certain way or I don't tell my daughter, 'Go do an experiment.' I let them do what they want. I provide tons of materials and books and opportunities to go places, but I don't say, 'Now we're going to go do this.' I don't think kids need as much direction as some parents try to give them."

Let's face it. Many of us are downright amateurs when it comes to having fun with a child. "Your idea of fun may not be your child's idea," says Lovejoy. "Kids are attracted by the worms they see in the soil. They're attracted by the bumble bees. They're attracted to the fact that they can take a cutting of geranium, stick it in the ground and it will grow. They're attracted to the magic, and it's all magical to them when they're out there experiencing it."

So you go out in a spring rain and collect earthworms from the driveway and throw them into the garden. You let the kids roll in the mud like pigs. You let them intentionally crash their kites. And if you're still having trouble with the whole fun concept, choose a theme for the interest based on something your child loves—a book, a movie, a character, a meal.

"Maybe they love Beatrix Potter's writings," says Lovejoy. "Go through the book and pick out those plants that Beatrix Potter writes about and do a Peter Rabbit garden. Or maybe you read *The Secret Garden* and you do that.

"One of my most popular gardens is a pizza garden shaped like a pizza," she continues. "I also grow sipping gardens with different plants kids can use to make tea; in the center grow straws, natural straws made out of lovage stems."

Kevin Nierman incorporates themes into his annual exhibits of students' ceramic works. One year students made tiles for a show at the Oakland Museum, which was sponsoring a tile symposium; another year they made creatures for an enchanted forest, which was displayed at a local ceramic supplier's gallery; and yet another year they made teapots that were displayed in a public window in the downtown area.

Even a dull aspect of the interest can be injected with enjoyment. "No kid wants to be told, 'Let's go out and weed for six hours this glorious Saturday morning,' " says Lovejoy. "With our family, we had what was called a ten-minute plan. I'd say, 'Okay, we're all responsible for ten minutes today,' and we'd run out and pretty soon the ten minutes would be more than ten minutes. Or I'd say, 'We're going to have a weeding contest. Who can fill this bucket up first?' It was always a good time."

Before you get all high and mighty that your child is pursuing an interest, remember that you're not really pursuing it if you're not exploring it in all its glory, from highbrow to lowbrow taste.

Twelve-year-old Julie adores Shakespearean poems and plays, especially scenes featuring witches. But she also adores watching the television show "Buffy the Vampire Slayer."

Her mother is not one to disagree. "Frankly, so do I," she says.

REWARD THE EFFORT

As their children's interest in nature grew, Kris and Peter rewarded each of them with a pair of professional quality binoculars. "They got them as gifts in recognition of the fact that they're interested in a serious way in the outdoors," she says. "We give them responsibility, and with their particular interests, they fulfill their obligations."

When eight-year-old Jesse completed 100 miles of trail hiking, his parents had a trophy cup engraved with "Mountain Hiker Award—100 miles—Jesse Oberlin, Age 8, October 2001" and presented it to him at a special dinner celebration.

Can you imagine the feeling this boy had that night? Small

gestures such as an award, a certificate, or a special night out can drive a child to want to take his interest further. Indeed, even in this technological age, children still get a big kick out of being recognized with something as simple as a certificate printed out on a home computer. And for a child who eschews competition, a trophy bestowed upon him by his family fills that void.

Aside from a trophy from their parents, children with interests can be rewarded in more public ways. Nierman not only holds annual exhibits of his students' ceramics works, he hosts a party prior to each show. "We have an opening with treats and drinks for the kids," he says. "It's important to have the shows because it allows the children to see their work in a greater context."

OUTSIDE REWARDS

With your child's permission, seek rewards outside your control. Having used her love of writing to publish a newsletter aimed at raising money for the local humane society, twelve-year-old Amanda wrote about her experience for the McDonald's Millennium Dreamer contest. She was one of 2,000 students chosen worldwide to spend a week in Disney World in Orlando, Florida, to celebrate the achievements of children who were making a difference all over the world. "It was truly the experience of a lifetime for both of us," says her mother, "and very inspirational for her."

If your child is eager to share the fact that he has an interest, consider calling your local newspaper to see if they're interested in running an article on your child. Give the editor a "hook" he can use to write such a piece. Perhaps your child won a competition or spoke before a group on her interest.

An article in a local paper may even propel your child and her interest to places you never imagined. Having read about Cole's interest in birds in a couple of local news articles, a Montessori school teacher suggested he give a slide lecture at a retirement home where her mother was a patient. Cole agreed, and discussed local birds, seagulls, and songbirds with the group.

When the head of a nearby retirement community heard about the success of that lecture, he asked Cole to give a local-bird lecture at his facility. It was so popular that he asked Cole to give a lecture every year. On one of his return lectures, Cole discussed owls, and was lent four live specimens from an ornithologist.

A word of caution when it comes to seeking outside rewards for your child: It's those awards we don't have control over that can cause the most heartache.

During Kyle's middle school graduation, a variety of awards were given out, including departmental awards. Though Kyle had consistently gotten A's in history and social studies, and his teacher marveled at Kyle's ability to "keep him on his toes," the social studies departmental award went to another student.

After inquiring about the award, Terry discovered why Kyle hadn't won: It was available only to students who were in the top percentile of their class.

"I said that's a shame, because it's this type of kid who really needs the award," says Terry. "It broke my heart. The principal said, 'You're right.' She'd been on the job two years and said, 'It's a policy I inherited and I'm going to change it.' "

HANDS-ON IDEA

Some children would prefer their interest remain a well-kept secret only family members are privy to; other children want the world to know about it. If your child belongs to the latter group, look for outlets that will make his interest known.

Children's niche magazines often encourage youngsters to submit photos, drawings, or poems, and local newspapers are often interested in profiling young people's hobbies.

Don't overlook adult magazines, either. Eight-year-old Lily has had her poems published in an adult poetry magazine. And ten-year-old Noah had his collection of South American fabric wall hangings featured in a national collectibles magazine.

A BLAST FROM THE PAST

As the two of you push forward, every once in a while look over your shoulders. The more you review what you've done, the greater appreciation you'll have for what you're doing.

Consider keeping a scrapbook noting your child's achievements. Include the certificate you printed out for your child, the photograph of Henry wearing his first pair of hiking boots, the drawings of gargoyles Caroline drew, the card from Grandpa praising Jeremy for catching his first fish—anything that relates to the interest.

A wall in your child's bedroom dedicated to the interest can accommodate items that won't fit into a scrapbook. Call it "My Interest Wall." Hang on the wall framed pictures of the clouds your daughter photographed. Install a shelf to display the knots your son tied. Add a bulletin board to tack up related items.

TIME TO REDECORATE

The more a child sees reminders of his interest, the more he'll think about it. The more he thinks about it, the more he's likely to entertain creative ways to pursue it.

Hillary's pottery is displayed throughout the house. Steve and Chris display their dinosaur paraphernalia in Chris's bedroom. Susan tacks onto the refrigerator the latest drawing of the fort her son is designing and keeps a pencil and pad on the kitchen island where Dylan can update the work in progress. Every time Dylan opens the fridge, he can't help but see the drawing of his fort.

Rachel maintains a home office in which she publishes a homemaking newsletter. Having seen her mother working, Amanda took her interest in writing to a higher level and published her own newsletter.

Set aside places that remind your child of his interest and provide space to pursue it. It can be a refrigerator door to display pictures of forts in progress and a kitchen island to work on the designs. Or it can be a shelf in the family room to display wind-up toys and a small table nearby to tinker with them. These areas are what gifted-child experts call "interest development centers." Though the term typically refers to areas set aside in a classroom for students to pursue interests, these centers can easily be set up in the home environment as well.

GOING WHERE FEW CHILDREN HAVE GONE BEFORE

In exchange for apprenticing his friends' daughter Laurel in falconry three or four days at a clip, Ken's daughter Meghan stays at Laurel's house for several days, riding the horses that Laurel's mother trains. On one recent trip, Ken allowed Meghan to bring her falcon, Chad.

The two teenage girls rode horses through fields and flew Chad—at one point losing the bird and eventually finding him. "It was exciting and wonderful, and they'll never forget it," says Ken.

Hand your child all the trophies and certificates you want (and by all means, do so), but getting the green light to pursue an interest in ways typically limited to adults is the ultimate medal of honor. Never mind that Meghan is one of a handful of children steeped in the sport of falconry. Add to that her recent outing and you have a child enamored of her interest.

Pursue activities outside the typical age range considered appropriate for your child. Certainly, you should feel comfortable with the activity and your child's ability to participate in it. But remember that within their areas of interest, children often exhibit a maturity beyond their years.

HANDS-ON IDEA

If your child is interested in the environment, consider involving her in an environmental survey program. Such programs give children responsibility, expose them to important issues, and give them hands-on experience. Here are three such programs:

- The National Audubon Society runs Project FeederWatch and Project PigeonWatch through the Cornell Lab of Ornithology.
  birds.cornell.edu
- The U.S. Geological Survey Patuxent Wildlife Research Center, Laurel, Maryland, runs FrogWatch USA.
  www.mp2-pwrc.usgs.gov/FrogWatch/index.htm

MOVING TO THE NEXT LEVEL

You might look at where you are now with your child's interest and wonder, How will I ever get to the point where my child is doing the kinds of things most kids his age can only dream of? It's a matter of progressing gradually, taking baby steps and giving your child more responsibility each time she proves herself in one area.

Julie's parents allowed her to keep progressing, and she continued to impress and amaze them. They may have started out reading their daughter passages from Shakespearean plays, but their daughter was the one who ran with it, surpassing anything they could have thought possible.

They were impressed by their sixth-grader's ability to emcee her school variety show. But they were wowed by her performance in an adapted version of *Macbeth* performed at a two-week summer day camp with The Shakespeare Theatre.

"Julie played Lady Macbeth in the 'unsex me' scene—and she electrified us," says Susan, her mother. "She understood the Shakespearean text, did it well, and improvised gestures beautifully and appropriately."

With seven-year-old Cole's interest in birds only strengthened through coloring books, his parents signed him up for an owl-banding expedition and later a survey program in which he gathered data on robin migratory habits. "That kind of hands-on stuff makes a big difference in their interest level," says Cole's mother Kris.

Interestingly, for Cole, the project wasn't hands-on enough. "I had to sit at my seat at the table and watch out the window at my bird feeder for a period of time every day," says Cole, who adds that he was more "interested in going out and being in contact with bird life."

The interest would move to a higher level of skill when Kris involved her son with their local Audubon chapter. "We needed to take him to the next step," she says.

Interests often take a nose dive in the teen years. To avoid this, move your child's interest along to the point where he is pursuing it in ways typically limited to adults.

INFINITY AND BEYOND

Your child is pursuing her interest at a level you never dreamed possible. Regardless, you continue to try to further it.

Despite their level of proficiency, as children mature the interest can get stale or be associated with activities they did as mere youngsters. That's why it's important to continually research off-shoots and subsets of the interest.

Meghan still flies her falcon, but she has also gotten involved in breeding prey, including pheasants. "That's turning into being one of her great loves," says her father.

Pat is encouraging her daughter Katie to explore other possibilities related to her love of clogging, such as duo events.

Hillary, too, is branching out within her interest. In addition to creating ceramic pieces on a potter's wheel, she is learning to apply Raku firing methods to her creations.

One way to keep the interest attractive is to put an entrepreneurial spin on it. Cole had such a bumper crop of pumpkins when he was ten that he approached a local health food store with the proposition of selling them. "He made fifty dollars from his extra pumpkins and still had all the other ones he normally gives to friends and family," says his mother. "For him, gardening is now a money-making possibility."

Indeed, Cole continues to seek markets for his crops. In fact, the owner of a local gourmet store has agreed to consider selling Cole's unusual crop of pumpkins—blue ones and a deep red-orange flat variety known as the prototype for Cinderella's carriage pumpkin.

There's really no limit to how or to what extent an interest can be pursued. When you find yourself getting too comfortable with your child's interest, think of this quote from Ralph Waldo Emerson: "The only sin is limitation."

What You Need to Know About Pursuing Interests—Part II

- Consider all types of reading materials, even—and perhaps especially—those outside your child's age level. All printed matter that may captivate your child's imagination is appropriate, as long as you are comfortable with it.
- Count yourself lucky if there aren't aisles of toys and games geared toward your child's interest. Then get creative and go out there and find your own resources.
- Show enthusiasm for your child's interest.
- It takes a sense of humor and a child's idea of fun to pursue interests.
- From home-computer-generated certificates to trophies to a dinner in their honor, tangible forms of support express what words alone can't.
- Devote an area in your home to encouraging your child to think about and pursue her interest.
- When you feel your child is ready, allow her to pursue her interest in a way typically limited to adults. Children with strong interests often exhibit a maturity beyond their years.
- Getting to the point where your child is doing the kinds of things most kids his age can only dream of is a matter of progressing gradually, taking baby steps and giving your child more responsibility each time she proves herself in one area.

- Interests are forever evolving, which is why it's important to continually research offshoots and subsets of your child's interest.

• *Stepping Out* •

Like many younger siblings, three-year-old Katie wanted to do some of the things her older sister did. So when her sister took a dance class, Katie wanted to go too.

Other than that reason, her mother Pat "didn't notice anything special that made me think I had to get her into a dance class."

It soon became evident, however, that Katie liked to dance. "Every year, I'd ask Katie, 'Do you want to do dance again next year?' and she never hesitated," says Pat.

Loud and Fast

For six years, Katie studied tap and jazz dance. Then a new instructor came to the studio and offered clogging, a loud, fast, precise form of dance with roots in Irish step dancing. "She was intrigued and signed up for the class right away," says Pat.

Katie and clogging clicked. "Clogging is really loud, really fast tapping," she says. "It's loud because you have double taps on the heels and toes of the shoes."

Not only was she attracted to its lively pace, she also enjoyed its competitive nature. "She loves to be part of a team and compete," says Pat.

"I love to perform and be onstage," says Katie. "With regular dance class, you don't get many chances to perform—usually just at the recital at the end of the year. With competition, I get to perform a lot more during the year."

There are many things Pat likes about clogging. "This is something she is good at, she enjoys it, she gets to travel and meet all kinds of people, it's great exercise, and it gives her wonderful self-esteem and confidence," she says.

Pat also appreciates the fact that costumes are more modest than in other dance forms. "There isn't that emphasis on being sexy that you see in other kinds of dance," she explains. "It's more about precision and energy and showmanship. It's a very family-oriented activity, and we like that as well."

Indeed, in addition to her parents, Katie's sister attends competitions and wears a T-shirt that reads, "My sister is a Doll," which refers to the name of Katie's team, the Dynamite Dolls.

"My grandmother has one, too," says Katie, who notes that her grandmother also sent her flowers when she competed on the national level. "There was a teddy bear and flowers in a mug with dance shoes on it," she says. "That was great. I had never gotten flowers before."

Moving On

Just as Katie was breaking into clogging, her family moved to another state. It would be two years before she would begin clogging again.

After the move, Pat and her husband searched around for a clogging team in the area. "Mom looked all over for a team and couldn't find one," says Katie. "I kept bugging her, saying I wanted to clog."

Eventually, the couple found a regional competition. "We saw one team perform that seemed very exciting," says Pat. "I tracked down a parent to find out where they were based.

"It was about thirty miles away—not a long distance for this area," she continues. "So I talked to the director, and Katie started with the team right away."

Tough Break

Four months after she returned to clogging, Katie broke her ankle while playing softball. "I shouldn't have suggested that she play softball the second year," says Pat.

While clogging and softball are both noisy, fast, competitive sports, Katie opted out of softball to avoid injuring herself again. Put simply, she says, "I wanted to dance more than I wanted to play softball."

Today, Katie practices twice a week with her team, which is a nationally ranked competitive clogging team. She also recently completed a workshop with two of the top dancers in the country. Referring to the workshop, Pat says, "When I asked if she wanted to spend six hours on a summer Saturday clogging, she said, 'Cool!' "

In addition to driving her daughter to twice-weekly practices (more if a competition is coming up) and out-of-state competitions, Pat helps make costumes and fundraises to cover expenses. Among the necessities required for competitive clogging are practice gear, a team jacket, dance bags, curlers, makeup, glitter, tickets to shows, and shoes, which, according to Pat, are a "major investment."

Pat has also become a clogging educator. "There is a tremendous lack of knowledge about clogging in the general public, so I'm constantly explaining what it is that takes up so much of her time," she says.

Katie, too, finds herself explaining her interest to classmates. "A lot of people at school still don't understand what clogging is," she says. "They're always asking me if it's dancing in heavy wooden shoes like Dutch people wear, and if I wear big 'poufy' skirts. I tell them, 'No, we wear tap shoes and dance in leather pants!' "

She adds: "Tomorrow I'm going to clog for our talent show. Maybe then they'll stop saying that."

But explaining is one thing; seeing is another. When Pat has explained clogging to Katie's friends, "they think it's pretty cool," she says. "Once they see it, they're amazed."

Limitless Enthusiasm

At this point, you might think that Katie has exhausted all possibilities within her interest. But she hasn't.

She's expressed an interest in competing in duo events, says Pat. "So we're talking to her team director about this extra training," she says.

Katie's excited at the thought of performing duos. "That

would be cool because I like to dance with my friends," she says. "I did a solo competition once and didn't like it at all. I got so nervous, I forgot my whole routine. I was so glad when it was over."

She's also planning to study clogging at summer camp with the Bailey Mountain Cloggers, a company of student dancers at Mars Hill College, in Mars Hill, North Carolina. "They are the best team in the country," says Katie. "That will be so much fun."

As with many children with interests, Katie's enthusiasm knows no limits, which is exactly the way it should be.

8

Pitfalls

Few interests are pursued without encountering bumps along the way. Rather than throw up your arms in frustration, learn from those who have been there.

Just about every parent I spoke with hit a snag at some point. Some worried about deflecting criticism from peers. Others wanted to find a mentor who could take the interest to a higher level. Still others found it difficult to get started, whether for lack of time or lack of resources.

But they didn't give up. In fact, in their drive to help their children pursue their passions, these parents became semi-experts themselves within the interest. It just goes to show that not only can pitfalls be overcome, but by rising above them, you, too, can grow by leaps and bounds. Based on my interviews, here are the most common pitfalls.

My child isn't ready to pursue an interest

If you find yourself putting off pursuing an interest because your child "isn't ready," you need to do a reality check. Perhaps *you're*

161

the one who isn't ready. Have you heard yourself utter any of the following?

- "My child's too young." No child is too young to pursue an interest. The activities you'll do to pursue the interest with your young child may be at times tedious and repetitive. But that's where you come in. Get creative and try to move the activity in another direction or to a higher level. Introduce a new book or propose relinquishing to your child some of your responsibilities related to the interest.

- "It'll be less work when she's older." Helping a child pursue an interest will always be work, no matter the child's age. If Ken had waited to pursue falconry with his daughter until she reached the legal age in California for doing so, he would have lost some ten years pursuing the sport with her. What's more, Ken might have encountered greater obstacles had he waited until Meghan was older.

- "She wouldn't appreciate the effort." Some parents I spoke with hinted that not all their efforts to nurture their child's interest were appreciated.

Children need to recognize the sacrifice you're making. Sure, it's rewarding to watch your child's interest blossom. But it's also important that she thank you for your efforts. After all, no matter how you try to simplify the process of pursuing an interest, it still involves time, resources, and planning.

Pursuing interests is an activity that offers a perfect opportunity to teach your child about appreciation and sacrifice. You sacrifice your time and energy for your child so he can pursue his interest, and he appreciates your effort; in turn, your child makes certain sacrifices to allow you to pursue your own interest, and you appreciate his effort.

- "It's too dangerous at his age." Children are often attracted to interests that involve some risk. But with the proper parental oversight, these dangers can be minimized and even avoided.

Sierra and her brother Bryce have spent weeks riding llamas with their parents in the wilderness. Chris received a sword when he passed a drum test. Meghan has flown falcons since she was a young child. Cole has banded wild owls.

If you're having trouble finding an interest, consider hobbies typically reserved for older children. Archery is one. Fencing is another. Start pursuing it via books. Go to tournaments. You need to set rules and stick to them. By showing your child you trust his judgment not to do anything unsafe, you'll engage him.

There's no time to pursue an interest

Pursuing interests forces parents to prioritize the time they spend with their children. On a weekly basis, would you really miss one less hour of television or one less play date? That's all the time it takes to pursue most interests.

"Our kids have a lot of free time in the afternoon," says Kris of her two children, Cole, eleven, and Lily, eight. "Peter and I do not have them out every day of the week taking a lesson somewhere. They have a lot of time in the afternoon that's unscheduled."

The parents with whom I spoke spend lots of time with their children. "People used to say, 'What programs are they enrolled in this summer?' " says Kris. "We'd say, 'Nothing.' Slow down their schedule if you're interested in nurturing a special interest. If they're going in fifty different directions, they won't be able to do that."

Parents whose children develop a strong interest often find themselves torn between following the interest to the child's full capacity and maintaining ties with extracurricular activities. Katie's passion for clogging involves three hours of practice a week with her team, which is a forty minute drive from her home, and extra practices when a competition is nearing.

I don't know anyone who can help us pursue the interest

Routines and traditions are important for children. But they can limit our exposure to the same group of people. As a result, we become close-minded and our world shrinks.

When you're with your child, make it a priority to talk to different people. If you're at a dog show, ask a handler how he got started. If you're at the library and the stamp club is meeting in an adjoining room, go in, observe, and see if it's appropriate to ask the leader a few questions. Join a book group. Attend a kite festival and ask a participant for suggestions in getting started in the sport.

We often don't realize just how small our world is until we see others whose world is full of people with various backgrounds and interests. As a home-schooling parent, Kris formed a local home-schooling group. Unlike parents who home-school for religious reasons and form groups around that theme, Kris sought a more diverse group. Her group includes artists, farmers, wildlife rehabilitators, and musicians. "People have pretty intense focuses in our group," says Kris.

Make it a point for you and your child to seek out people with diverse interests. By doing so, your children will grow up accustomed to spending time with adults and able to listen and absorb concepts and ideas many children never do till they're older.

Peter, Cole's father, struck up a conversation with a patient in the dentist's office. Today that person, a respected poet, teaches Peter's children poetry.

By example, show your child how to ask questions and strike up conversations. Because you'll be with your child at all times, you'll be the judge of whether the person is on the up-and-up.

That said, be careful with whom you share your child's interest. Even well-meaning adults make comments that can dampen if not squash an interest forever.

Aunt Ethel's giggle or Uncle Ed's snide comment can wash away months of careful nurturing. If your child wants to share her interest with someone, a simple comment such as "She's very proud of her interest," said with a serious tone, should be enough for any adult to understand.

When Cindy Ross and her husband decided to share their passion for backpacking with their young children, they were told it was impossible and that they'd live to regret it. Ross offers this advice in her book *Kids in the Wild: A Family Guide to Outdoor Recreation*: "There will always be people who try to scare you out of doing something. They project their own fears into the situation. Know your stuff, know your limitations, and don't be afraid to turn a deaf ear to folks like this."

I don't want my child to be labeled "different"

One mother whose four-year-old son had a strong interest said to me: "He never came across as the odd egghead type." You can't fault her for saying that. After all, the tendency in our society is to label a child different if he doesn't pursue typical childhood activities.

As early as grade school, good looks and sports ability begin to determine popularity. It's often not until children leave the school system that they discover that the rules of school don't apply. In fact, many times high school outsiders become the more successful and admired adults.

Emphasize to your child that it's okay to be different. Children labeled "science nerds" five years ago are respected among their peers today.

Parents themselves often make their children feel self-conscious about their interests. I find that addressing a child with a matter-of-fact demeanor no matter what they say makes them feel confident about expressing their feelings. Instead of raising your eyebrows, keep an even keel and say, "That's nice" or "What made you think of that?"

My child is obsessed with his interest

In preschool, Julie played Sleeping Beauty by lying on the floor and pretending to be asleep. "Sometimes she'd carry it a little too far and her daycare provider would get exasperated, telling her to get up, that she'd played Sleeping Beauty for long enough," says Julie's mother Susan.

Some children become so enamored of an interest, they need to have limits imposed as to where and when they may pursue them. Susan imposed limits on where and when her young daughter could act out her favorite fairy tale scenes. Judy limited her son's penchant for collecting by requiring that he get an after-school job to pay for the items.

Children often go through a stage during which they want to constantly pursue their interests. This stage usually diminishes over time. In the meantime, set limits and impose rules to keep the interest in check.

Now sixteen, Terry's son Kyle is no longer the history buff he was at the age of three. "He's no longer obsessed by it," she says. "The interest is still there, but it's not a predominant part of his life at this point."

My child doesn't want to pursue the interest anymore

Pat's daughter jumped at the chance to spend six hours on a summer Saturday clogging.

Susan doesn't have to work at keeping Julie's interest in acting alive. "She does it herself," says Susan.

Your child may not show this amount of enthusiasm. In fact, she may start to show signs that she no longer wants to pursue it. Rather than allow the interest to fizzle, take action. Consider all aspects of the interest you're pursuing, as well as those aspects you're not pursuing.

Perhaps you're pursuing an aspect of the interest that no longer appeals to your child. If it's kites, perhaps it's not as straightforward as flying them. Maybe the interest lies in designing and crafting them. Perhaps kite-making will evolve into a love of studying how different cultures and tribes used kite flying as a spiritual act.

Return to the chapters on pursuing interests and see if there isn't something you haven't tried. Are you on a fast track with the interest? Are others involved? Have you done anything spontaneous with regard to the interest? Are your child's friends giving her grief over it?

Ceramics artist/teacher Kevin Nierman keeps his students' interest level high by putting them in charge of their work. Students are not forced to participate in Nierman's annual exhibit, and if they do participate, they are not required to produce a piece that fits with the yearly theme. "Sometimes a student doesn't like the theme," says Nierman. "So they make whatever they like, and we make it work in the show."

It's that ability to be flexible that makes the child want to pursue her interest. "Oh, I can do it the way I want to?" a child might ask. That's appealing.

If your child's pleas to stop pursuing the interest finally get to you, remember never to abandon the interest-development process itself. Continue to expose your child to different experiences, and a new interest may emerge.

If your child balks, do what I do: insist she do something related to the pursuit of interests. One mother once told me that trying to get her children to go somewhere different was like pulling teeth. She asked me, How do you get your son to go to a museum or a gardening show? I told her the deal is this: On weekends, everyone in the family gets to do something that interests them. He gets a turn, but so do his parents.

The frustration level is too high

When an interest takes hold of a child, the tendency is to want to know everything about it. That can lead to frustration. "I get very frustrated when I can't find any answer because that means I have to wait a very long time before I can meet someone who knows the answer," says eleven-year-old Cole.

Cole manages because he not only has bird field guides and other reading material; he has also, with the help of his parents, established a group of experts he can call on with a question. In addition, he's been taught to feel comfortable about approaching those experts. "I'm quite confident because I want to know a lot about birds," says Cole.

Children also get frustrated when too fast a pace is set for them or they aren't successful at what they set out to do. Slow it down and create projects in which your child is sure to experience a positive outcome.

Of course, you'll always be there to help. "When a kid can't get something smooth, I'll do it," says woodworking teacher Richard Starr. "I smooth over the rough places metaphorically too."

How do I know when an activity related to my child's interest is over his head?

You don't. That's why it's important for a parent to be present when pursuing an advanced activity related to the interest. When a parent helps his child accomplish an advanced task related to the interest, the child reaps enormous benefits in terms of knowledge and self-esteem.

Eleven-year-old Cole was excited to participate in an owl survey—even one that involved tracking the birds in the New England woods in winter from seven to ten at night. He was less enthusiastic about the second part of the survey, which had to be conducted during the hours of ten P.M. to midnight.

Cole's parents have always insisted their children complete projects they start. So Cole went on the second survey, and even the third, which ran from midnight to two A.M. He was accompanied by his father on all three surveys, and also by his mother and sister on the second survey.

Not only did Cole complete the project, on the second leg of the survey he and his family were treated to an unusual series of calls between two owls.

My child loses patience with those who know less about the interest than he does

Being around adults and developing a rapport with experts can make children feel like adults themselves. As a result, they may come across as disrespectful and insolent.

In elementary school, Kyle often knew more about history than his teachers. "He's not patient with people who don't know as much as he does about a certain subject," says his mother Terry. "So at times he's had teachers he hasn't gotten along with that well."

Indeed, some children become so comfortable around adults, they consider themselves equal to their elders. "It was cute when she was five, six, seven, eight years old," says Ken about his thirteen-year-old daughter Meghan. "But at nine, ten, eleven, twelve, thirteen years old, people don't see that as so."

With the right comments, children can be brought down to earth. "Children need to be in their place," says Ken. "She has had a harder time with that as she's gotten older. I tell her, 'Meghan, you have to learn what is appropriate and when you can speak.' . . . I say, 'It's not that you're not correct, but you have to realize your position in society.' "

There are so many ways to pursue the interest that I don't know which to choose

Susan and Stan encouraged their daughter Julie to pursue her love of acting. But they were careful not to steer her into certain areas. "We don't want her to be a stage kid, so we haven't pushed her into auditions," says Susan. "We want her to be a well-rounded person."

Many parents might have done the opposite. They might have figured that was the correct action to take, since many child actors got their start that way.

When it comes to pursuing an interest, put lots of faith in your own feelings and observations, and avoid following the path that everyone else takes. It's easy to be brainwashed into thinking that pursuing an interest means performing certain activities in particular ways.

"In some ways, the rebirth that we see in gardening is a direct result of marketing," says Sharon Lovejoy. "Everybody gets those shiny catalogs and wants their yard to look like that . . . It's got to look like the magazines and be pruned and orderly, and the thought of a child running amuck in their garden is probably terrifying to a lot of parents."

Ask yourself if you're pursuing an idealized aspect of the interest rather than a realistic one. Have you considered the many niche areas within the interest? There may be areas you have never heard of. Research all areas of your child's interest by visiting your local library and bookstore, surfing the Internet, and talking to people knowledgeable within the interest.

After nine-year-old Ben and his father read a book on stargazing, Ben's eyes lit up when John, his father, suggested they do a little stargazing of their own. The next day John purchased a $200 telescope. It took a Saturday to figure out how to work it, and once they had it working neither knew what to look for.

A more logical way to pursue the interest would have been to use the book they had and their own eyes to locate specific stars and constellations; download a monthly star chart from an astronomy web site, and again using their eyes, see what they could find; stargaze using John's binoculars, which can pick up many objects found on sky charts; visit the web site of their local astronomy club to find dates of stargazing parties open to the public, then attend one; and look into one of the growing number of amateur telescope making groups and explore that area of astronomy.

My daughter spent a lot of time with her grandfather pursuing her interest—since he died she's lost a lot of her passion

For a child, death can be devastating, especially when it involves someone who has acted as a mentor in pursuing the interest. Still, a child's interest shouldn't have to die with the person who helped nurture it.

Chris's grandfather helped to nurture young Chris's interest in historical reenactments by playing Sousa music and marching throughout the house with his grandson. Since Chris's father Clark had participated with them, it was possible for Clark to help his son continue his pursuit of the interest following the death of the grandfather.

Pursuing an interest in the absence of a grandparent or mentor who helped nurture it is one way to remember and honor that special person. By keeping the interest alive, you're keeping the memory of the deceased alive too.

My child's friends have started rolling their eyes when she starts talking about her interest

As part of her rediscovery of gardening after the death of her grandmother, Lovejoy dug a small pond and surrounded it with cuttings. "Some of my girlfriends saw it, and they thought it was strange," she says. "I think the difference was that, to me, it was natural."

"Natural" is the operative word here. Interests can become such an integral and routine part of a child's life that it seems strange not to pursue them. Peers may chide and tease, but like most kids they grow tired of it.

"For Meghan, it's like, 'Yeah, she's the bird girl,'" says her father of his daughter's interest in falconry. Hillary's friends "know that I just do it," says Hillary of her interest in the potter's wheel. Bryan might have told his friends that his collection of dollhouse furniture was his sister's, but it didn't stop him from collecting the pieces.

For those children who do care what others think, parents must watch closely for signs that their children's interests have crossed the fine line between cool and uncool. To participate as a drummer in historical reenactments, Chris is required to wear traditional eighteenth-century-style clothing. Such a requirement wasn't an issue when he started at the age of seven. But it may become one as he approaches the age of thirteen.

Clark has taken several steps to keep the six-year-old interest alive. He has cut back on the number of reenactments in which they participate, indulged his son in his new interest of basketball, and purchased a drum set "where he can branch out if he wants," he says.

Even young children aren't immune to their peers' social judgments. Three-year-old Kyle's interest in history was an issue from the "get go," says his mother Terry. But, interestingly, approval and acceptance of Kyle's interest became easier as he got older. "Now, in high school, a lot of kids know about history and are interested in it," says Terry. "But in preschool and elementary school he [had] to find other common ground."

People have said my child's a genius—is she?

Probably not. Children with deep-seated interests often find themselves reading at levels beyond their age and spending more time with adults than children who don't have interests. The inclination is to label these children "whiz kids."

"People look at our kids and say they're geniuses," says the mother of two children, both of whom have interests. "That's nice to say, but our children are not geniuses. They're extremely bright. But most children are smart and love to learn."

Julie's interest may be Shakespearean acting, but to her parents, she's like any preteen. "Julie loves to read, listen to pop music, go to the movies—in many ways she's a typical young adolescent," says her mother Susan.

Among the parents I interviewed for this book, none labeled their child a genius. They have said, however, that their children are strong learners, because they have been supplied with the time and resources to pursue their interests.

My child wants to compete within his area of interest—I'm afraid he'll get discouraged if he doesn't win

Ceramics artist/teacher Kevin Nierman holds an annual exhibit of his students' creations. At his first show, an attendee offered to purchase one of the pieces. "It started a buying frenzy," says Nierman. "For the next year that is all the kids talked about: 'How much do you think I can get for this pot?'"

Not surprisingly, Nierman now enforces a no-sales policy at his shows.

Competition can rear its ugly head in places you'd least expect it, as in Nierman's case. In many cases, however, competition is an integral part of an interest.

Sure, some children can handle the ups and downs of competition. Katie loves clogging partly because it's a competitive sport. Julie accepted the fact that she lost out to an eighth-grader for a big role in the school play. "She handled it well and is happy to have a small part; she knows she'll learn a lot," says her mother.

Vikram's love of geography earned him first place in a state geography bee. But he didn't make it to the finals in the national competition. "He did lose his passion for competing when he didn't win in the nationals," says his mother. Fortunately, the experience didn't dampen his passion for geography.

It's up to parents to know their children's competitive limits. Talking about the pros and cons of competing is helpful, as is assuring your child that there is no pressure to compete.

I try to correct my child's mistakes—my wife says I hover

Nierman has been teaching ceramics to children for more than fifteen years. "I've seen it all over the years, all types of parents, and as I've grown as a teacher, I have felt more confidence in saying, 'Please, let's back off and give him some room,' or 'Let's not say anything about the way they're holding their hand on the wheel. Let's see what happens,' " he says.

"I had one woman whose mother is an art teacher on the East Coast," he continues. "This grandmother came out and was watching her grandson and said, 'Oh, you're doing this all wrong and da-da-da.' The boy was upset and so the mother came to me and she said, 'Look, my mother, who has been teaching for X amount of years, said that you're doing this wrong.' And I said, 'Okay, rule number one: There's no right or wrong way here. That's the first rule in clay. Second, you never tell a child when they're making art that they're doing it the wrong way.'

"She agreed with me. She and her son went out and talked about it. She explained how Grandma teaches differently than Kevin, and that was that. I was really pleased."

Allow your child to make mistakes. As long as she isn't getting injured, it's okay. If you need to say something, lessen its impact. "Maybe there's a better way to do that" is preferable to "You did it wrong again!"

When it comes to school, my child's interest is sometimes a source of annoyance

Kyle has loved history since he was three, so it was only natural that he'd want to share his interest with his kindergarten peers at show-and-tell. His selection? A book on the assassination of John F. Kennedy.

"It was one of those Easy Reader books for fifth- or sixth-graders," says Terry. "But I thought the kids in kindergarten wouldn't know who Kennedy was and might not want to know about assassination."

Unfortunately, Kyle's second choice was also cause for concern. "The next thing he wanted to bring in was a newspaper article on the Shroud of Turin," she says.

By the time elementary school rolled around, Terry found herself having to decide whether to explain her child to his teachers. "In third grade I thought, 'I'm not going to go in and set preconceived ideas about him.' Sure enough, two and a half weeks into the school year she called me in and said, 'Your son turned in a paper that I consider inappropriate.'

"It was some paper on the presidents, and he'd written about Kennedy," she continues. "His opening sentence was 'President J. F. Kennedy had sex with women who were not his wife.' I said, 'Well, he reads *Newsweek*.' There'd been an article on it. I hadn't seen the paper, or I would've said we don't need to include that. He's saying, 'Well, it was in *Newsweek*. What's the problem?' "

In middle school Kyle would often test his teachers' resolve. "He would get bored," says Terry. "I got calls from his social studies teacher in eighth grade saying, 'Kyle's got to stop raising his hand and asking these questions.' "

Though Terry's ride with Kyle through his school years was often bumpy, she continued to nurture her son's interest. The payoff came in small but highly rewarding moments, such as when Kyle's eighth-grade history teacher told her how much he appreciated Kyle's interest.

"He said, 'Kyle really keeps me on my toes,' " says Terry. " 'I drive to work in the morning thinking, What's Kyle going to ask me today? Will I be ready?' So a lot of times it's personality. And his, too, in terms of not realizing what the teacher has to deal with."

Your child's teacher may be so overburdened with instructing the classroom that your child's interest may not be fully appreciated, and may even become a source of anxiety. Don't get insulted. Express to your child why it may exasperate her teachers.

Then give the interest lots of attention at home. When appropriate, allow your child to weave her interest into school reports and essays. Just remember to check her work before she submits it to her teacher.

What You Need to Know About Avoiding Common Pitfalls

- The time to start pursuing an interest with your child is now. Waiting till she's older, stronger, smarter, less whiny, more polite, or what have you, is an excuse, not a reason to avoid pursuing an interest.
- Making time to pursue an interest may require cutting back on play dates and extracurricular activities. But even one hour a week is enough to pursue an interest. And, once the interest takes hold, you may find your child asking for more time to pursue it.
- When you're with your child, make it a point to talk to a variety of people. Doing so will expose your child to different interests and give him the confidence to seek information related to his interest from others.
- If your child's interest draws criticism from her peers, emphasize to her that it's okay to be different. If that doesn't work, keep her interest something the two of you pursue together, apart from classmates.

- Some children become so enamored of an interest, they need to have limits imposed as to where and when they may pursue it.
- If your child starts to show signs that she no longer wants to pursue her interest, consider new aspects of it that you could pursue. Oftentimes, the most attractive aspect of an interest is the least well known.
- If your child gets frustrated with his interest, slow it down and seek activities related to it with which he's comfortable.
- Some children become so knowledgeable within their areas of interest that they become like little adults, speaking down to or interrupting real adults. Let your child know he's still a kid and needs to respect his elders.
- Grandparents make ideal mentors for a child with an interest. However, it's important to stay involved with your child's interest in the event of the grandparent's death.
- Children with deep-seated interests often become strong learners, reading at levels beyond their age and seeking experts who can answer questions related to their interests. Encourage them, but avoid labeling them geniuses.
- Just about every interest offers with it the possibility for your child to compete. Though some children thrive on competition, others take losing quite poorly. Know your child's competitive limits, discuss the pros and cons of competing, and assure her that there is no pressure to compete.
- Making mistakes is an essential part of the interest development process. So stand back, grit your teeth, and let your son mess up. Then ask, "How could we have done it differently?"
- Not all your child's teachers will appreciate her interest. Some may even ask that she keep it out of the classroom. Don't get insulted. Express to your child why it may exasperate her overburdened teachers. Then give the interest lots of attention at home, and allow your child to weave her interest into school reports and essays.

• Soaring to New Heights •

Like many seven-year-olds, Cole enjoyed watching birds peck from feeders hung from tree branches. "Cole was always watching the birds out back and at my mother's house when she had bird feeders out," says Cole's mother Kris.

Recognizing the beginning of an interest, Kris and her husband bought their son Audubon field guides and audiotapes. They also purchased Peterson Field Guide Coloring Book—Birds, *which features intricate line drawings of birds as well as detailed information on different species.*

Today, eleven-year-old Cole's fascination with birds continues. "The best thing about birding is, it's so complex: birds' behavior, their anatomy, how they build their nests, why their eggs are certain colors," he says.

It isn't long before his own questions have him pondering possible answers. "Robin eggs are light blue, but other birds lay pure white eggs," he says. "I'm wondering if the robin eggs match the color of the pine trees, but then the white eggs sort of stand out."

Hands-on Time

As Cole's knowledge and interest grew, so too did his capacity and desire to learn more. "He developed an extraordinary level of education about birds," says Kris. "I thought he [was] at a point where he need[ed] hands-on experience."

The next step came about when Kris read in a newspaper that a local Audubon chapter was seeking experienced birders to attend a slide-show presentation on saw-whet owls to be followed by a banding expedition. She called and was told her son was too young.

"I said to the woman running the thing, 'If he doesn't get some hands-on, it will squelch an interest,' " says Kris. "She thought it was amusing, and when I told her the extent of his knowledge, she said, 'Fine.' "

Cole and his father not only attended the presentation; Cole was the only person in a room full of adult birders who recog-

nized a trick question planted by the ornithologist into the discussion to measure the knowledge of her audience. "She was so impressed she invited him to come back and do songbird banding," says Kris.

Cole's field work soon expanded to include data collection for Project FeederWatch, conducted by the Cornell Lab of Ornithology. "To be part of something where you're doing scientific work—not technically challenging, but was real work . . . was important and it made a . . . big difference in their interest level," says Kris of Project FeederWatch.

At the ripe old age of nine, Cole was invited to give a slide presentation on local birds at a nursing home, followed by a second invitation to give the same lecture at a retirement community. He recently gave a presentation on owls featuring four live specimens provided by the Chewonki Foundation, a nonprofit environmental educational organization.

"The people at Chewonki are so receptive for him to get hands-on experience," says Kris.

Father and Son in Ca-Hoots

Cole knows a great deal about many birds. "Chimney swifts can't perch; they can only hang onto a vertical surface," he notes. "Someone once told me they look like flying cigars."

But owls remain his greatest passion. "Owls are definitely my favorite bird to study because they're nocturnal, which means people hardly ever see them," says Cole, who then describes the call of a saw-whet owl—"like a series of whistles"—a barred owl, and a great horned owl—"long, deep hoots."

Cole and his father have also participated in an Audubon-sponsored statewide owl survey in which they traverse the Maine woods for three hours on three different nights. On the first survey, Cole was accompanied by his father from seven to ten p.m.; on the second survey, which lasted from ten p.m. to midnight, his mother and younger sister joined them; and on the final survey, from midnight to two a.m., father and son traversed the woods.

Cole's job was to play tapes of owl calls and record live calls *along with current cloud cover and temperature. "The owls might call when it's cloudy and might not call when it's clear," says Cole. "On my last survey, dad and I went out, and when we played the barred owl call, a saw-whet started hooting, and a few stops later, once dad played the tape, three barred owls started hooting like crazy at once.*

"I'm not sure if my data is enough," notes Cole, acknowledging that there's still much to learn about birds. And while that may be true, he continues to inspire and teach others.

"Dad says he's learned a lot from me—so has mom," he says. "I say, 'Hey, Dad, look at that hawk up there. It's a red-tailed hawk.' He goes, 'It is?' And he gets out his binoculars and looks and he says, 'Hey, you're right.'"

9

Special Interest Groups

As we've learned from the families profiled in this book, age is often not a limiting factor in a child's ability to pursue an interest. In fact, children are capable of some fairly advanced activities within their areas of interest. We've read about young people banding birds, throwing clay on a potter's wheel, playing Lady Macbeth, and drumming in historical reenactments.

We've learned, too, that interests know no gender. Girls have rock collections and boys collect dollhouse furniture. Girls practice falconry and boys garden.

Unfortunately, many of us forget this fundamental fact. We apply labels to boys and girls, to toddlers and teens, and to children with disabilities. Consequently, we limit children to our preconceived notions about what they are and aren't capable of doing and what they should and shouldn't do.

Fortunately, interests don't stereotype. They sneak up on their unsuspecting quarry, grab hold of their attention and seemingly never let go. In other cases, they are dangled enticingly in front of a child by a caring parent who sees the germ of an interest and wants to nurture it.

The experiences and comments of those interviewed in this book serve as a valuable reminder that parents need to keep an open mind when it comes to interests. Though short, this chapter reinforces the notion that every single child is capable of enjoying an interest.

BOYS AND GIRLS

It's amazing how early in life children begin to avoid the opposite sex. One year, boys and girls play together in the sandbox; the next, they know if they mix they will be ostracized—by both adults and children.

Pursuing interests with children is a great way to nip this situation in the bud. Start by choosing an interest that reflects your child's preferences, not gender. Maybe your daughter likes to make miniature furniture from sticks she's collected. Perhaps she'd like to pursue woodworking.

As a woodworking teacher for thirty years, Richard Starr dismisses the notion that the art appeals solely to boys. "My impression is that girls tend to be good at this stuff," he says. "Woodworking is carving and sculptural stuff, and although it's not [something] girls do more than boys, there's all kinds of opportunities to build more than just cabinets and shelves."

Others interviewed for this book have had similar experiences. Ceramics teacher Kevin Nierman has had a female student make war machines from clay. Sharon Lovejoy has seen boys attend garden festivals dressed as beneficial insects. Kris marvels at boys' interest in flowers. None of them question children's decisions to pursue the interest in their own way, and neither should you.

RATED E FOR "EVERYONE"

Noah had a collection of colorful wall hangings started for him when he was spending much of his day lying in a crib. Today, the ten-year-old still cherishes and collects the wall hangings. Along the way he's even taken the initiative to start collections on his own.

Lovejoy started taking her son into the garden when he was ten days old. "Every day we would go out," she says. "We would stop at the wind chimes, and we'd blow on them or touch them. I would take Noah's little hand and brush them across the tops of herbs, trying to sort of get all their senses, from the sound of the bells to the feel of the wooly lamb's ear and the smell of the mint."

Take advantage of the fact that your young child delights in just about everything. A collectible that's pleasing to look at and a plant that's soft to the touch will awaken your child's passions.

Venture out with your baby. As founder of Heart's Ease Gardens, in Cambria, California, Lovejoy recalls putting on annual festivals that attracted children of all ages. "We had a child who was three months old dressed like a fairy, because the family comes and spends the day," she says.

TODDLERS

Parents often lament the repetitive nature of toddler-hood. Young children want to read the same book over and over, they ask the same questions, they become fixated on certain topics. We savor the day when the behavior stops. Then we complain that they have no patience and jump from topic to topic in rapid-fire succession.

Interests recall toddler days, when fixation was the norm. Children with interests will read the same books over and over. They'll regale you with facts you've heard from them several times. They'll push you for answers to their questions, and they'll never tire of asking you to help them with activities related to their interest.

What do we do? Invariably, we try to circumvent their line of questioning. Or, worse, we scold them for their repetitive behavior. In effect, we squash the beginnings of an interest.

Terry still finds it difficult to believe that her son developed a love of history when he was just three years old. "Sometimes I'll think he couldn't have been that young," she says.

"But soon he was interested in early American history and Lincoln," she continues. "He heard about the assassination. I was pregnant with my second son, who's three-and-a-half years younger than Kyle. I remember going into my OB appointment and had to take Kyle, and he kept trying to tell the doctor about John Wilkes Booth, or 'Boof,' as he pronounced it."

The trick to nurturing interests at this age is to live for the moment. Cindy Ross discovered that with her two young children. "Kids in general live in the present," she writes in her book *Kids in the Wild*. "What they see along the way is more important than the destination, and parents must be willing to give up goal-oriented 'hikes' for a while in exchange for their children's company."

Also, maintain a positive attitude. "Don't always say no, no, no," says Lovejoy. "Kids learn respect when you quietly explain to them, 'If you step on that, you won't get any tomatoes from it because it will be squished and it can't grow.' They learn that if they don't water, things die. They learn that if they beat up on a plant, it will die, and it's just a process of constant learning every day."

YOUNG CHILDREN

Whoever said "an elephant never forgets" never met a young child. Just out of diapers, they have an uncanny ability to remember conversations, events, and off-the-cuff remarks. The downside is that you have to be careful about what you say to and around them; the upside is that interest-related conversations and activities will long be remembered.

"We don't get to see our granddaughter that often, but she never forgets what we do," says Lovejoy. "She'll say, 'Can we go out? Can I water the plants?' She's not even four yet, so it sticks."

She adds that older children also tend to have long memories. "I worked as kind of a mentor for school science projects, and kids who I worked with one year the next year would say, 'Hey, Ms. Lovejoy, is that licorice plant still growing out there?' "

Note, too, when your young child delights in one of the hundreds of activities young children are typically drawn to, such as listening to music, dancing, or playing in the sand. Rather than chalk up the early interest to a phase all children their age go through, consider ways to nurture it into a lifelong interest. Perhaps it isn't a phase. Maybe the child really does like the activity and would take it further if given the chance.

ADOLESCENTS

Pursuing interests with teenagers is about patience and understanding on a level different from that with young children. Amanda has been writing poems and stories since third grade. As an eighth-grader, her stories have gotten longer and more involved. But as she reads and absorbs other ideas, she has difficulty inventing her own. "She has a hard time focusing on her own ideas, in contrast to the ideas of others," says her mother, Rachel.

Rachel is optimistic that the situation is a phase her daughter needs to work through. In the meantime, to keep Amanda motivated, Rachel is introducing her to the writings and biographies of different authors. "Her world view is changing from that of a child to that of a young woman," she says. "I know she will find her voice again in time."

To encourage adolescents to pursue an interest, put some space between you and your children. Give them responsibility with restrictions. Encourage them to read about their interests and teach you a thing or two based on what they've read. And always encourage them to follow their own instincts rather adopting the typical herd mentality.

Resist the urge to use your child's age as an excuse for not pursuing an interest. Lovejoy has seen urban teenagers who spent their free time playing video games transformed into entrepreneurial gardeners. "What has been happening in a lot of cities, not just L.A., the kids are raising small plots of tomatoes and hot peppers and stuff," she says. "They sell them at a farmer's market or they make something from it, with mentors, and they sell them through school or through various organizations."

Lovejoy has seen female teens dress as garden sprites to celebrate nature. She's also seen her own teenage son pull away from gardening. "Teenage times were hard," she says. "But it ended up paying off in the long run."

How did it pay off? "When he moved away to go to college, we went to visit—it was a pretty dismal bachelor pad," says Lovejoy. "He said, 'Come outside, I want you to see something.' He had planted a moonlight garden. We used to go out in the evening and wait for the sphinx moths to visit the fuchsias. I guess he wanted that magic."

Involve your teen in planning interest-related activities. If she likes to cook, consider a bicycle tour that takes participants to various inns where they work in the kitchens with chefs. Let her research tours and plan the itinerary within an allotted budget.

If your child has had an interest, it may start to soften in the teen years. She may not be as vocal about it and may pursue it less often. And because of her age, others may not be in such awe of her achievements. As a high school junior, Kyle still loves history, but it doesn't draw the kind of attention it did when he was three. "He doesn't feel like he's the expert in history anymore," says his mother.

Still, try to keep the interest a part of your teenager's life. Fourteen-year-old Amanda doesn't publish her newsletter or write as many stories as she once did. But she continues to write in the journal she received in third grade, and her mother nurtures her interest in other ways.

SPECIAL-NEEDS CHILDREN

The only thing ceramics teacher Kevin Nierman wants to know about new students is whether they have a medical condition that requires special measures to ensure a safe, enjoyable place to work. "I have some kids . . . I don't even ask what's wrong with them," he says. "Sometimes their parents volunteer and sometimes they don't."

One young student comes with his father to the studio every Saturday. "He can't focus on one thing for more than maybe two minutes, maybe not even that," says Nierman. "But he has this fabulous father who is willing to come with him and gives him just enough room to be very creative about what he's doing and yet not destroy or hurt anybody else in the studio or anybody else's work."

Nierman allows the student to use the potter's wheel in a non-traditional way. "His father puts a lump of clay on the wheel, and we let him stick his fingers into it," says Nierman. "He loves to gouge out pieces of clay and cut and chop, so he's creative—some amazing pieces of art, actually."

Interestingly, Nierman has shown the magic that can happen when special-needs children meet up with teenagers who have interests. The result is a mentor relationship that fulfills the needs of the teenager to demonstrate responsibility and knowledge, and a child who can demonstrate mastery and skill.

For two years, Nierman has had a mentally and physically disabled student. "If she presses too hard with her fingers, it hurts her," he says. "I have been fortunate enough to have one of the other teen students volunteer—this is going on the second year now—to come and be with her in each class so that she gets extra attention in terms of being able to help her press the clay down and create whatever it is that she's trying to do."

It's especially important for special-needs children to find an interest that highlights their strong points. Terry's son Kyle had a mild case of sensory integration dysfunction, which affected his fine-motor coordination.

"He had difficulty discriminating certain sensory input through his fingers," says Terry. "He hated doing crafts and coloring. [For him, it was] like working with mittens on. Since it was difficult for him, he gravitated toward other things, like reading."

Lovejoy has worked on community gardens designed to incorporate the requirements of special-needs children. She has installed raised beds and widened pathways, then lined them with decomposed granite to make them wheelchair accessible. The modifications add to the costs, and she's had uphill battles obtaining financing for such features as ramps and Braille labels.

Lovejoy recalls working as a consultant on a community garden that included a tree house she wanted to make wheelchair accessible. "There was a lot of hullabaloo because it would make it more expensive," she says.

One night at a meeting of community members who gathered to discuss the garden, Lovejoy asked the children to help plan the garden on large pieces of butcher paper. While they worked on the floor, a child with muscular dystrophy sat at a table and struggled to draw a picture of a tree house.

"I had been fighting about the tree house during the day," says Lovejoy. "[The boy] could barely talk, and they had the microphone up, and he said his dream was to have a tree house. And I said, 'You know what? You're going to have your dream, because you're going to have one right here in this garden.'

"People were crying. He was crying. It was one of the neatest things in the world. All they had to do was [install] a ramp that came up from the third level of the garden and rolled out into the treetop, and it worked for him."

Cindy Ross has seen how the outdoors can transform a special-needs child. She has written about how the parents of a child with spina bifida used a llama to carry their son for four or five days every summer into the backcountry, how another set of parents whose son has cerebral palsy used a bike trailer to accommodate their child and his wheelchair; and still another pair of parents who took their son camping despite a condition that required him to have a special diet administered around the clock.

Of the latter child, Ross writes:

These outings have given Kurt a much broader base of experience. He has seen dolphins close up in the Gulf of Mexico, and moose and beaver in wild rivers. He loves it out in the wilds. It has built self-reliance and independence in him, which is so important for every child but especially important for a special-needs child whom the world tends to look at as handicapped.

Unlike a book, interests do not have a beginning, a middle, and an end. Interests have only a beginning. They are forever evolving.

Remember this as you pursue an interest with your child. Live for the moment. Enjoy every small conversation, cherish every new discovery and share in the disappointments. It's these snippets of time spent together that are the most memorable.

• Travel Plans •

For Vikram, subway rides were never about arriving at a final destination. He took what many riders consider a chore to places few parents of preschoolers could imagine.

As a preschooler living in Manhattan, Vikram liked trains. That led to an interest in the subway, which he would ride with his mother and younger brother. "Riding the subway became a great way to spend a rainy day," says his mother Meena. "For one token, we could explore different neighborhoods."

As they rode the subway, Vikram would follow their path on a map. Eventually, he memorized the entire subway system and enjoyed giving directions to passengers.

"I was aware of his interest and tried to find ways to help him explore it," says Meena. "I would say, 'We're going from this point to that point. How should we get there?' I always took the lead from him."

Meena is a big believer in the idea that young children have strong instincts. "By the age of five, they know what they like and dislike. In many cases, children's instincts are clearer, purer than those of adults. It's important to listen to them. It makes them feel good that what they feel and believe means something, and that they don't have to bend to an adult's will."

A Big Interest in Small Countries

Visits to various neighborhoods led to a desire to learn about different ethnic groups. "He became interested in the cultures, politics, economics, foods, you name it, of other countries," says Meena.

That interest, in turn, led to a fascination with geography. "My parents have helped me pursue an interest in geography by finding interesting books for me and talking about world affairs with me," says Vikram.

Indeed, Vikram pores over atlases and reads adult-level history books, despite a disability called oculocutaneous albinism, which affects his ability to see. What a person with normal vision can see 200 feet away, Vikram can see only at 20 feet. His vision will not deteriorate over time, nor will it improve.

Vikram has developed a fondness for small countries, including Kuwait, Qatar, Bahrain, San Marino, Liechtenstein, Kyrgyzstan and Tajikistan. "These countries are interesting to me because there is not that much information that you can find out about them," he says, adding, "and not many people know about them."

Vikram's fascination with small countries led him to create his own: Indoguay. It is shaped like Cyprus, has its own language, and it travels—it has been in the Arabian Sea and the Red Sea. He and a friend even created an architectural style for the country, which they call "neoclassical Japanese."

"The buildings look very similar to pagodas, only they are more curved and are made of different colored marble," he says. "The tiers are usually black marble, while the walls are green or white. The insides have glass and pink-and-white marble."

High-Speed Journey

Vikram was such a voracious reader of geography books that Meena became concerned his interest was overshadowing other aspects of his life. "Sometimes it worried me," she says. "I tried to get him interested in other things. Maybe it has to reach a certain point, a saturation point."

Her fears subsided when Vikram entered middle school. "In elementary school, he would spend five to ten hours a week on his passion," she says. "Middle school is a different world. His homework load is substantial and there are more activities, and he wants to participate in all of them."

Meena was also concerned that her son's passion was being tainted by the lure of competition. When Vikram was in fifth grade, he competed against about a hundred students in grades five through eight in a state geography bee sponsored by the National Geographic Society.

"We let him know that his winning or losing didn't matter to us, and that he would always have our support," says Meena. "If he lost, we said [the letdown] wouldn't go on forever; if he won, the euphoria would also not last forever."

Vikram placed first in the state competition, but did not make it to the finals in the national competition. "I don't think I like geography as much as I did," he says. "I think that the competitions partly ruined the interest."

Travel Plans

Today, the fourteen-year-old is gravitating to history, specifically Asian history. "If I could do anything related to my interest," he says, "I would become an executive of a corporate firm and create a charity to help people and nature all over the world."

Meena credits her son's resiliency with her early approach to sparking his interests. "We exposed our children to as many different experiences and people as possible without getting stressed out about it," she says. "They saw us enjoying these things and doing it together as a family.

"When I told my son I would be interviewed for this book, I asked him to tell me what I did right with him," she continues. "He said, 'You never pressured us. No matter what we did you never told us what to do, within certain limits. You always backed us up.'"

10

Take a Hike

Some parents are so passionate about their interests they can't imagine putting them on hold while they raise their children. Such was the case for long-distance hikers Cindy Ross and her husband Todd Gladfelter, who despite arguments from other hikers that it couldn't be done, managed to log 2,000 long-distance miles in the first three years of her two children's lives.

Here, Ross describes how she found her passion, and how she and her husband worked to instill it in their children. Ross and Gladfelter are the authors of *Kids in the Wild: A Family Guide to Outdoor Recreation* (The Mountaineers Books, 1995). Ross is also the author of *Scraping Heaven: A Family's Journey Along the Continental Divide* (Ragged Mountain Press, 2002), in which she describes how over five summers her family traversed the 3,100-mile footpath running along the crest of the Rocky Mountains from Canada to Mexico, using llamas as kid-carriers and packers.

How did you get involved in hiking and backpacking?

It started when I hiked the Appalachian Trail in 1978. That was my first long hike.

What made you do that?

I lived within forty-five minutes of the Appalachian Trail, and I had been a member of a hiking club since I was fifteen because my parents didn't hike. My father hunted and we went to his hunting camp for our family vacations, but he never really hiked.

I met this long-distance hiker on the trail who was doing the whole thing, and I was fascinated by it. It was just kind of like a dream in the back of my head. I was going to art school in Philadelphia at the time and decided I needed to get out of the city, and my best friend said she'd do the trail.

[With hiking], you are either totally obsessed with it and fall in love with it and can't wait until you can go out and do another long hike; or you never go out there again, because you realize that it's so big and important but you can't change your lifestyle so that you can have that kind of freedom. For [me and] my husband, whom I met later and who was also a long-distance hiker, it became so important that we wanted to create a lifestyle where we weren't dictated [to] by a nine-to-five job.

After we hiked the Appalachian Trail, we went on to hike the Pacific Crest Trail that goes from Canada to Mexico. We came home and decided to build a log home from scratch. We bought land, raised food, and had no debt because we did everything ourselves. We decided to work part-time so that would equal one full-time job, and it would be the kind of work where we could leave when we wanted.

The long hikes put us in this frame of mind of loving our freedom and independence over loving material things and money. We were poverty level for years. We lived on $10,000; we made $15,000 and saved five every year and still went hiking every year. Now we're better than that, and we can travel to other countries. But it never felt like a sacrifice.

How did having children affect your hiking?

We started to backpack with Sierra when she was three months old. We went on long trips with her, and we were fine until we got our son and then we couldn't do it and we didn't know what to do. We ended up buying mountain bikes and bike trailers and doing long rail trails. We bought canoes and started paddling long distance. But that didn't satisfy us because it wasn't remote. It wasn't the high mountains.

It wasn't until we met this man who told us about llamas, when Bryce was an infant and Sierra was two, that we got back into the mountains again to hike the Continental Divide Trail.

But it's funny, because about ten years ago I was at a long-distance hikers' convention, and I was standing up there saying, "Look, you guys have to believe us that you can have kids and continue this." They were terrified to have kids! And now they're starting to, and we were really the first long-distance hikers to say, "Okay, they're coming along. It doesn't matter how hard it is—we're going to figure it out."

You have basically involved your children in your interest since they were infants.

Everyone used to say to us, "It's too bad they won't remember this," or "It's too bad you can't give them to somebody." We said, "We're not doing this to broaden our kids—not when they were six months old. We're doing it because we love it and it makes us happy and we can't live any other way." They're just really along for the ride, whether they're riding in a bike or riding on the llama.

But it turned into something we don't want to do without them now because they bring so much more joy into it and a different perspective. Plus, they have come to realize that they need it to be happy too, on some level. It doesn't have to be hiking, but it has to be time out there in the wilderness.

How has the interest shaped your children?

We home-schooled for a couple years because I didn't want the school system telling me that I could only travel in the summer. We put Sierra in third grade halfway through the year and Bryce in first grade.

My daughter had problems with some of the kids and the groups—twenty kids the same age in her face. She liked different people of different ages from different cultures and different backgrounds who liked to do different things. This stemmed from us being out there and traveling and meeting different people.

She doesn't buy into the whole "You have to look like this in order for us to accept you." She gets her feelings hurt, but she's not going to change. She has high self-esteem because that whole life out there makes you feel independent and confident. When my kids were five years old, they learned to read the land, figure out where water was, how to go cross-country.

Even though you don't need those skills in normal life, it gave them a good sense of themselves and confidence. They could go into society and not feel like they had to be like everyone else. Now, it does make a problem with my daughter because she isn't like everyone else and she learned that in third grade. I said, "Well, no one's like anybody else. Everyone's different. You just kind of stick out a little more."

My daughter is leaning toward the sciences because of the things we saw and did out there. I'm interested in everything and I'm always writing articles and I'm pretty vocal as far as sharing things. I make sure I point out everything to them, whether it's "Do you see that light? That light is orange because the sun is setting. That's a different color light than during the day."

I'm always trying to share what I see with them, to open them up and broaden them. I don't want them to go through their lives foggy, with their eyes closed. I see my nieces and nephews, and they act like their spirit is dead at fifteen. I don't get it. I don't know if it's computers or what, but my kids have never been like that, and I think it's because they see the bigger picture from living out there so much.

When my daughter has time, she goes out and studies and does experiments on her own. She'll pick flowers and put them in water or sugar water or different kinds of stuff to see how they grow. She takes notes, and she's stalking animals with binoculars.

She's got this sense about finding things. One time we were out West, and we were camped near the Anasazis [Indians], their land, and I said, "We gotta go, we're packed up." She says, "I have to find an arrowhead." I said, "Sierra, we're leaving." There was no indication there was anything there. And she said, "Just give me one more second. Oh, here it is, I found it." And it was this obsidian bird point [arrowhead]. It was so delicate. She knew she would find it and she found it.

How has the outdoors influenced your son?

My son will draw out there all the time. He doesn't draw anything that he sees. Everything is in his head.

I introduce my kids to many different experiences, mostly outdoor experiences, but I let them go. I don't try to have my son draw a certain way or I don't tell my daughter, "Go do an experiment." I let them do what they want. I provide tons of materials and books and opportunities to go places, but I don't say, "Now we're going to go do this." I don't think kids need as much direction as some parents try to give them.

How do you keep their interest in the outdoors high?

Take all your cues from them. My daughter and I were chasing this flock of turkeys the other day, and she's looking at the footprints and she said, "I'd like to make a cast of those footprints. Can we do it now?" I said, "I don't think we can do it now. I think you need plaster of Paris. Let's go look it up in a book and find how to do that."

Another time we went to this star party in a state park in Pennsylvania where there is the darkest night sky east of the Mississippi. Four hundred astronomers go there every new moon and show you the unbelievable things in the heavens from every telescope. My daughter was whining, "I want to bring my girlfriend." I said, "I don't want to bring your girlfriend." She asked, "Are we going to spend the whole weekend away?" I said, "I'll go myself." "No, we don't want to miss anything," they'll say, because they know it's wonderful.

Does your daughter have a hard time making friends who are interested in what she does?

She's got two friends at school who are kind of into the outdoors. But most of the kids play with their friends in the school-yard or have a friend over every now and then on a Saturday.

A lot of my kids' friends are our friends. They are different ages. Some are single guys or older people or just different people who, for whatever reason, they don't have kids or they can't see their kids because they're divorced. They don't talk down to my kids. They'll do things with them and show them things.

Do your children's friends accompany you on hikes?

I'm not big on taking other kids along because then the whole dynamic of the family changes. [M]y daughter doesn't treat my son as well, and they really have a close relationship. From being out there together so long, they've learned to play together.

Do you bring what you know into their classrooms?

We have a twenty-four-foot teepee in which we have a big Native American Thanksgiving dinner party with a fire and wild foods. When Sierra was studying Native Americans, we brought the teepee to school and set it up outside and brought drums that my husband made from skins and made food for them.

I'll give slide shows and things like that. The school is happy about that, which is why their principals let me take my kids out for two months at a time.

Do your children ever not want to participate in a hike or an outdoor recreational activity?

Oh, yeah. It's before we go. When we get out there, they're

thrilled to death. It's just, you know, "I don't feel like getting in a car," or "Do we have to drive that far?"

I can keep them quiet because I say, "Look, it's my job [to write about the outdoors]." They know they have to do it, but they swim with manatees. They've done so many neat things because of my job.

In Kids in the Wild, *you detail your efforts to keep your children entertained on long car trips.*

I wrote that book when they were such little kids, and we've really learned a lot about entertaining them. And they know how to entertain themselves. Sierra will be twelve. She only watches a movie like two times a month. Other than that, they have to entertain themselves. They read, draw. When we went to Thailand, they made up eight songs that they composed themselves, then made a video of it when they came home. They did that in the van as we drove around Thailand and we never said, "Why don't you make up some songs?"

What suggestions do you have for parents who want to get involved, say, in the outdoors and their child shows little or no interest?

They need to start as early as possible. Once kids get old enough, they think they know what they like—and they do know what they like, they just don't know what they haven't been exposed to.

If they're older and you want to introduce them to it, then be sensitive to what the child likes. Maybe they like to paddle better than they like to ride a bike, or they love to ride a bike and they hate to hike.

My kids like some sports better than others. Sierra doesn't like to hike as much as she loves to ride. When we were out West, Bryce only got on that llama when he was so tired he couldn't walk anymore. Sierra and I horseback ride all the time because she likes to ride. You have to find out what they like and then do that with them. There are so many outdoor sports that it doesn't have to be hiking. It can be anything. And then, where do they want to go? What do they want to see? Do they like animals? Do they like the weather better—would they like to see Florida instead of New England? That lets them be the boss.

Having seen their parents pursue their interests, do your children understand the importance of having interests?

My kids see that we're doing what we love, so they do what they love. If my son can't draw about four hours a day, he loses his mind.

Some children start collections based on their interests. Do your kids have collections?

My daughter collects everything. She has a huge rock collection and seashells and feathers.

Does she display them a certain way?

She has setups. She took a pottery course, and then we went to Virginia to do some Raku firing with my friend. We've got two whole countertops [filled with them]. Furniture in the living room had to be cleared off for this setup of some twenty-five pots.

When you're home, how do you keep the interest in the outdoors alive? It sounds as though your kids do it on their own. But are there any things you do? Do you sit around the table and discuss the next trip? Do you get a map out?

No, they don't even know until the day we're leaving.

Last weekend, we went to a star party. I picked them up from school and said, "We're going upstate this weekend. We're going stargazing." Or I'll say, "Okay, the moon's full tonight, we're going hiking tonight."

"Oh, I don't feel like going hiking," they'll say. I say, "Too bad, the moon's full. We're going hiking. You'll have a great time."

I'll spring this stuff on them all the time because this is what I want to do and they want to do it, too. But they're at the age where they think they need to say something or maybe they want to read their book because they're obsessed with their book and I go, "You can read your book anytime. The moon's full, let's go."

I do it to make everybody go out there and be together, because as a family this is the best time we have. I know a lot of people who love these sports and don't do it anymore because it's work. But I never wanted to do it without them. If I went by myself, my husband couldn't go, so the other choice is everybody goes.

In your book you write about special-needs children and the outdoors.

They see so many limits in their lives. Bringing them outdoors opens up another whole world for them. [B]eing outside broadens them, and even if they can't get out of a wheelchair, they've got the whole sky, birds, smells, sound. It gives them more freedom. That's important for anybody, but especially for kids who have so many limits in their lives.

You're taking fly-fishing lessons. Are you planning to introduce your children to that sport?

That's the reason I started. Sierra has been crazy about fish since she's been born.

My husband said he has no interest in fishing and doesn't want to sit there and be bored. So I figured I'll learn to fly-fish because you can move and can walk up the creek. I've been taking lessons for three years and writing stories about it. I got Sierra her first pair of waders, and she's got a spin-casting rod.

Bryce will swim and lie on a blanket and read a book. He could not care less about fishing, because if he can't get a rod to work, he's frustrated. But Sierra is out there screaming, "Oh, my God, look at the fish. I'm going to catch one, Mom, I know I'm going to catch one!" After twenty minutes, she couldn't catch it, because these fish are caught constantly, so she went over with her mini-bait bucket and her net and spent the next two hours trying to catch minnows, which she caught.

What advice can you offer parents who want to share a particular interest or hobby with their children?

Make time for them. What's important to them is important, and what you think you need to do, whether it's the dishes or your phone call or your e-mail, is not as important as your kids.

In five minutes they'll be gone, and you will have lost your chance to stimulate them or nurture a relationship or maybe give them this wonderful interest that could make them happy the rest of their lives. Just take the time to listen. Sometimes it's subtle as far as what they like to do, but if you see a spark, just forget about what you think is so important yourself and go be with them.

• *It's No Act* •

Two-year-old Julie was lying in her crib at naptime when her mother heard sounds on the baby monitor. It was Julie. She wasn't fussing; she was reciting the introduction to one of her parents' favorite television shows. "Space . . . the final frontier," Julie babbled.

"As a family, we loved watching 'Star Trek: The Next Generation,'" says Susan, Julie's mother. "Quite a giggle to hear those oh-so-serious platitudes about the Enterprise's *continuing mission coming from a toddler."*

Julie was truly of the "next generation" of kids, because her parents also shared with their daughter their love of the Bard. Shakespeare's Queen Mab speech from Romeo and Juliet *is one of Susan's particular favorites.*

Julie's introduction to the Bard also exposed her to characters feared by most young children: witches. She took an instant liking to her father's rendition of the "double, double, toil and trou-

ble" witches' incantation from Macbeth, and memorized the
fairy tale "Rapunzel."

"Then she decided she was going to play the part of the
witch," says Susan. "We were amazed how at the age of three she
could mimic a witch's cackling.

"Now as a thirteen-year-old, she adores 'Buffy the Vampire
Slayer,'" she adds. "Frankly, so do I."

From Lines to Roles

It wasn't long before Julie moved from memorizing lines to
acting out parts. At day care, she liked to play Sleeping Beauty.

As Julie entered elementary school, Susan and her husband
Stan realized their daughter was interested in acting. But they
questioned whether she was attracted to acting or being a movie
star.

They leaned toward the latter. "We were wrong," says Susan.

"On what we thought was the off chance that she was interested in acting," she says, "we found opportunities to play small
roles in high school renditions of dramas that called for children." Among those roles was a nonspeaking fairy in A Mid-
summer Night's Dream and a thieving Cockney boy in My Fair
Lady.

"She loved being in those productions," says Susan. "In retro-
spect, I suspect her love of acting really took root then."

Pulling Back—a Little

By third grade, soccer and a growing workload at school
prompted Julie to stop acting in those productions. Her parents
nevertheless kept her interest alive in other ways.

They attended movies as a family, critiquing the films. "I love
watching the actors perform, especially if they are cute," says
Julie. "I like to see how well they do, and if it is something new
for the actor. I like hearing the script and trying to figure out
where they might have changed words or added more."

And just as Julie watched "Star Trek" with her parents as a

toddler, she was allowed to attend select R-rated movies with them. (Julie saves ticket stubs from the films she's seen, and has some eighty in her collection.)

"My parents think I'm more mature than some kids, and that I can handle it," she says. "Also, a lot of the Oscar-nominated movies are R-rated, so I can figure out what to root for."

Julie's parents also take her to plays. As a third-grader fresh from reading The Diary of Anne Frank, Julie was treated by her parents to a Broadway revival of the play. Living not far from Washington, D.C., they also attend plays at The Shakespeare Theatre, where Julie saw Othello, which starred Patrick Stewart, whom she first encountered on "Star Trek."

At the end of the performance of Othello, Stewart exited past Julie's box seat near the stage, turning toward Julie and smiling at her. "She cried, literally wept for joy afterward," says Susan. "He also sent her a handwritten note, prompted by my writing to him to say how much we all appreciated his performance. That note is framed in a place of honor in Julie's bedroom."

Later, Julie would return to the stage in her school's annual variety shows. When she was in sixth grade, she and a friend emceed the show in which they wrote a comedy script introducing thirty-four acts.

"They brought down the house," says Susan. "Stan and I were surprised and impressed."

It's for Real

According to Susan, the "Omigod-she-really-wants-to-act moment" came when Julie was twelve and attended a two-week summer day camp with The Shakespeare Theatre.

"Julie played Lady Macbeth in the 'unsex me' scene, and she electrified us," says Susan. "She understood the text, did it well, and improvised gestures beautifully and appropriately."

In fact, the role proved to be Julie's most memorable. "Lady Macbeth is so complex and there is more to her than it seems," she says. "I liked figuring out why she wanted to do what she did."

The performance marked a turning point in her parents' perception of their daughter's interest. "That's when we knew that she really wanted to act, and that she had significant talent—and vowed to do whatever we could to help and encourage her."

Today, Julie continues to audition for roles in school plays, and will be in her middle school production of Fiddler on the Roof. *She is looking forward to participating in The Shakespeare Theatre's summer camp production of* Othello. *"I would love to be Desdemona," she says.*

To hear Julie's enthusiasm is to know just how passionate children can be about their interests. "I love almost everything about acting," she says.

Of course, like any new teen, Julie also loves a lot of other things, including soccer and socializing. Her mother is mindful of that fact of teen life, and acts accordingly.

"Listen to what your child is saying, and try to take an interest in whatever she is interested in," she says. "Ask her what she thinks, ask her opinions. Scout out available opportunities. But in the midst of all this, don't overprogram her. Give her time to lie on her bed, stare at the ceiling, listen to music, and otherwise just be."

11

Molding Young Artists

As a boy growing up in Michigan, Kevin Nierman says of himself, he was "somebody who didn't fit into a structured environment." Fortunately, his mother was sensitive enough to that fact that she nurtured his passion in the unstructured world of ceramics. Today, Nierman is an internationally known artist recognized for rebuilding ceramic creations he has purposely demolished.

Nierman shares his interest in ceramics each week with some 200 young students at his Kids 'N' Clay Pottery Studio, in West Berkeley, California. There, children ages five to eighteen express themselves using clay.

"The way I look at it is that they come here, and they have enough creative juices to last a lifetime," he says. "All I need to do is sort of stay out of the way, give them technical information and a little bit of structure now and then, and I just find they take off."

Based on his fifteen-plus years as a ceramics teacher, Nierman describes how to encourage children's creativity and the role adults should play in the process. "We are their coaches and cheerleaders," he says. "We're there to help them figure out how to make whatever it is that they're feeling and seeing."

How did your childhood influence your becoming a ceramics artist?

I grew up living around artists. My mother was a painter, and although I have five other siblings, none of them became working artists. She certainly was encouraging in terms of allowing us to have materials around. We were pretty much given free rein of the backyard and garage in terms of paints and wood and nails and you name it.

Describe your school years.

I went to public school in Michigan and hated every minute of it. Ceramics was my saving grace—the fact that I was allowed to create whatever I wanted.

At some point, I guess I was twenty-two, I took an eight-week ceramics course—I had moved to Florida by then—at a local pottery studio. That was it. I found my true love. I ran home and built my first potter's wheel. I bought a little kiln and put it in the vestibule of my apartment.

I started making pots and making pots and making pots. I'm essentially self-taught in that I never did any more schooling after that.

And that became your career?

It took a long time to make enough money and to figure out how to make it work, but essentially I never stopped doing clay. I never made much money on it. I always had to clean houses and gardens and do whatever I needed to do to keep working with clay, but from that point on, I didn't stop.

Then I did a workshop in Southern California with a Native American potter. There were a couple of women there who were talking about a backyard pottery studio they had and how they taught children. I had always really loved kids. I said, "That sounds like fun." And they said, "You should go do that. You should go home and invite your neighbors."

So I did, and it grew until now we've got almost two hundred kids a week at Kids 'N' Clay Pottery Studio. I consider them artists-in-residence. I had maybe one student in sixteen years who didn't like clay.

How long is the program?

It's open-ended and ongoing. When a space opens up, whoever is waiting can get in.

The ages?

The ages are from five to eighteen. We stop at the end of June and do a summer camp, weeklong for four weeks. Then we take August off.

How is it different for a five-year-old coming in versus a nine-year-old? A preteen? A teen?

To me, it's no different, partly because of the way I've structured the program. I introduce the five-year-old or the twelve-year-old to the studio, and I tell them it's their studio. Then I give them the options: They can hand build, sculpt, go to the potter's wheel—whatever it is they want to do. They can sit there on that first day as far as I'm concerned.

I start them by just feeling and touching the clay. Then if they want to build a cat or a cheetah, we start rolling out clay, a slab, and building a cheetah. The teenagers are a little more excited to go to the potter's wheel right away. The young ones are more apt to wait half an hour or do a project by hand and then run over to the wheel when they feel more comfortable. It totally depends on the child, though.

What if they're unsure of what to make?

I have a book which has some of the projects we've done over the years. The kids are free to get that whenever they want. I have several other notebooks with pictures of animals and planes, and everything I can think of. They can get ideas, or maybe they want to see what a cheetah really looks like and make it more like what this book says a cheetah looks like. I also have lots of ceramics magazines around of other people's work.

Say a child has been here three years and he comes to me and says, "What should I make?" I say, "What is it you want to make?" I'll give him suggestions, and we'll try exercises. We'll go to the yard, we'll look at texture, we'll think of a lot of things, but what I find is that they want me to tell them what to make because that's the way it is with every other aspect of their lives. But not with creativity. It's harder for them to have an open program. But the result is that it allows them to access deeper creative urges.

Young children love animals. What do your teen students like?

The teenagers tend to be more independent. If they're not interested in the wheel right off, they might sculpt. They often want to be left alone for the first class or two and just sort of feel their way into the clay. They may make some small sculpture. At that age, they have more of an interest in working with their hands.

A lot of parents expose their children to new things with good intentions. But somewhere things go wrong. For example, my son likes clay, so I bought him a child's potter's wheel. But it frustrated him, and eventually he lost interest. What did I do wrong?

That's why I like having an open program. What happens is a kid will start, say at five years old, and she'll try the wheel. I make certain on the very first time that she's successful.

How do you do that?

I do a real hands-on thing so that I'm in front of them at the wheel, and this would have helped with your child. In *The Kids 'N' Clay Ceramics Book,* I write about how the adult can help the child be successful. All they have to do is figure out the hand motions, and they've got it.

I know this because last week I had a new student. I said, "Have you ever worked with clay?" and she said, "Oh, yeah, I've worked with clay and it was wonderful." I said, "Where?" She said, "I bought a little wheel, I bought that little wheel, that twenty-five-dollar wheel, and I made pots." They were really tiny pots, of course—that little wheel doesn't have a lot of torque. Somehow she figured it out. That's what I've noticed about kids—it completely depends on the child, and what the adults are expecting.

It seems as though the idea is to help them just enough so they can achieve what it is they want to create.

I am here to help this child remain open to his or her creativity. That's my first job. My first job is not to teach them clay; it's to make certain they stay open to their creativity.

I believe that it's vital and important because that's what happened to me. I didn't make it in a normal school setting. I barely got out of high school. But I had a passion. I had art. I had to be creative about how I was going to work my life. I was fortunate it worked out. Otherwise, I would have been on the street.

I love that so many parents, at least here, are aware in some way that their child is interested in clay.

Is that how most come to your studio?

It's one of two reasons. Either the parent knows about the value of art and that their child isn't getting enough art in school; or, more often, the child says, "I want to do clay."

The thing about clay over other mediums is that it is the most generous, wonderful, accepting medium. I ask, "Why do you like clay so much?" They'll say, "I can make anything out of it, unlike a cardboard box or something," or "You can start with a blob and end up with something."

There's got to be a degree of frustration. For example, what if a child comes in and wants to make a tiger. But the tiger doesn't come out like the image they had of it.

I had a five-year-old girl [who] made a cheetah with the staff. This was her first class.

The way we work it is that we help them a lot with this. So they're rolling out a slab of clay, and they put bunches of newspaper inside to create a hollow body form, and the child learns to score and slip on pieces of clay for the legs and what have you. It turned out somewhat large, maybe thirteen inches long and seven inches tall. The front legs were bent back and were awkward looking, and she knew it. It didn't match her vision. To me or others, it might have been fine. But it didn't match her vision, so she started to cry.

We talked a little, and I said, "What do you want to change about it?" And she said, "Those legs." Luckily, it was still not completely dry, although it had sat out all week because she had said she was done with it. So I said, "Let's see what we can do. I don't know if this will work, but we can try. It might be too dry and we might not be able to change this, but I have a hunch we can."

So we cut off the legs, put more water on it, scored and "slipped" it (applied a mixture of clay and water), and she got the legs on it that she wanted. Her vision then seemed complete. The tail she wanted changed as well. She had a really strong idea.

You were smart enough—and patient enough—to go back and help her with it. If she had made that project at home, her parent might have said, "You should have said that a week ago when it was still wet."

We are their coaches and cheerleaders. We're there to help them figure out how to make whatever it is that they're feeling and seeing.

We're not there to tell them to make a cheetah. We're not there to tell them to make a cheetah orange instead of purple. We're there to help them figure out their vision. That's our job at Kids 'N' Clay, and sometimes it's really hard and sometimes it doesn't work.

What do you do when it "doesn't work"?

When things get bad with some kids, I bring them to my studio and show them my work. I tell them that I was making something and I wanted it to be a certain way, but it got a big break in it, and I called the person I was making this bowl for and I said, "It has a big crack. How would you feel if I glued it back together?" The person agrees and I glue it back together, and it turns out more wonderful on some level than originally planned. It has more character. It has more feeling. I explain to them that this is sometimes the way it is with clay, because so many things can go wrong.

Parents will read this and run to their nearest ceramics studio to enroll their child. What's the difference between a studio such as yours and the many ceramics stores that cater to a young clientele?

The difference is that you're working with wet clay here. There you're working with an already fired object, and you're accepting that it's a bowl already. You're accepting that it's a cat already, and it looks like what it looks like—and somebody else made it. Those are great. Anything to get people painting, doing something creative, is terrific, but it's limited for some people in that you don't start with your original vision and follow it through.

Also, for children specifically, one of the most thrilling things is making the object. After it's done, it's a lot less interesting for many children to finish through with painting and glazing. It's so thrilling to create this thing, and then to have it painted and finish it is not quite as thrilling. We often have to work at getting them to finish their work.

For parents who don't have a studio like yours near them, can they do this at home?

That was the whole intention of my book. Parents can set up a corner in the bedroom, kitchen, den, garage. Get a little table and a board with a piece of canvas on it so the clay can be worked easily. Then go to the local ceramics supplier and ask for a smooth, low-fire clay and low-fire, nontoxic underglazes and glazes. They do need to have access to some firing facility, but in most major towns, they can find it.

If a child loves ceramics, how do parents know how much to expose their child to it?

What I found over the years is that some parents will say, "My child loves this so much. Can we do three classes a week?" Some times I'll say yes. But depending on how the child is in the class, how interested, sometimes I'll say, "I don't think it's such a great idea."

What I've noticed is that children who get a lot out of the program come over a longer period of time and gain in skill and confidence, thereby being able to create more of what it is of the vision that they have. They progress over a period of time.

If there's too much access too quickly, kids burn out. Their interest isn't there. Partly, it's the way I've structured it. I ask them to tap their own ideas. I won't say, "Let's all make a cup today. Let's all make a bowl." They're being forced to continually develop and grow, in this case, in ceramics.

Do you suggest that parents nurture the interest outside of class?

Sure. We have our own exhibits every year. We had it at the Oakland Museum last year. Also, whenever something interesting comes to town, I put up flyers about it. If there's an opening somewhere, I'll suggest it to specific kids. Some kids are more interested in pottery versus sculpture.

What do you say to a parent who says, "I want to get a wheel at home"?

I've helped a lot of parents buy wheels. I have one girl who was sixteen and had been coming since she was a kid decide she wanted her own studio. So I helped her set one up in her basement. Every once in a while she teaches the neighbor kids and continues to do her work.

I have another girl who has been coming since she was little, and she would much prefer just to be here, to be in the studio setting here, and do it only on Saturdays. It depends. But if the child is just starting, I tell them don't bother. It's expensive to buy wheels.

Your mother played an essential role in your passion with ceramics. How did she do that and how might other parents do the same?

If I was having a problem with something, she'd say, "Well, what if . . . ?" That's the way we worked it, and that's the way she structured my life, which may or may not have been fantastic, but it worked for me. She did that in all aspects of my life, and what it did for me, somebody who didn't fit into a structured environment, at least not the ones that I was encountering, was that it allowed me to be more creative about finding my way, thereby staying with what I loved and finding a way to keep doing what I loved, which was working with clay.

The Kids 'N' Clay Pottery Studio was the result of my knowing on some deep level that children are more remarkable than we give them credit for, and that they can access places inside themselves to problem solve in ways that are important.

The way I look at it is that they come here and they have enough creative juices to last a lifetime. All I need to do is sort of stay out of the way, give them technical information and a little bit of structure now and then, and I just find they take off.

• An Intentionally Incomplete List of Interests •

No list of children's interests could ever be complete, and this one is no exception.

Interests incorporate such an infinite number of pursuits that it would be futile to try to list them all. Rather, what I've done is to compile a list of broad interests.

As you read through the list, look for interests that might appeal to your child. Then research specific niche areas within those interests.

For example, if your child likes to take pictures, research all the many possibilities related to photography. Enthusiasts can focus on certain subjects, such as wildlife, portraits, or architecture, or limit picture-taking to certain types of cameras, such as pinhole, digital, toy, or subminiature (aka "spy") cameras.

Keep your eyes peeled for niches that would likely appeal to children. What child wouldn't be interested in spy cameras? A child interested in dogs might be drawn to the exciting, fast-paced sport of agility training. A passion for rocks doesn't necessarily have to translate into rock collecting. Perhaps it lies in flintknapping, which is the ancient art of making stone tools.

Also, consider combining interests. A love of kites and photography can be combined. It's called kite aerial photography, and involves the use of large kites to lift cameras up to 500 feet above the ground. The idea is to consider interests from all angles, be creative, and open your child's eyes to the unlimited possibilities out there.

Acrobatics	Armor
Amateur radio	Aviation
Acting	Backpacking
Animals	Balloon sculpting
Antiques	Basketry
Aquariums	Beading
Archery	Beekeeping
Archaeology	Bell ringing
Architecture	Birding

Boating/sailing
Bookmaking
Calligraphy
Camping
Candle making
Canine training
Canoeing
Carpentry
Cartooning
Climbing
Cloud gazing
Coastlines
Composting
Cooking/baking
Costumes
Crocheting
Cycling
Dancing
Decorative painting
Dinosaurs
Doll making
Drawing
Dyeing
Embroidery
Environmentalism
Equestrian sports
Falconry
Fishing
Flower pressing
Foreign languages
Fossils
Gardening
Garden railroading
Genealogy
Geography
Glass painting
Ham radio

Heraldry
Herbs
Hiking
History
Historical reenactments
Juggling
Jewelry creation
Karate
Kites
Knitting
Knot making
Lace making
Macramé
Magic
Martial arts
Mask making
Mazes
Metal detecting
Miniatures
Mobiles
Models
Model railroading
Mosaics
Music—playing an
    instrument
Nature
Needlepoint
Oceanography
Origami
Paddling
Painting
Paper airplanes
Papermaking
Period games
Photography
Plant and wildlife
    identification

Poetry
Pond life
Pottery/ceramics
Prints/printmaking
Puppetry
Puzzle making
Quilting
Radio control
Costumes
Robotics
Rocks, gems, minerals
Rocketry
Rock polishing
Rubber stamps
Sand castles
Sculpting
Seed collecting
Shelling
Shields
Singing

Scrapbooking
Sewing
Sports
Stargazing
Stitching
String figures
Table tennis
Theater
Topiaries
Trail riding
Travel
Ventriloquism
Volcanoes
Weaving
Wetlands
Wildlife
Woodworking
Writing
Yo-yoing
Zoology

12

Blossoming Interests

Sharon Lovejoy's passion for gardening was nurtured at a young age by her grandmother. The experience left such a strong, lasting impression that Lovejoy went on to nurture her son's interest in gardening, as well as that of her grandchildren and hundreds of other youngsters, including special-needs children and inner-city teens.

Using theme gardens that are easy to grow and designed to be played in, Lovejoy demonstrates that nurturing a child's interest is about learning to see the world through his eyes. "The most important thing is to cultivate wonder before you cultivate seeds," she says.

Lovejoy is the author and illustrator of *Roots, Shoots, Buckets & Boots: Gardening Together With Children* (Workman Publishing, 1999); *Sunflower Houses: A Book for Children and Their Grown-Ups* (Workman Publishing, 2001); and *Trowel and Error* (Workman Publishing, 2003).

You were introduced to gardening through your grandmother.

That's right. It only takes one person. I always tell people, if there's just one person, one grownup, to go out and enjoy the garden, to experience it—not to say we're going to go out and work in the garden, but just to go play—that's all it takes.

After [my grandmother] died, I didn't garden for a little while. Then when I was a teenager, I had all this knowledge. It took a while to realize that it was all flowing back from the years when I was one and seven. It just sticks with kids. Now they realize that a child's brain between the ages of one and three is developing incredibly. So, I think you can't take a child out in the garden too soon.

My friend, who is involved with children's gardening, says once they reach eight or nine, if they haven't gardened, it's hopeless. But I don't agree. I've seen kids in Los Angeles who are really problem kids, who began gardening and realized they could grow things that they could eat and grow things they could sell, and it changed their lives.

Why did you start gardening again?

It was a release and a freedom for me, and it was a way to be alone. I took the back area of my parents' flat lot. We had lived in the hills, and I loved the hills.

When my grandma passed away, we moved to a flat, ugly, barren area, and I just started first by wanting to dig a pond. And I dug a pond –a small pond, sort of a mud hole—and I started making cuttings of things. I remembered how we had done cuttings of geraniums, and I separated some bulbs. It gave me a sense of freedom, and it gave me a sense of respect for myself, and accomplishment, too.

Did you share that with your friends?

Some of my girlfriends saw it and they thought it was strange. I think the difference was that, to me, it was natural because I had grown so much of what I ate. It was like having an outdoor classroom every day of my life until my grandmother died. It was the most wonderful rooting and foundation for anyone. I always say that all knowledge is rooted in wonder, and she gave me that essential sense of wonder that stayed with me all my life. I tried to give that to my son, and I've tried to give it to every other child I have come in contact with.

Is that why you decided to focus on involving children in gardening?

I felt like kids were getting out of touch, and I was worried by what I saw. We go cross-country a few times a year. In the late sixties and early seventies, we'd see kids playing outside at night, chasing fireflies and kicking the can and playing hide-and-seek. As the years passed, there were no people outside. It was as though a bomb had gone off. People weren't sitting on the porch or anything. I attribute it to television.

In about 1978 I worked as a naturalist at the Morro Bay Museum [of Natural History, Morro Bay, California]. Kids didn't know anything. They didn't know that catsup came from tomatoes. I asked, "Where do you think carrots come from?" and they would say, "I don't know, the market, the truck."

When I showed them carrot seeds, they were astounded. And when they planted them, they were more excited than if I had given them a handful of dollar bills. As they grew them, they realized that there's this untapped fountain of excitement and wonder, and it's not hard to get it started.

That's what I wanted to do—jump-start it. Then I realized I couldn't do it just teaching classes at my garden and herb shop or just going to schools. They say that the pen is mightier than the sword, and it is true. I learned that I could reach hundreds of thousands of kids by writing and aiming it to parents or to grownups to share with them.

When did you begin working with children?

In addition to the museum, I also had a business, Heart's Ease, a community garden in our little town [of Cambria, California]. I only had a quarter acre, but it was rich and right in the matrix of town. It was pure luck that I got it.

My husband and I bought it. We had just gotten married. We bought it from Angela Lansbury, the movie star. She could have sold it to people with more money who would have knocked it down and built a little shopping mall. I sent a packet of things that I had been doing with kids through the years and said, "My dream is to have a community garden in the center of town. I don't want to knock the little old building down. I want to plant every inch of it."

She believed in my dream and carried the note on the property. She actually came up and had her brother-in-law's memorial funeral service in our garden. We turned it into this fertile, wonderful teaching garden, and we were able to reach thousands and thousands of kids.

Is it still there?

When I started writing full time and not working at the business, I started traveling and teaching on the road. A dear friend who was in education for twenty years bought it and is continuing on with the festivals. The garden is much reduced because my husband and I did so much and nobody can afford what we did in our little plot. So it's probably half the size, but it still entertains lots of people.

What's the age range of the children who come to the festivals?

From newborn up into teenage years. The girls in teenage years love to dress up like garden sprites. And it's not even the costumes that are important; it's just the whole aspect of a celebration of music and art and fabulous little fairy foods in the garden with all these kids who are enjoying the garden.

Did your son grow up gardening?

Yes, but when he got to be a teenager, he didn't love it. He pulled away and complained.

To develop the community garden, we had a lot of heavy work—hauling rocks and laying gravel trails—and he griped about it. But when people started coming and appreciating it, he'd say, "I planted those there."

Now he and his bride have a tiny little postage-stamp garden, and they love it. They say things to me like, "How come in this whole neighborhood, we're the only place that has butterflies and humming birds and bumblebees? Nobody else does." I'll say, "Look around. You planted it and they came."

What attracts children to gardening?

Kids are attracted by the worms they see in the soil. They're attracted by the bumblebees. They're attracted to the fact that they can take a cutting of a geranium, stick it in the ground and it will grow. They're attracted to the magic, and it's all magical to them when they're out there experiencing it. It's so neat to watch my granddaughter visiting the plants in the middle of the pond or looking at the salamander in the ferns. Kids are so disassociated from nature that it's really a magical experience for them. They need to get dirty.

How can parents help their children develop an interest in gardening?

Start small. If you want your kids to garden, it has to be the sort of manageable thing that isn't hanging like a big lead weight over their heads. I love to have small plots of ground or little container gardens. One of the things that I emphasize is [the importance of] playhouses or hideouts. Nothing you build, but things that you grow and can use as your own secret space.

There are so many parents all over who realize that for our kids to have value, to value the earth and respect it and take care of it, they have to be taught at an early age. So people are tackling these projects as groups or families, and they are gardening with their kids. They may only grow one tomato plant, but that's the beginning.

That's what matters—small. Small is the most important

thing. No kid wants to be told, "Let's go out and weed for six hours this glorious Saturday morning." With our family, we had what was called a ten-minute plan. I'd say, "Okay, we're all responsible for ten minutes today," and we'd run out and pretty soon the ten minutes would be more than ten minutes. Or I'd say, "We're going to have a weeding contest. Who can fill this bucket up first?" It was always a good time.

What mistakes do parents make in trying to get their kids involved in gardening?

They make it too overwhelming. I have a list of plants that are easy for kids to grow and that are what I call "personality plants." They're multifaceted. They're not just pretty flowers. They attract humming birds or bumblebees or butterflies, I try to pick plants that maybe were used as toys, as jewelry.

I usually start with potted things. That works well because you're pretty intimate when you're growing something in a pot. You can do it indoors in the winter. You can [force] bulbs in the winter. You don't just grow a beefsteak tomato; you grow little green marble-sized tomatoes and little teeny golden currant tomatoes. Make it interesting, make it small, and make sure they're interested in it, and keep it in an area where they can enjoy it. Don't keep it out of reach or far from the house. Make it an area they walk past every day.

Find something your kids love. Maybe they love Beatrix Potter's writings. Go through the book and pick out those plants that Beatrix Potter writes about and do a Peter Rabbit garden. Or maybe you read *The Secret Garden,* and you do that. One of my most popular gardens is a pizza garden shaped like a pizza. I also grow sipping gardens with different plants kids can use to make tea; in the center grow straws, natural straws made out of lovage stems. Plant a spaghetti garden. Grow spaghetti squash and tomatoes and bell peppers and basil and oregano.

In the gardens I had downtown—well, they're still there, they're twenty years old—I knew that there was going to be a big toll paid by the plants because of the thousands of kids that came through there. So I engineered it for kids. I made twisty, turning paths with scented things so when they were running through there they would brush against them. I made signs that tell what the plants do. I made a five-senses garden. Each area had a stake in it that named the sense—touch, taste, smell, sight, or sound—and the kids would stop along the way and sample them.

Part of the problem is when you go to a nursery, and you're presented with run-of-the-mill varieties.

One of the neatest resources for gardeners is mail order catalogs. At the end of *Roots, Shoots, Buckets & Boots,* I've got pages of free catalogs. It's a neat experience for kids to send away for them. Allow kids to cut them up and write down what they want. Or the parents can write it down.

When you go to the nursery, have an idea of what you want. Maybe you've gone to a botanical garden or a nursery and gotten an idea of what interested the kids, or the kids read a book and saw that they can make their own pizza with these edible things that we use as toppings and sauces.

You make the process interesting. I always post things on a bulletin board or on the refrigerator: a drawing of the garden the kids wanted or pictures of the plants they wanted. Make it part of the mainstream. Keep it in the forefront. It sounds like work, but it isn't. It's easy and fun, but the parents have to enjoy it.

And it doesn't necessarily have to be parents. Gardening is coming into schools more and more, all over the world. I spoke at an international conference in Sweden, and educators from Japan and Greece and Spain and Italy and England were all saying that our kids spend much of their lives in school and the schools look like prison yards. So all over the world, they're ripping out asphalt and cement and planting plants.

Have you worked with special-needs children?

A garden that we put in downtown was a special-needs garden. Everything was wheelchair accessible. The only thing I didn't have the financing for was getting someone to do special labeling for the blind. All the pathways were covered with—my son, my husband, and I did all the work—decomposed granite, so it was wheelchair accessible. Every entry was wide enough for wheelchairs. We utilized a lot of large terra-cotta containers filled with plants so people could wheel right up to them.

Let's talk about mentors. Where do you find them?

I find that people involved in Waldorf, Montessori, and homeschooling have no problems. They have mentors coming out their ears. Where you find your problem is in the suburbs where both parents are gone [from the home], or in inner cities where there may be [a single] parent who is gone most of the time.

The solution to that is YMCA and 4-H and organized groups like Big Brother, Big Sister. I wouldn't have gone out in my parents' creepy backyard when I was fifteen and dug a pond and planted calla lilies if I hadn't done it when I was a kid. I had a mentor when I was a kid and that's what formed me.

Older kids are good mentors, too. You still have to have sort of an overseer because it can get pretty wild sometimes with kids throwing weeds and tossing tomatoes at each other. It gives older kids a sense of importance. They're almost like docents.

What if a parent knows nothing about gardening, but wants to get her child involved in it?

The way the parent finds out is by going out and piddling around, going to a botanical garden, arboreta, public gardens, nurseries, or reading *The Secret Garden*. You have to be interested in it or your kid's usually not going to be, unless he's around someone who is—and that could be a fabulous kindergarten teacher who's growing sunflowers, starting them in the classroom. You just have to watch your kids and read their responses.

How much time should parents spend nurturing their child's interest in gardening? Should they be out there every day?

For a few minutes, yes. That's important. You don't say "Saturday is garden day" because gardens are a way of life. They're not a one-day-a-week thing. They're something that you don't nurture every day, but that nurtures you every day.

So you incorporate it into your routine.

Every day you go out and wander through to see what's going on. You pick a dead flower and you know when you pick that dead flower you're going to get three more in its place. Kids love to deadhead. They even like the word "deadhead." It's a way of life. It's not just a hobby. Well, it can be a hobby, I guess, but it changes your life. I think it softens everybody up.

You have to look at everything through a child's eyes even when you're ninety. Go out for ten minutes a day.

Go out there and be there. The most important thing is to cultivate wonder before you cultivate seeds. Once you do that, you'll be able to cultivate seeds.

Afterword

Throughout the nearly two years it has taken me to complete this book, I've naturally kept an eye peeled for any and all information I could read about children's interests.

Early in my writing, information on the topic was scarce. But as I neared the end of the project, I noticed more was being written about interests. Discussions on the effects of interests on children were popping up in letters to the editor in the *New York Times*, in short pieces in parenting magazines, and even outside my son's school.

While it's heartening to read and hear this dialogue, it's been even more gratifying to be a part of the interest-nurturing process in my own home.

In some ways, I've come so far. I know more about my son's interests than I would have had I never taken on this book-writing project. Two years later, he is still engrossed in the simple act of drawing imaginary creatures in a way that remains true to his own vision.

The more I learn, however, the more apparent it becomes that exploring interests can be an incredibly long process. That's because the more we explore, the more we realize there is to explore. For example, my son's interest in the natural world has broadened from a fascination with animals and insects to one that includes hiking, fishing, gardening, and wildlife rehabilitation.

We'll explore each of these areas together. Who knows where a strong interest will emerge? But that's part of the fun—exploring and learning about his interests with an emphasis on going slowly and enjoying the ride.

Resources

Interests Detailed in This Book

Reading about interests pursued by some of the children profiled in this book may have inspired you or your child to want to give one a try. If so, then the following information can get you started.

Birding

The Cornell Lab of Ornithology is a nonprofit membership institution whose mission is to "interpret and conserve the earth's biological diversity through research, education and citizen science focused on birds."

"Citizen science" programs involve thousands of people of all ages and backgrounds who participate in Project FeederWatch, Project PigeonWatch, birdhouse monitoring, the Christmas bird count, and the house finch disease survey. To learn about these projects, visit www.birds.cornell.edu.

Ceramics

In addition to writing *The Kids 'N' Clay Ceramics Book* and teaching at his Kids 'N' Clay Pottery Studio, in West Berkeley,

California, Kevin Nierman runs a website, www.kidsnclay.com, which offers resources for purchasing related materials, as well as photos of young artists at work and their completed pieces—inspiration for any aspiring ceramics artist.

Clogging

In addition to promoting clogging, the Clogging Champions of America strives to "make sure the beginner clogger will get to enjoy competing as much as the clogger who has been in it for years." Its website provides updates, highlights and information on clogging events; www.ccaclog.com.

Clogdancing.com includes a message board; clogging news from around the world; and a directory of instructors, teams, clubs, and organizations.

Falconry

The North American Falconers Association provides a recommended reading list for beginner falconers, as well as a list of state wildlife agencies that regulate the sport; www.n-a-f-a.org.

Geography

Each year thousands of schools in the United States participate in the National Geographic Bee using materials prepared by the National Geographic Society. Schools with students in grades four through eight are eligible; www.nationalgeographic.com/geographybee/index.html.

Historical Reenactments

The Brigade of the American Revolution has nearly 3,000 men, women, and children enrolled in more than 130 separate units that recreate the life and times of soldiers of the American War of Independence. Its website contains a schedule of historic reenactments, archives, and related organizations; www.brigade.org.

The Field Music of the American Revolution stages weekend-long shows that portray the weapons and battle tactics of the Revolution. Its website contains pictures from events, a calendar

of upcoming events and links to regional units; www.fieldmusic.
com.

Shakespearean Acting

The Shakespeare Theatre offers two-week summer sessions
for children ages ten to seventeen. The Washington, D.C.–based
group is designed to "enhance young people's understanding of
Shakespeare's language through performance"; www.shakespearedc.
org/campshak.html.

For information on the Shakespeare Theatre, visit www.
shakespearedc.org/tinfo.html.

Collectibles

Here are three books on introducing children to collecting,
each geared to a different age range:

Ages 3–5: *Hannah's Collection* by Marthe Jocelyn. New York:
Dutton, 2000.

Ages 4–8: *Collect This: A Cool Guide to Collecting for Kids*
by Donna Guthrie and Christy Zatkin. New York: Price Stern
Sloan, 2001.

Ages 9–12: *Collecting Passions: Discovering the Fun of Stamps
and Other Stuff From All Over the Place* by Susan McLeod
O'Reilly and Alain Masse. Toronto: Key Porter Books Limited,
2001.

Publishers

National Association for Gifted Children
1707 L Street NW, Suite 550
Washington, D.C. 20036
202-785-4268
www.nagc.org

Though most of this group's offerings are geared specifically
toward gifted children, its *Parenting for High Potential* quarterly
magazine is a good read for all parents who want to nurture children's interests. A one-year subscription is $25.

Creative Learning Press
P.O. Box 320
Mansfield Center, Connecticut 06250
888-518-8004
860-429-8118
www.creativelearningpress.com
   Publishes "The Interest-a-Lyzer" booklets that enable parents
and teachers to assess a child's interests. The full line of booklets
includes:

"My Book of Things and Stuff" for kindergarten through sixth
grade.
"The Primary Interest-a-Lyzer" for kindergarten through third
grade.
"The Interest-a-Lyzer" for fourth through eighth grades.
"The Secondary Interest-a-Lyzer" for high school students.
"The Primary Art Interest-a-Lyzer" for kindergarten through
third grade.
"The Art Interest-a-Lyzer" for fourth through twelfth grades.
"My Book of Things and Stuff" is available for $14.95; all other
booklets are available in sets of thirty, ranging in price from
$15.95 to $29.95 per set.

   A subscription to a magazine that features children with interests is a great way to encourage your child to pursue his or her
own. Consider the following:

Boys' Life
1325 W. Walnut Hill Lane
P.O. Box 152079
Irving, Texas 75105-2079
972-580-2366
www.boyslife.org
   Boys' Life is a monthly magazine published by the Boy Scouts
of America. Targeted to boys six to seventeen, the magazine features articles on the interests of boys. A one-year subscription is
$18.

New Moon: The Magazine for Girls & Their Dreams
P.O. Box 3620
Duluth, Minnesota 55803-3620
218-728-5507
www.newmoon.org
　　The bimonthly magazine for girls eight to fourteen includes
profiles of girls with interests. Past issues have profiled a young
cartoonist, a girl who participates in reenacting medieval feasts,
another who is a belly dancer, and a girl who is interested in astronomy. A one-year subscription is $29.

Grass-Roots Groups

Putting Family First
www.puttingfamilyfirst.us
　　Based in Wayzata, Minnesota, this group jump-started a national movement in 2000 to give high priority to family time and
activities. Its website offers advice on starting a Putting Family
First movement in your community, and contains news clips, research, and recommended reading.

Parents United for Sane Homework
www.sanehomework.com
　　P.U.S.H. is a group of parents and educators who are con-
vinced by research studies, their own schooling, and children's
school experiences that the current "pile on the homework" ethic
in elementary school is wrongheaded and harmful to children.
The website offers approaches for confronting the homework
load in your school district, activities to do in lieu of homework,
and downloadable articles on the topic.

Bibliography

Bensen, Vidabeth. "The Art Interest-a-Lyzer." Mansfield Center, CT: Creative Learning Press, 1997.

———. "The Primary Art Interest-a-Lyzer." Mansfield Center, CT: Creative Learning Press, 1997.

Cohen, Dorothy H., and Stern, Virginia, with Balaban, Nancy. *Observing and Recording the Behavior of Young Children.* New York: Teachers College Press, 1958, 1978, 1983.

Csikszentmihalyi, Mihaly. *Flow: The Psychology of Optimal Experience.* New York: Simon & Schuster, 1994.

———. *Creativity: Flow and the Psychology of Discovery and Invention.* New York: HarperCollins, 1996.

Eysenck, Hans. *Test Your IQ.* New York: Penguin Books USA, 1995.

Griffith, Mary. *The Unschooling Handbook: How to Use the Whole World as Your Child's Classroom.* Rocklin, CA: Prima Publishing, 1998.

Hall, G. Stanley. *Aspects of Child Life and Education.* New York: D. Appleton & Co., 1921.

Hebert, Thomas, Sorenson, Michele, and Renzulli, Joseph S. "The Secondary Interest-a-Lyzer." Mansfield Center, CT: Creative Learning Press, 1997.

Johnson, Neil. *National Geographic Photography for Kids.* Washington, D.C.: National Geographic Society, 2001.

Keno, Leigh, and Keno, Leslie. *Hidden Treasures: Searching for Masterpieces of American Furniture.* New York: Warner Books, 2000.

Lovejoy, Sharon. *Roots, Shoots, Buckets & Boots.* New York: Workman Publishing, 1999.

———. *Sunflower Houses: A Book for Children and Their Grown-Ups.* New York: Workman Publishing, 1991.

Lutterjohann, Martin. *IQ Tests for Schoolchildren: How to Test Your Child's Intelligence.* Briarcliff Manor, NY: Stein and Day, 1977.

McGreevy, Ann. "My Book of Things and Stuff: An Interest Questionnaire for Young Children." Mansfield Center, CT: Creative Learning Press, 1982.

Nierman, Kevin. *The Kids 'N' Clay Ceramics Book: Hand-building & Wheel-Throwing Projects From the Kids 'N' Clay Pottery Studio.* Berkeley: Tricycle Press, 2000.

Oswald, Diane. *101 Great Collectibles for Kids.* Dubuque: Antique Trader Books, 1997.

Otfinoski, Steve. *Coin Collecting for Kids*. Norwalk, CT: Innovative Kids, 2000.

Renzulli, Joseph S. "The Interest-a-Lyzer." Mansfield Center, CT: Creative Learning Press, 1997.

———, and Rizza, Mary. "The Primary Interest-a-Lyzer." Mansfield Center, CT: Creative Learning Press, 1997.

Ross, Cindy. *Scraping Heaven: A Family's Journey Along the Continental Divide*. Camden, ME: Ragged Mountain Press, 2002.

———, and Gladfelter, Todd. *Kids in the Wild: A Family Guide to Outdoor Recreation*. Seattle: The Mountaineers Books, 1995.

Starr, Richard. *Woodworking with Your Kids*. Newtown, CT: Taunton Press, 1990.

Taffel, Ron, and Blau, Melinda. *Nurturing Good Children Now*. New York: St. Martin's Press, 2000.

Index